------------------

# Saving
# St. Germ

# Saving
# St. Germ

Carol Muske Dukes

VIKING

VIKING
Published by the Penguin Group
Penguin Books USA Inc., 375 Hudson Street, New York, New York 10014, U.S.A.
Penguin Books Ltd, 27 Wrights Lane, London W8 5TZ, England
Penguin Books Australia Ltd, Ringwood, Victoria, Australia
Penguin Books Canada Ltd, 10 Alcorn Avenue, Toronto, Ontario, Canada M4V 3B2
Penguin Books (N.Z.) Ltd, 182–190 Wairau Road, Auckland 10, New Zealand

Penguin Books Ltd, Registered Offices: Harmondsworth, Middlesex, England

First published in 1993 by Viking Penguin, a division of Penguin Books USA Inc.

10 9 8 7 6 5 4 3 2 1

PUBLISHER'S NOTE
This is a work of fiction. Names, characters, places, and incidents either are the product of the author's imagination or are used fictitiously, and any resemblance to actual persons, living or dead, events, or locales is entirely coincidental.

Grateful acknowledgment is made for permission to reprint excerpts from the following copyrighted works:
    An Introduction to Recombinant DNA Techniques, Second Edition, by P. Hackett, J. Fuchs, and J. Messing (Menlo Park, CA: Benjamin/Cummings Publishing Company, 1988).
    Letter from Mileva Maric to Albert Einstein from The Collected Papers of Albert Einstein, Volume I (The Early Years, 1879–1902), translated by Anna Peck, Princeton University Press.
    Women in Science by Marilyn Bailey Ogilvie, The MIT Press.
    "Power" from The Fact of a Doorframe, Poems Selected and New, 1950–1984, by Adrienne Rich. Reprinted by permission of the author and W. W. Norton & Company, Inc. Copyright © 1984 by Adrienne Rich. Copyright © 1975, 1978 by W. W. Norton & Company, Inc. Copyright © 1981 by Adrienne Rich.
    Rosalind Franklin and DNA by Anne Sayre, W. W. Norton & Company, Inc.

LIBRARY OF CONGRESS CATALOGING IN PUBLICATION DATA
Muske Dukes, Carol.
Saving St. Germ / by Carol Muske Dukes.
p.  cm.
ISBN 0-670-84047-5
I. Title.  II. Title: Saving Saint Germ.
PS3563.U837S28   1993
813'.54—dc20      92-50351

Printed in the United States of America   Set in Sabon
Designed by Ann Gold

*This book is dedicated to Dr. Leona Ling of Biogen Inc., Cambridge, Massachusetts, and to Dean Gerald Segal, Professor of Chemistry, University of Southern California:* sine qua non.

*And to my daughter, Annie Cameron,* ditto.

Unlike the rest of the body's cells, a germ cell
has one-half of each of the twenty-three pairs
of human chromosomes, since at fertilization,
the sperm and the egg each contribute their
one-half of a complete set of chromosomes to
the newly conceived being. Thus, when the
germ cell is being formed, it "picks" pieces
from the bearer's paired chromosomes.
Somewhat like a diner at a Chinese restaurant
picking some dishes from Column A and
other dishes from Column B.

          —*Genome*, Jerry Bishop and
          Michael Waldholz


OPHELIA: . . . They say the owl was a baker's
daughter. Lord, we know what we are, but
know not what we may be.

          —*Hamlet*, Act IV, Scene 5

# Acknowledgments

Much of the technical and general scientific information in this novel derives from the following books and articles: Malcolm W. Browne, "Mirror Image Chemistry Yielding New Products," *The New York Times*, August 13, 1991; Gerald Segal et al., "Chirality Forces," *Journal of American Chemistry Society* 109 (1987); Richard Lewontin, "Doubts About the Human Genome Project," *The New York Review of Books*, May 28, 1992; Christine de LaCoste-Utamsing and Ralph L. Holloway, "Sexual Dimorphism in the Human Corpus Callosum," *Science*, June 25, 1982; Martin Gardner, *The New Ambidextrous Universe*; Marilyn Bailey Ogilvie, *Women in Science: A Biographical Dictionary with Annotated Bibliography*; Edwin A. Abbott, *Flatland*; Christine Battersby, *Gender and Genius*; Desanka Trbuhovic-Gjuric, *Mileva Einstein: Une Vie*; Richard P. Feynman, *QED*; Stephen Hawking, *A Brief History of Time*; Eve Curie, *Madame Curie*; Fritjof Capra, *The Tao of Physics*; Francis Crick, *What Mad Pursuit*; James D. Watson, *The Double Helix*; John Stachel, ed., *The Collected Papers of Albert Einstein, Volume 1: The Early Years: 1879–1902*; P. B. Hackett et al., *An Introduction to Recombinant DNA Techniques*; Harriet Zuckerman et al., eds., *The Outer Circle: Women in the Scientific Community*; Judith Stone, *Light Elements: Essays on Sci-*

*ence from Gravity to Levity*; P. C. W. Davies and J. Brown, eds., *Superstrings: A Theory of Everything?*; John D. Barrow, *The World Within the World*; Thomas G. West, *In the Mind's Eye*; Anne Sayre, *Rosalind Franklin and DNA*; Jürgen Renn and Robert Schulmann, eds., Shawn Smith, trans., *Albert Einstein, Mileva Maric: The Love Letters*; John Gribbon, *In Search of Schrödinger's Cat: Quantum Physics and Reality*; Jerry Bishop and Michael Waldholz, *Genome*; Paul Davies and John Gribbon, *The Matter Myth*; Philip Frank, *Einstein: His Life and Times*; Abraham Pais, *Subtle Is the Lord: The Science and Life of Albert Einstein*; and *Science News* (many issues).

The list of individuals to whom I am indebted for technical information, explanations, general assistance, and moral support is long. It includes the following: Professor Marilyn Ogilve, University of Oklahoma, Professor Emeritus James Warf, USC, Professor Gerald Segal, USC, Professor Howard Taylor, USC, Professor James Ellern, USC, Dr. Leona Ling, Biogen Inc., Professor Richard Lewontin, Harvard University, Professor Robert Hellwarth, USC, Professor Heather Weber, USC, Professor Lawrence Singer, USC, Dr. Karen Segal, USC, Professor Ellen Quandahl, USC, Dr. James Husman, Andrew Fishmann, M.D., Tom Hellwarth, Lee Shallat, Lerri Atwater, Van Ling, Gloria Walther, Susan Dubs, Holland Taylor, Catherine Bos, Martha Millard, Marty Shapiro, Dawn Seferian, Adrienne Rich, . . . and *special* thanks to Zachary Santos (for the red language!), to Richard Rothstein for the two stand-up jokes from his act, to Bruce Lagnese and Lynne McMahon for patient, nonstop reading and kind encouragement, to David Dukes for love and support, for making my writing possible, and to Erik Jackson for immense help, especially his uncanny ability to read pages of terrible handwriting and produce flawless typed manuscripts at record speed.

# Part One

I do not believe that the human brain is to be
blamed for the fact that man cannot grasp infinity.
He certainly could do that, if in his young days,
when he was learning to perceive, the little fellow
had not been so cruelly confined to the earth, or
even to a nest, among four walls, but instead was
allowed to walk out a little into the universe.
     —Mileva Maric
      *The Collected Papers of Albert Einstein*

## Chapter 1

After the children were taken away, we were seated outside on white folding chairs under a large blue tarpaulin. "To keep the pigeon poop off our heads," I heard another parent murmur as the crowd streamed past. Above, at a remove from human discourse, the devious birds perched and plotted, chortling, their heads clustered like feathered bowling pins, nesting aggressively in the downspouts and eaves of the Lower School roof. I watched the principal, followed by her assistants, stride to her place behind a makeshift podium festooned with rich maroon bunting; the bunting's Gothic gilt letters spelled out "Sillitoe School." The principal gazed (falling silent, we followed that pointed gaze) out over the rolling grounds: four acres of Marathon grass growing lush about the stucco-and-redwood classroom buildings. As silence fell, the last of the parents hurried to their seats before the podium.

I found myself hanging back a bit, staring at the doorway through which the children had disappeared. Above, a breeze worried a rainbow windsock in the shadow of a spiteful Chinese elm, which for the last hour had been showering sap balls on the heads of the parents.

That was it: things just seemed to drop from the heavens at Sillitoe. Its templelike calm bespoke gifts from above, or from a more lateral direction: hands unobtrusively signing tuition checks, eight thousand per annum. The Lower School grounds were landscaped with self-conscious abandon: a number of muscled climbing trees shouldered each other over a montage of dirt paths, conversation pits, fortlike hedges. Two Dr. Seuss–ish palms, skinny and straight as telephone poles, towered over the other trees. Everywhere I looked sprang up the programmed implements of joy: redwood seesaws and sandboxes, balance beams and rocking horses. By contrast, we parents, squeezed tight in rows on our metal folding chairs before the podium, looked deprived and curiously passive—testimony to the drab and discredited teaching traditions that had produced us and preceded this more flamboyant, self-aware pedagogical era. I slipped into the third seat of a row near the rear.

Sillitoe, you see, was known as a wonderful school. And I had come, like all these other parents, to hear about it.

"We are a wonderful school," the principal whispered into the mike. Her name was Allegra Shatner, she said in a strengthened voice, and she was gratified to see us all here today.

I felt a sharp pain in my chest, put my hand over my heart, and inhaled carefully. I found, in trying to concentrate on Allegra Shatner, that I was afraid of her; in particular, I feared her clothing. Allegra Shatner was a large, imposing woman in a black-and-white leather zebra-striped jacket with fringed sleeves. She wore black-and-white cowboy boots and ribbed white leggings, and her jewelry was of a kind one associated with bodyguards: heavy gold chains, jaguar heads with garnet eyes, a great brass quetzal over her chest. Her hair was also large, the dull orange of a turkey wattle, wrestled into a pugnacious chignon, a huge trapped bundle, ballistic in its restraint.

I tried to calm myself by running through some bonding hoops in my head. To soothe a headache when I have no aspirin handy, for example, I build the Kekule structure of the painkiller acetaminophen, $CH_3CONHC_6H_4OH$. It relaxes my mind to assemble the skeletal structure of Tylenol or Excedrin, I pop the bonds together mentally like sparkling Tinkertoys, building only the electrons in covalent bonds, as is traditional—then build again, unabbreviated, the complete formula, including the carbon atoms in the original ring and the hydrogen atoms attached to them, a kind of chemical mantra. Though, usually, mantras aurally *soothed*, my mantra was visual and alarming: images of chemical dissolution, the world coming apart.

Breathing carefully, I refocused on Allegra Shatner, already deep into her explanation of how today's screening process determined eligibility for Sillitoe's famous kindergarten.

"I feel for you all," Allegra intoned into the mike. "There are two hundred of you here today, and a week ago we had another parent group of two hundred—and there are only *four* spaces available in the kindergarten at Sillitoe this fall. And we take only the cream of the cream, by which I mean, the cream of the cream for *us*—the children most suited to our program. Our teachers are in there right now with your kids, isolating that cream."

I glanced around at the rows of silent worried parents. The tarpaulin above us riffled a little in the breeze and occasionally a pigeon crash-landed on one of the tarp posts, remaining to tremble above, convulsively cooing.

I looked back at Allegra Shatner, who sighed and shook her head at the upturned faces before her. "It's *tough*. I wish I could be more encouraging, but numbers are numbers."

Anxiously, I checked to see if my name tag was still stuck just above my left breast: ESME CHARBONNEAU TALLICH.

A tan woman in a rose-colored suit on my right placed a white styrofoam coffee cup in the grass near our feet, and as I glanced down, I saw that one of the gummed-back name tags had stuck to the heel of my shoe. I strained to read it: BRANDON.

There was an audible intake of breath in the mike and the audience straightened up expectantly. "We are looking for the independent child, the motivated, creative child who can function completely on his own. Who can listen and follow directions."

Allegra stared dramatically into the faces before her: two hundred cowed, well-heeled parents. "Let me give you all an example."

I began hooking up a few mental atoms. This time, desiring a cigarette, I constructed the chemical architecture of nicotine. The pain in my chest grew, pushing outward in concentric circles.

"My own little girl attends Sillitoe— What am I saying, '*little girl,*' she is in the Upper School and her class is near graduation! For her senior project Brittany decided to do something on the homeless. She plans to go right down there to Fourth and Wall and interview some of these less fortunate people, ask them how they got into this situation. She believes that there are a lot of fascinating stories, I mean exciting, TV-drama-caliber stories, hiding down there and, as a journalist, she can bring them out. *Of course* I'm concerned for her safety—perhaps she'll have to stay in the car and shout out her questions—but she'll do a terrific job of it. She's a Sillitoe girl. That says it all."

I heard the sound first, since I'm most familiar with the source. It was an eerie quavering note, somewhere between a groan and a pigeon's wobbling cry, and as it grew louder, the birds flew up, flapping their hideous wings and raining poo on the tarp. Allegra Shatner paused and looked up, smiling nervously. "What is that noise?"

It rose and fell like an air-raid siren. As I stumbled out of my row, I noticed the woman in the rose suit staring at my foot. I walked quickly in the direction of the school, BRANDON flashing at my heel.

"What is the problem here?" Allegra Shatner asked as I hurried by, but I did not look up at the podium. My eyes were on the schoolroom door, through which Ollie had disappeared nearly forty minutes earlier—and from which Ollie now burst, lowing, a teacher at her heels.

"Sweetheart," I whispered, and Ollie pulled away from the teacher, her eyes wide, her face chalk-white, her mouth wrenched open, vibrating with sound.

"Come here," I said, "it's OK." But Ollie stopped suddenly, hung her head, then glanced guiltily up at the teacher, who stared severely down at her. The teacher, a slim, heavily made-up young woman, turned to me.

"We were taking Polaroids," the teacher said—and when I looked quizzical, "we *have* to *remember* what these kids *look* like somehow!" "She"—she glanced down at Ollie's nametag—"*Olivia* got frightened for some reason."

"It's all right, Ollie." I held out my hand and Ollie stared at it, then slowly put her palm inside.

"She hates to have her picture taken," I said. "She's like a Bedouin."

"She was extremely agitated." The teacher looked accusingly at me. "She didn't talk at all during the interview."

"She doesn't like to talk," I said. "She hardly ever says a word." The teacher and I stared at each other. "Unless of course she's really stimulated by her environment." There was a pause. I slung my bag over my shoulder and turned away, my hand in Ollie's.

"Well," I said, "I guess Ollie's made the decision for us here. You'd better get back in there. Really, you don't want to miss any dairy products."

She blinked, then turned her back on us.

We walked together across the thick grass. Allegra Shatner stared in our direction. I waved as we headed for the parking lot. The chemical formula for Quaaludes slowly began to form in my mind.

Ollie stopped several times to pick up acorns or pine needles, a bottlebrush blossom. She was humming under her breath. She knelt down and investigated a tiny castle of nearly fossilized pigeon shit, but then looked up at me and left it behind.

# Chapter 2

I take my daughter to the doctor. We park in a large, spiral-shaped parking structure, then board an elevator, which stops at a huge lobby, then rises again and lets us out on the eighth floor—a long hall leads to the Pediatric General Specialists Group (after a colon, the logo reads: A CORPORATION). The corridor is soundlessly carpeted, track-lit, with a series of recessed niches. Inside each niche (they appear at equal intervals) is a time-lapse photograph of an ongoing lunar eclipse—time and space overlap as we move down the hall.

Ollie glances sideways at the photographs. They are an attempt to teach, among other things, perspective—but the moon is viewed through the usual haze of clichés. Though the satellite camera is trained directly on its surface and the camera is suspended in space (the laser lens on its retractable stem, focusing, zooming in, deftly probing like a hummingbird's beak), the moon still appears to be *above* us, curiously flattened, despite the fact that its craters and volcanic peaks come into sharp contrast prior to obliteration by the earth's shadow. The eye learns to see what it expects to see.

Ollie stops to stare at one of the photographs and suddenly her small figure looks iconlike, framed by the plaster window. Once, as a college student, hosteling through Brittany, I came across one of those seaside churches (Perros-Guirec?) built on a cliff above the water. It was a village haunted by the Black Madonna. A local artist had sculpted his own faux assemblage, renderings of the famous dark patroness, whose likeness stood ensconced in a side chapel of the local church—where one wan ray of sunlight banded her forehead between four and five every day in the afternoon. The artist placed his imitations on the rock outcroppings that jutted from the natural stone colonnades marching to the sea. Inside each tiny parapet was a black madonna, each slightly different: a progression in the chalky stone. Some had smeared eyes; some had godly fear in their faces, some a sunflower's idolatrous cheer. I stayed a day or two in the town and I kept coming back to the church, haunted by those small dark figures, and then one portentous day, the Feast of the Assumption, August fifteenth—all the madonnas were gone. Just like that. The eye searched frantically but found just a series of absences suggesting . . . what? The artist must have known that until the madonnas returned, it would be impossible *not* to see them. And not as obvious *versions* of an "original"—or shadows of a white madonna. No, they were, standing there, mounted on their parapets above the regular shudder and hiss of the sea, intricate representations of the unexpressed— mockeries of the representational. It was simple, the eye had to explode pattern, try to answer the riddle of the unseen without thinking of it as the *missing*. That absence was part of the way to see them, to see what wasn't there, unchartable through set visual fields, the compass, the laser, the electronic simulator. I realized that was what I wanted to do: to see that moment of invisibility more and more clearly.

Ollie tugs my arm. "Mom. Go. Go now. This light is too *loud*."

———

In the posh waiting room, Ollie spun around silently, like a top, emitting a high wavery sound and I paged through *A Mother's Guide to Child Development:*

> Your baby is five! Do you believe it, Mom? Most child-development experts believe that at five your child should be capable of using words in comprehensible sentences. (That means putting key "subject" words in an order that makes sense!) They also believe that at five the child should be capable of an expanded attention span—he should be able to sit and play by himself for extended periods. *And* he should be able to recognize and identify correctly most primary colors, as well as a number of familiar shapes!
>
> Read to your five-year-old, then "quiz" him gently about what you just read together. You can actually *improve* your child's educational potential!

Beyond the door is a Kiddie Doctor of some renown. We've been to see him just once before this visit. As a famous child specialist, he is confident in his judgments; he leans back in his executive adjustable lounge chair, lacing his long slender fingers, contemplating the ceiling, talking about the behavioral habits of developing human beings. This doctor and I argue: I've been outspoken in my reactions to his analysis of Ollie. Ollie's "problems," though they sometimes seem like involuntary withdrawal or hyperactivity, are not, in my opinion, these states.

This doctor has suggested to me that my daughter has been exhibiting signs of emotional dysfunction, with hints of (but not) autism —because her silences are long and peculiarly stimulating to her, because her sudden flights of words and activity are inappropriate, often without context. I differed with his interpretation of these "signs." I had many reasons for disagreeing, but I had trouble explaining them to this person who mumbled into a bar-of-soap-sized tape recorder in his vest pocket as he interviewed patients. Once, as he began earnestly murmuring to his pocket in front of us, I reached over, pulled the tape recorder out of his vest, and clicked it off. His hands flew to his breast as if I'd stabbed him. His mouth fell open.

I sat, shaking, in front of him, holding up the tape recorder like a prize.

"When you whisper to this tape recorder, it makes me feel as if you're not listening to me."

He kept his hand, Napoleon-like, over his heart. He blinked once, twice.

"I *was* listening to you, Mrs. Tallich."

He slid his hand across his vest, then held it out, tentatively. I placed the tape recorder in his palm.

"I don't want to put my child on medication for as you put it, 'occasional symptoms.' "

He raised his eyebrows, which were silver, sculpted as his hair, and shook his head. The tape recorder sat, silenced, on the gleaming desktop between us. In the time-honored pose of shrinks, judges, or actors demonstrating a studious remove, he sat slowly back in his chair. He cuffed the side of his nose with his fist and stared at me.

He said nothing.

I said nothing.

Ollie said: "Blue blue blue . . . walk walk waves the shark."

His eyes, the brows above frozen in a spasm of disbelief, wandered to Ollie, swinging her legs from the tall chair. Eventually, they slid back to rest on me.

Now, as I drove out of the Valley, her humming beside me, I considered Ollie, the way Ollie fit into the world. When I wore my red glass beads, Ollie would crawl into my lap and finger them one by one. "Hot," she would say, "the beads are hot." Other kids might have pointed out more immediately apparent qualities of the beads. They were pretty, red, one could see through them—but I could follow Ollie's logic. The beads *were* hot, from resting against the jugular pulse, against the heat at the curve of the neck. Now she smiled at me, chattering about the bumps in the road as if they were alive.

Ollie said the odd thing, the unexpected thing. Ollie looked away from people as she spoke, she stared up at the ceiling, she stared at her sneakers. Sometimes she covered one ear and cocked her head as if she were intercepting a message from a satellite. She laughed occasionally, and she threw her whole body into laughing—making no sound at all. Sometimes she rocked back and forth on her heels in silence (this was the crucial behavior in the diagnosis of possible autism) but I saw that Ollie was not in a pathological trance, I saw that Ollie was thinking hard. Ollie was (for the purposes of being Ollie) functional. And what else matters? I thought hotly, as I changed lanes, remembering that day at the specialist's. The kind of kid she is, she is. I'll protect her, her different way of looking at the goddam storybook, the goddam model galaxy. I thought, burning, of Sillitoe's "qualifying" test—each child was asked to parrot back a mindless narrative, some computer-generated "listening text," verbatim.

I swung the wheel too forcefully and she slid sideways in the seat and looked up at me. I smiled reassuringly at her.

At times like this, I longed for the lab. I was calm there, when I was making calculations or working on soundless, endlessly reconstructible sequencing patterns. Glass beakers in sun, polymer ladders, dot-matrix readouts . . . dust motes in the slow dim fluorescent air, a scribbled page of equations next to a CATS coffee mug. Peace. Dreams. I rubbed the headache in my left temple, looking in the rearview mirror, driving south out of the Valley on the Hollywood Freeway and over the hill, exiting on Gower, following it past the drive-ins ("Home of the Whopper"), then the lots and studios where the sitcom taping signs were up: ALF, FULL HOUSE, DESIGNING WOMEN, and the studio-audience lines, long as Soviet food lines, wrapped around the buildings.

The crowds were in sweats, Rambo headbands, and neon spandex tights, spilling over the curb. I eased the car around a heavy woman with a "Roseanne" haircut, who stood in the street, laughing and gesturing to her companions on the sidewalk. A friend was photographing her. She put her hands at her studded belt and executed a kind of bump and roll with her hips. I honked once at her, gently, and she gave me the finger.

I glanced nervously at Ollie and she coughed and sank lower in the passenger seat.

"Are you sick? Do you have a temperature?" I reached across the seat and held my right palm against her brow.

Ollie turned her head away to look out the window. A bright red spot had appeared in the center of each cheek.

I stared glumly through the windshield at the thin brownish haze on the horizon. A toxic stew boiled in my head: formaldehyde, sulfur dioxide, hydrocarbons, acrolein, nitrogen oxides.

"Daddy," said Ollie suddenly, sitting up. "Daddy." She pointed at the bright metal bas-relief globe turning on top of the Paramount building.

I attempted a feeble stand: "You're sick, we should go *home*"— then, against my better judgment swung a quick left on Melrose and another through the rococo gates and into the Paramount lot, braking at the guard booth. There was a young guard at the gate, a small man who was working on resembling Paul Newman.

"We're here to see Jay Tallich. He's T.D. on *Drastic Measures.*"

The guard cocked his head at me and slowly smiled. He shifted his weight, hooked a hand in his belt, looked up to the heavens, arched an eyebrow, then scratched his upper lip. "Did he call your name up?"

"No, but I'm his wife. I think I remember what soundstage he's on."

The guard leaned out the other side of his booth and waved a van through.

He turned back to me with a dreamy look, humming a little. The hair under his cap was the color of clotting blood, as if his scalp had vacuumed up all the plasma from the capillaries in his face.

"Sorry, I can't just let you on. I have to call *up*. See if they left you a *pass*."

I smiled sweetly and ran one hand back and forth on the leather wheel cover.

"You don't *have* to call up. It's really no big deal."

The guard smiled too and hung his head a little. "Sure I have to. What am *I* here for then? It *is* a big deal. I'd say, in fact, it's kind of a *huge* deal."

His smile disappeared. I watched him work at a daunting expression. "People try to get in here all the time. But they don't get far."

I leaned out of the car window in a confidential attitude. I knew what I was going to do and I was shocked at myself, but not enough to change my approach.

Still smiling, I felt behind me on the backseat for my bag, pulled out my wallet, and flipped it open to a fan of ID cards. I held up my UGC Research Laboratories clearance badge and a card identifying me as a professor of biochemistry.

"Look, my friend, you got me. You're too savvy to try and bullshit. I'm going to tell you the real, frightening story. I'm a biochemist, an underground operative, in effect, a *spy* for Superfund Toxic Dump Cleanup."

I sighed and shook my head sadly, staring through the windshield. I could feel his eyes on me..

"Oh God, where to begin? Did you know that there are giant, illegal liposuction dump sites all over Los Angeles? Think about it for a second—have you *ever* wondered where all that fat they suck from jiggling thighs and bellies and buttocks actually *goes?*"

I looked around furtively, then leaned out the window, speaking sotto voce. "I'll *tell* you where it goes. You may not wanna look at it, my friend, but the reason we've been having so many earth tremors lately is because they're piping blubber by the pound under the ground surface of L.A.—soon we'll all be skateboarding on a layer of sub-cutaneous (subterraneous) *fat*. Hey, *don't laugh!*"

He shook his head, pawing the ground like a pony, his expression scornful. But he did look a little shaken. I saw him glance again, furtively, at my ID.

"Hey, I'll tell you *more*. The La Brea Tar Pits are an adipose swamp, a seething mass of old love handles, eyelids, and saddlebags—and *nobody knows*. I'm here today, posing as a visitor, but the fact is, you've got one of the biggest Blubber Depots in the city, right here on the lot, outside your Executive Offices, and my orders are to *check it out*."

We looked straight into each other's eyes. He moved his lips but no sound came.

"Do you think," I said, staring into the back of his head, "I'd be here at all unless the situation was really grave? Do you think I'd bring my *kid* into this?"

Then he got mad.

"This is not funny, lady. And you're not intimidating me."

As he spoke, I covered my mouth with my fist and pumped out the background music from *Jaws,* which Jay had recently gotten me to watch.

"Jesus. You're *weird*," he said. He rolled his eyes heavenward. "Why do I do it? Why do I put up with this kind of treatment?"

"Because you're a whopper," said Ollie suddenly from the passenger seat. "You're a whopper in the sky with diamonds whopper little

Lucy." She began humming atonally and kicking the glove compartment in front of her.

"Soundstage Thirty-two," I threw this out quickly, dropping my hand. "Ask for Paloma."

The guard stuck his head a little way into the car, glaring at Ollie, who crossed her eyes at him. I noticed, belatedly, that his nameplate read s. LUCY, and I suddenly got Ollie's joke. I'd been playing my old Beatles records for her lately.

"Your kid's real funny. You *train* her to do that?"

I shrugged.

"I don't care if people don't say 'please' or 'thank you' to me— *that* I don't mind. I *do* mind when people insult me outright."

His face had turned as brick-colored as his hair. Too late that face reminded me of dumb mistakes I've made my whole life, going too far with people who, as I should have been able to tell, didn't want to *get it,* or who didn't think my humor was funny. I would find myself blundering into sudden hostile depths awash in wreckage: missed punch lines, solemnly answered rhetorical questions, fundamentalist interpretation of my smartass one-liners.

"Whopper," chanted Ollie, "whopper whopper Lucy Lucy foolish."

"Please. Just let us *in.*"

"Whopper, diamonds, whopper . . ."

"I'm not myself," said the guard, running a hand across his eyes. "I been playing a *skinhead* in a waiver production and I'm not *myself.*"

Just then, miraculously, I saw a friend of Jay's, an assistant director, whose name I'd forgotten. He answered my wave and came loping over, figuring things out on the way.

"Sherman!" He threw his arm around the guard's shoulders. "This is our technical director's wife—you know, Jay Tallich? On *Drastic Measures?* It's OK to let her in." He pointed to his headset, wired to a walkie-talkie on his belt. "If you want, I'll get a special OK from the office." Sherman scowled and the director smiled dazzlingly. "Hey, we'll bend the rules just this once. It'll be all right." At last Sherman nodded, glaring at me, and two minutes later I was parking the car near a cement bank of terraced flowers. I got out with Ollie lagging after. We slipped into the maze of outbuildings and barnlike studios, passing the West Seventy-second Street subway stop in New York City, a Hopper-like 1930s gas station, a block of Western saloons near a hospital, its EMERGENCY sign neon red.

I thought, chastened, about the exchange at the gate as we walked. OK, I'd known as soon as we'd driven on the lot that Sherman was (in my husband Jay's terminology) an "actomorph," a would-be actor. I should have known better than to act *at* him. Acting "at" an actomorph receptionist could bring out the "Tara" speech from *Gone With the Wind*, could encourage the dental hygienist to abruptly crack stand-up jokes and palm an invisible mike while you sat, the inner lining of your mouth being sucked dry by the drool vacuum. It could elicit a Tom Selleck wink and heavy breath on your neck from the garage mechanic and an Ice-T rap as you tried to pay the baby-sitter or the reaction *I'd* elicited—fury. Nobody got madder than a would-be actor at being *upstaged*.

Ollie and I stared at a large flat of pure blue sky set on rollers, like a rebuke to the yellowish original above, then turned to the peeling posters on the prefab soundstage walls; L.A.'s Watteau-esque light flickered across the lovely peach-shaped breasts, biceps, tremulous lips. The faces dreamed, set in emblematic grooming: expressions quickened by the desire to express, not the self, but the self as *somebody else*.

Around a corner we found Soundstage 32, pushed open the frameless door, like a flap sheared from the particleboard wall. It was cavernous inside, hangarlike, with huge lights on tracks above.

Four- or five-tiered bleachers were pushed against one wall, and the bleachers were filled with people: visitors, fans, taping junkies. This audience was loud and restless, mostly young people in Madonna garb and soccer jackets. A hapless comic, the warm-up act, ran frantically up and down the bleachers, cracking jokes, soliciting hometown information and insults.

Ollie shrank away from the bleachers and, murmuring under her breath, turned her attention to the center of the floor, where human beings rode by on long-necked camera cranes, like chimps on the backs of giraffes. There were rolling boom platforms carrying sound equipment, each projecting a long boom arm with a dangling mike and an attendant who followed humbly behind the boom platform, making sure no cables got stuck. There were other people in earphones wandering about, whispering into mouthpieces. Thick black cables crisscrossed the floor like snakes. Ollie tripped over one and looked up at me, embarrassed.

"Whopper, whopper, whopper . . ."

Opposite the bleacher were brightly lit rooms, three-sided, missing the front wall, lit from above: a barroom, a drugstore, and a kitchen. The center room, the kitchen, was brightest lit. At the edge of a long radiance, a large sign printed in reflecting letters said DRASTIC MEASURES.

In the center "room" were the actors, dressed as Hell's Angels and their girlfriends. They wore leather jackets and boots, rainbow spiked hair, heavy metal crosses and skulls; their jeans were studded with gemlike brads. One of them had a huge fake wound on his forehead, dripping red gore. Ollie stared at the fake blood. Makeup people milled about, touching up the actors' faces; the actors ignored them, sipping coffee, talking over their heads or around them.

I looked about, intimidated, for a familiar face. I had been on this set only once before, on blocking day, when the actors memorized their final positions for the three cameras and their angles. There were far more people on the set now.

I hurried forward, towing Ollie, stepping gingerly over cables and props. A painfully thin woman in earphones, with very black frizzy hair and heavy theaterish makeup, hurried by.

"Paloma!"

The woman blinked, then focused on my face.

"Is Jay in the booth, Paloma? We'd like to join him."

Paloma looked annoyed, then saw Ollie and smiled. Her wolflike face relaxed.

"Hi cookie, hi sweetie. How old are *you*?"

"Whopper!"

Together Paloma and I watched Ollie collapse on the floor and hunch over, struggling to put her mouth on her shoelace. Paloma looked bewildered.

"Can we go to the booth?" I repeated. My headache was worse. I should have known better than to indulge Ollie. Out at the gate, I'd remembered Paloma's name and face only by chance. She had worked with Jay before, I'd met her on another set, some months earlier, but my memory for "industry-related" people (as Jay put it) was generally very bad. Through some chance synapse stimulation the exotic name had popped back into my head. I smiled gratefully at her, but she wasn't looking at me.

Paloma glanced at Ollie, a little worried frown on her face. She tapped reflectively at her headset with her long red nails.

"You're Jay's wife, right?"

"Right."

"Um, I don't know what to say . . ."

"Whopper, whopper, whopper!"

"I'm sure it'll be all right."

I watched in horror as Paloma's fire-engine-red lipstick broke down before my eyes into its chemical ingredients: dye sucked from the glittering bloodred irises of rabbits, sluggish castor oil, fats, sheep piss, wax, and lanolin, that mixture of high-molecular-weight esters and alkanes dredged from petroleum. As the woman's lips moved, I saw the coating twist alive, deconstructing again, as if I'd turned up a microscope's power, into the color-producing atoms—chromophores and auxochromes—teeming like a nest of insects under Paloma's nose. Dizzy, I stepped back, almost colliding with a boom platform.

She began another conversation with her earphones. "I'm sure it's OK," I heard myself say again. Paloma, still looking annoyed, motioned for us to follow her.

The director's booth was located in a trailer right next to the soundstage. In this very cramped space, a wall of TV monitors rose, and before this wall three people sat: the director seated in the middle with the assistant director and the technical director on either side of her.

Ollie and I followed Paloma, who pointed toward a row of plastic chairs against the opposite wall. It was air-conditioned in the booth, but the atmosphere was heated, kinetic: the director, a woman with shaggy blond hair, spoke to the floor crew through her headphones, turning script pages and snapping her fingers each time she wanted a camera angle changed. Jay recorded the change, counting out loud, and the picture on the monitors jumped, altered. Jay had told me that this finger pop was directors' shorthand: she snapped, the story got told.

I stole a glance at Jay, sweating beneath his headphones even though it was cold in the booth. He hadn't noticed us. He kept counting as the snaps came: "One ninety-five, one ninety-six . . ." I saw the producer suddenly—how could I have missed him? The producer was a tall rangy Kris Kristofferson type in faded leather and denim; despite his relaxed garb, he emanated discontent, a petulant expression on his broad face. "Let's *go* . . ." he kept repeating, sotto voce. "What's holding us up here? My actress is losing *energy*."

I watched Ollie watching the monitors—the same scene, two actors about to embrace, viewed from three different angles on nine screens. One screen displayed, close-up, a young woman with a desperate expression frozen on her face. The other revealed a handsome long-haired man in a leather biker outfit, holding a gun to the young woman's temple, grimacing cruelly; the last showed these two people locked together in a death embrace, which quickly dissolved as the director called out, "Cut." The two moved swiftly away from each other, their expressions growing identical: twin raptors, starved. The young woman rubbed her eyes and bleated, "Cherry Diet Coke? OK, Roz? With ice? OK? Two more minutes under these lights and I'm beef fuckin' *jerky*!"

I laughed and Ollie stared up at me, then laughed too, silently. The producer glanced in our direction, but did not laugh.

Jay turned around and saw us. He looked surprised, then slightly irritated.

"What are you doing here? I th-thought you were at that school interview thing over in the Valley."

"We were. It's all over."

Jay stood up. He was a tall man, but appeared slight. He had shaggy brown hair and an earring and his eyes were sad. He had a very slight speech impediment, a glimmer of a stutter.

"Ollie," he said softly. "C-come here and meet Lee."

Ollie held both hands up in front of her face and counted her fingers aloud. "One, two, three . . ."

Jay glanced, embarrassed, at the director, who was pulling off her earphones and turning toward them, smiling.

"*Ollie*," repeated Jay. He looked at me, expecting me to do something, to make Ollie respond. I shrugged. Ollie slid to the floor and hugged her knees, still counting.

I stood up and put out my hand to the director, who had a pretty, freckled, Huck Finn face. Her name was Lee Shallat.

"Hello," I said, my voice cracking. "Sorry to interrupt you but we were driving right by on our way back from the Valley." I paused. "This is my—our—little girl, Ollie."

Ollie was completely silent now, rocking.

"She's sh-shy," said Jay to the room. "Really a shy kid."

The director smiled down at Ollie, reaching into her shirt pocket, pulling out a stick of gum. She knelt down, unwrapping it, and offered it to Ollie. Ollie, miraculously, peeked out at her, then reached for the gum.

"Nothing like a little bribery to overcome shyness," the director said, winking at me, then turning, distracted, as three people approached her at once, asking questions.

Jay touched my shoulder and I smiled at him, but he did not smile back. He coughed and looked away. Then he smiled downward, into his shirt collar. A voguish black woman in a sarong and a Batman sweatshirt brought him a plastic cup of coffee and he seized it and took a gulp, coughed, and set it down.

"Break's over," a voice called. "Places."

"What's the matter with Ollie now?" he murmured, his mouth still in his collar.

"She's tired. She doesn't feel well actually."

"Then what the . . . h-hell are you doing here?"

I picked up the coffee cup and took a sip. "We came to see *you*. We thought you'd be delighted."

"Jesus, Ez, gimme a break. I'm trying to work here. You know this is no place for her. Especially when sh-she's . . ."

"So *weird*?"

"Did I say that?"

"No, of course not. You didn't have to."

Jay grimaced, then bent down and lifted Ollie's face in his hands.

"B-bye-bye, Olls. Daddy's got to go back to work now. I'll see you later, OK?"

Ollie put her hands back over her face.

"Thirty-three, thirty-four, thirty-five . . ."

Jay stood up. He looked at me, an unfathomably sad look.

"See ya later."

I took Ollie's hand and pulled her gently up and walked her over to the monitors. I put my hand on the director's shoulder. She turned away from her mike, grinned, shot us a thumbs-up.

Jay walked us to the door, waved, then sprinted back to his chair. Someone was calling him.

Outside, Ollie crumpled into a small heap on the gravel.

"Come on, Ollie," I croaked, exhausted. "Get up. We have to get you home."

Then I looked more closely at what she was doing. "Fifty-one, fifty-two . . ." Ollie proudly held up her fingers for me to see, then snapped them, once, twice, just like the director.

"Fifty-three," Ollie added, and snapped again. She paused, her thin little face upturned, spattered with light. Her grey eyes were very clear.

"This is count and count TV pictures, Mom," she said. "They snap—and then a number. The picture jumps. It moves ahead. Do you see?"

# Chapter 3

On Thursday I explained the molecular effects of equilibrium to my Organic class at UGC, working at the blackboard. I wrote: "1. Changes tend to occur in the direction of lower potential energy with the evolution of heat energy. 2. Changes tend to occur in the direction of greater molecular disorder."

Next I considered, in chalk, the acids, strong and weak, swerving suddenly to a discussion of the environment. Lately I had been trying to make my lectures as topical as possible, since my students seemed so innocent of any political thought. These days I was feeling more and more like a famous professor I'd had at Harvard: trying to inject notions of morality into chemistry. It wasn't really my style, but I felt a need to *startle* them.

"You know what's wrong with the world?" I cried out suddenly, turning from the blackboard. "And please note that the world I'm talking about is roughly synonymous with the scientific community —I'm talking about the absence of any connection between chemical research and the end products of research—like industrial chemical waste—and questions of social consciousness. In the case of gene manipulation or proliferation of combustible hydrocarbons, we have entered controversy without any program of ethical inquiry."

I paused. "Do you agree? Disagree?"

The faces in front of me were affectless. They had all stopped taking notes. I shook my head at them, but went on, undefeated, searching for a concrete example.

I wrote:

$$CO_2 + H_2O \rightarrow H_2CO_3(aq)$$

on the blackboard and got them to think through a series of equations that broke down sulfur oxide to sulfuric acid, or nitrous oxide emissions combining with water to give nitric or nitrous acids, all of which produce acid rain.

I wrote:

$$H_2CO_3(aq) \rightarrow H^+(aq) + HCO_3^-(aq)$$

I drew a picture of a lake with pointy waves, whitecaps. I told them it was a lake like any lake in upper New York State or New England, a typical one with no fish left in it. I talked about eastern Canada, about U.S. pollution entering its rain. I drew several large fat raindrops on the board, whiptailed as tadpoles. How does acid rain come to be? I asked in a very bright voice. The term, I said, did not simply mean rain with a pH of less than 7, did it? I asked for the pH of normal rainwater and wrote "5.6" on the board. Then I wrote "!!!!!!!!" after it. Then I drew a frowning face and circled it.

I began to feel tired. What was I doing, trying to be Q, the crusader? I just wanted them to consider the facts. "As you can see," I said, "normal rainwater is well within acid range, and this acidity is from dissolved carbon dioxide, coming from the small amount of carbon dioxide naturally present in air.

"Now, however . . ." I paused theatrically, then flipped off my left loafer and struck an empty desk with it. The shoe hit with an enormous bang. Everyone sat up. Everyone listened. "Now, however, data collected over the last twenty-five years show that rain and snow in

North America are considerably more acidic than pH 5.6. Fish are *dying*," I said directly to a startled boy in the front row. "Goddam fish are dying!" I drew an enormous cigar shape with fins and a gaping mouth, from which bubbles spiraled upward; then I drew large X's where the eyes should have been. The bell rang. I wrote "DEAD FISH" next to the cigar shape.

"We'll continue our discussion of acid rain next time," I said. "In the meantime, review your strong and weak acids. Get your goddam notion of equilibrium together." I kicked off my other loafer and it ricocheted off my desk sideways and bounced off the corner blackboard. A fat boy hurried out of the classroom, protecting his head with his chemistry text.

A favorite of mine, a girl named Rocky, gave me a high sign on the way out. "Hang on, Prof, tomorrow's Friday!" she called out.

I drove home. The house was dark when I walked in, but I could hear voices in the back. I snapped on a lamp and the hall light, and switched on the overhead light in the kitchen as I entered. It was an off-the-normal-schedule day—Jay had had to pick up Ollie from nursery school, because I'd had a meeting after Organic with my grad students.

I found him standing in the middle of the kitchen floor, looking as if he'd been crying. On the floor, nearly under the kitchen table, Ollie sat comfortably, her little legs in red corduroy pants stretched straight out, a large cardboard box over her body. This box was her "TV" —she'd insisted that I paint it to look like a television set with knobs and dials and a cutout screen for her face. She sat within and watched things carefully through her "screen." Occasionally she would imitate a quiz show host and cry "Let's spin the wheel!," utterly spooking me—but mostly she was silent. She followed me from room to room in this box, crashing gently into things, then backing up, humming, self-contained as a turtle.

Jay clenched his fists and glared at me. "I want a di . . . divorce," he said in a strangled voice.

I crossed in front of him, lifted the TV box gently from Ollie's head, then knelt and kissed her hello. Then I stood up, opening drawers and cupboards, putting an apron on, lighting burners, opening the refrigerator.

Jay stalked over, pulled me roughly by the arm. "Did you h-hear what I just said?"

I shrugged free. "A divorce? Now just what difference would a divorce make to me? Today is—what—the *second* time you've had to pick Ollie up this year: I mean, *who* would *miss* you?" I paused and looked at him. *"Us?"*

Jay's lip curled. He tried to speak, but couldn't. He closed his eyes and pushed air out from between his lips but no articulate sound came. The fierce expression on his face grew mild as he breathed. I watched him will his face and body to relax.

"Sh-shit," he said, and exhaled lengthily. Then he grinned at me.

I gestured at him with a small copper-bottomed pot. "Jesus. You can't cook. You can't *talk*. What the hell good *are* you?"

The pot slipped suddenly out of my grasp, hit the floor and reverberated, gonglike, on the linoleum, spun wildly, then rolled leisurely over to Ollie, wobbled to a stop in front of her. Ollie applauded delightedly, then lifted the TV back on her head.

Jay shot me another smile. I smiled back. He got up, crossed the room, and put his arms around me. "OK," he whispered into my ear. He was still breathing carefully, as if he were counting exhalations. He said it all at once: "Forget the *divorce*. I want a w-w-*wife*."

Ollie trundled by us in her box, making her way to a little polished pedestallike table in the corner where she and I had piled up a motley cache of geological specimens: chips of red roof tile and stucco bits from the collapsing garage next door, three spherical stones, a trilobite from a museum shop, a sharp-etched skeleton of a fish embedded in shale, a sprinkle of driveway gravel, two bottle caps, a green cat's-eye marble, a lump of creosote, a brain-shaped blossom of pumice.

Ollie sang happily to herself. Little bursts of flatulence accompanied her progress.

Jay stared after her.

"R-raisins. I gave her too many, I g-guess."

Ollie lifted off her box, sighed deeply—then picked up each specimen, held it up carefully to the light, peered at it, kissed it, then flung it thoughtfully to the floor.

He wouldn't let go of me and I felt awkward standing aimlessly within his embrace. He put his face into my hair.

"I want a wife," he repeated, into my hair, his warm breath in my ear.

Lately I'd noticed how our marriage derived its information about itself from hyperbole. Lately it was: "I want a divorce"; "I'm going to *kill* myself!"; "I can't *breathe!*"; translating to quite pedestrian literals: "I need your attention now"; "I'm tired and hungry"; "You were *mean* to me." Overstatement had numbed our power to affect each other. *And* Jay was, more than I, given to the dramatic. This was partially a function of his personality but also a natural result of listening to too much bad television dialogue.

I waited out his lips on my ear, thinking about dinner. Jay laughed softly; the sound made me stand up straighter. He had a wonderful luxurious laugh, like a ripe fruit being peeled, slowly: a long, tropical, smoky rind, spiraling around me.

I pictured the two of us standing there, wrapped around each other. Jay—tall and lanky, the planes of his thin face against mine, his wide blue eyes, lidded, head tilted downward. And me, not quite so tall, my red hair pulled back in a hasty elastic-bound ponytail, nose sticking out, eyes moving over his shoulder: Where was Ollie, what time did the battered kitchen clock say, what would I put on the table?

Jay sensed my internal commotion and pulled back, looking at me. He shook his head.

"N-*nice,* Esme."

He let me go, an injured look on his face, turned and flipped open a high squeaky cupboard, gingerly lifted out a bottle of vodka. He opened the dishwasher and took out a spotted glass, blew on it, and raised it to me.

"I'm going to mix a drink. You want a little shot of $H_2O$ and $CH_3OH$?"

I plucked little pasta bow-ties and wheels, multicolored, from a covered glass lab beaker I kept near the stove. With the other hand, I put a pot filled with water on the stove to boil.

"No, thanks. I'm not in the mood for a methanol cocktail."

I heard him open the refrigerator and rattle the ice cube tray.

"So, OK, I *missed* one! What *is* it?"

"I don't know—*wait:* $C_2H_5OH$."

The ice cubes dropped into the glass.

"Shit," he said. "That's probably *potassium chloride.*"

I turned around to look at him. He stood, slouched against the counter, head cocked, stirring his drink with his left index finger. He winked at me and cocked his right index finger at me like a pistol.

"*Gotcha,*" he said.

It made me uneasy that he was plowing through my old chemistry textbooks, my biochemical short courses. Not because he'd learned that potassium chloride injected intravenously would stop the heart and leave no trace in the bloodstream—that struck me (in my morbid moments) as useful and cautionary uxorial information, a Merck Manual family kind of fact: but because I was under a not-entirely-benign scrutiny.

I shook the pasta bow-ties onto the counter, then opened the refrigerator and took out a half-full jar of ready-made pesto with Paul Newman's face on it, considered it skeptically, then poured a small dollop into a pan. I turned to the fridge crisper and took out tomatoes, slightly withered basil leaves, and a ferny knot of parsley, to beef up the sauce. I began to chop tomatoes on a pine cutting board shaped like a galloping pig.

Jay was on the hunt for *material*. By day he was a technical director in television but by night he stood hustling for yuks in a surgical spot: he wanted to be a stand-up comic. He tried out his routines wherever they'd allow him on stage. He'd done every kind of gig from bar mitzvahs to the Café Blah Blah in the Valley. Once he'd even filled in at the Improv. It happened that he was pretty awful. For such a delicately constructed man, with such technical prowess, to have no sense of timing, to be so *slow* with audiences was unexpected and disheartening. But no one, especially me, had the heart to tell him. Let him have fun, everyone said. Of course *they* didn't wash the flop sweat out of his Arrow shirts. The fact was, almost *anybody* I knew was funnier than Jay. He'd become desperate. And it wasn't a matter of his stutter. When he stood up in front of a microphone, his stutter disappeared. The truth was that onstage, he just got boring.

Sometimes I thought he was amazingly brave, the rest of the time I found myself resenting his vampirization of our intimate moments, the intrusion of his need for reassurance into every level of our lives. It had become difficult to tell joke-trolling from the real thing. Sometimes he seemed so obsessed that I'd become uncertain about his displays of emotion: were they *real*, or rehearsed?

I'd come late to a friend's birthday party at a restaurant—the friend had asked Jay to perform on the small supper-club stage—and walked in on my own words: an argument with my mother I'd had a week earlier on the telephone. People were chuckling, and Jay was holding an imaginary receiver to his ear, cocking one hip: "But, *Mother,* that's the *wrong end* of the microscope!" Right after that he started doing Science Send-ups; he had a stable of characters, drawn from among my academic colleagues and professional acquaintances. He started doing *me*—or a burlesque version of me, mocked up and lab-coated and throaty. I was the Mad or Absent-minded Scientist; he was the Long-suffering Husband.

I stirred the sauce, thinking about the night before. I'd gotten out of the bath and wandered into the living room, still steaming, wrapped in towels.

Jay's recorded voice soared: "How'd ya like t-to have a k-kid who talks like this: [a pause] 'Sun hop top top the wind green'?" He repeated the string of words, then rewound the tape: Ollie's treble voice rose on the tape saying the same words, undercut by his. Finally he looked up and saw me. He clicked it off, stumbled to his feet, and came toward me, his hands out.

"Ez," he said, "it's not for a *routine*. I was just th-thinking *out loud*."

My damp turban unwound itself and I shook my hair free and ran a hand through it. I waited for a second, then opened my mouth, but he'd turned. He knelt down, popped the tape cassette out of the recorder, and flung it away. It bounced off a small palm tree in its terra-cotta pot in the corner.

"It doesn't matter!" he cried. "It's n-not what you think at all."

He stalked off. I stood there for a while, rubbing the towel through my hair. Drops of water fell on the carpet as I moved my head back and forth.

I didn't mind that he was making a tape and I knew it wouldn't be for a stand-up routine. It would be for Jay himself. It would be just Jay talking, talking to the air, the empty clicking spool filling nothing up with his sounds.

Talking about his daughter, who sat before her breakfast egg crying "Yellow" twenty times in a row, who followed her own feet around herself, around and around in faster, tighter orbits, who wore a painted cardboard box over her head, who chewed her clothes and talked to the sink. "Dream tub," she said. "Sugar puppet. Drink. Drink. Drink."

I could understand how he'd pour his words onto celluloid, into any receptacle for his terror; what I couldn't fathom was the silence between us about her. We could not find a path to the familiar descriptives, the words that could represent bent twigs, stacked stones, *trail markers* to the place where she started, this unprecedented being. Where *we* could begin to talk about her. And yes, I believed that place was where language itself began, under the twisted tree in the ancient kingdom—far away from the petty despots of syntax, where each new word fell, gold and perfect, unalloyed from the mouth. Something told me Jay and I were not going to find this path.

I turned from the burbling sauce and prowled through the cupboards, looking for pistachios. I heard Jay behind me, filling his glass again. More ice rattle, then a shattering sound, cubes hitting the floor.

"Shit—doesn't anybody ever *defrost* this thing?"

"It's supposed to do it automatically."

I pulled a half-full bag of shelled pistachios from behind a Frosted Mini-Wheats box and shook a handful into the Cuisinart. I poured in some olive oil, added more basil leaves and two cloves of garlic and turned it on—just as Jay started to speak again.

He stalked over and snapped the machine off.

"I want to t-*talk* to you, Esme."

We faced each other.

Jay set his drink down and put his hands out again beseechingly.

"Tell me what's going on."

I leaned against the counter.

"I took her to that school interview," I said slowly, "and the school was frightening to her. *And* to me. I took her to the doctor—he wants her on medication."

"Medication."

"To control hyperactivity. But"—I turned around to stir the sauce—"she isn't hyperactive," I whispered, "and the doctor will only pay attention to what he calls her *symptoms* instead of what's amazing about her."

Jay snorted.

"T-tell me what's *amazing* about her."

I turned away and he grabbed my shoulder and spun me around to face him.

"Esme, t-tell me. Really." His face was scrunched up, as if he'd *sighted* me, with my quiver of heretical ideas, taking aim on the horizon.

"She thinks in very unusual ways. She figures things *out,* you know, how things work, and explains them in metaphors or verbal *shapes,* instead of . . . conventional language."

Jay set his drink down and put his arms around me.

"S-sweetheart. She's not *capable* of using conventional language. She can't put thoughts and words together."

He held me, swaying a little, and I swayed with him.

"Jay?" We listed together, leaning to the left, like saplings, two saplings, about to blow over in a high wind.

"She embarrasses you, doesn't she?"

He jerked away, pushing me off balance. Then he turned his back on me, hunching over his drink.

"Why can't you just *talk* about it, Jay, instead of *around* it?"

He whirled around.

"Because I'm not the problem, *she* is. I want to talk about *her,* what's wrong, what we can do about it—not *my* failings, what *I* do wrong."

He pronounced each word very carefully and touched himself on the chest, identifying himself solemnly. *Not the problem.*

"Come here. Taste this," I said, "tell me if it needs more garlic."

He opened his mouth obediently and licked the wooden spoon.

"What's that taste, that s-second taste?"

"Pistachio."

He licked again and nodded.

"I like it. Pis-t-tachio?"

"No one's the problem," I said. "No one."

"You *sure* you don't want a drink?"

I watched him refill his glass. Though vodka is supposed to have no smell, the room filled with a high anxious scent, distilled and astringent, lining the moist veil of tomato-oil-garlic. The scent of ethanol solution refining itself, I thought. Bubbling in the copper vat: spirits, pure spirits. I flipped the pasta wheels and ties, like tiny Frisbees, into the boiling water. I turned the Cuisinart dial.

The machine droned, E flat, and Jay hummed along with it, nodding. At the molecular level, his cells were humming too, taking an ethanol bath.

I found Boston lettuce in the crisper, rinsed some, tore the leaves into salad-size bites.

I turned the machine off. He was waiting.

"You're blaming *me*."

"No," I said, "there's no *blame*. It's just a fact, isn't it? You're *embarrassed* by her sometimes because she doesn't act like other kids."

"You're *blaming* me, Esme. All this s-stuff about n-not being home enough . . ."

I chopped some more tomatoes. The knife clicked against the board; I felt blindly with my other hand to stir the pasta sauce.

"Could you drain the pasta, Jay? The strainer. In the sink." He started, then moved slowly toward the stove.

"I think," I said, "I'd like to talk to my mother about Ollie. I remember so *little* from my early childhood—and she's so *reticent* when it comes to talking about the past—anyway, I thought maybe she could fill in some things. I've been thinking lately that the way Ollie acts is . . . a *tendency* toward a certain kind of behavior."

The strainer smacked repeatedly against the side of the sink.

"What complete and utter b-bullshit! You think it's genetic? Your *m-mom* is going to help you discover inherited tendencies?"

"Come on, Jay. It's my *field*. And it's *my* mother. Can you just help me think this through?"

"What about me? What about m-my genetic input? Where'd my genes go, to the laundry?"

His shoulders shook with laughter and he reached sideways, left-handed, for his drink.

I didn't laugh. I assembled the salad, mixed vinegar, oil, garlic, and mustard in a glass cruet. I remembered a half baguette in the freezer and fished it out, popped it in the microwave.

The TV backed into the room. Then it stopped in the middle of the floor, spun around, and backed out in reverse, Ollie's face framed by the screen, placid, her lips moving.

I poured the sauce over the pasta, grated some Parmesan. Jay reached plates and cups down from the cupboard. We went into the dining room.

"So what are *you* saying, Jay?"

"I'm saying, Esme, that she needs professional help and we've got to get it for her."

We set the table. I called Ollie. Jay went to get his drink, then sat down.

"Jay, listen for a second. When I think back I *remember*—I'm pretty certain I remember—acting the way Ollie acts. I remember *turning*. I'm sure I'd walk in circles—you know, you've seen me, I *still* do that when I'm concentrating on something. All my responses to things were . . . a little ritualized, disconnected. Very odd."

Jay took a long slow drink. Then he scratched his side, yawning.

"You know, Esme, all your responses to things are s-still very odd," he said.

He began to laugh and I sat down, exhausted, at the table and joined him. We put our heads in our hands and laughed.

Ollie appeared in the door and watched us. The TV had disappeared from her head and she had taken all her clothes off. She held a large yellow Big Bird in her arms. She farted again loudly.

"This bird just said to get to Sesame Street, Mom," she said. "But Ollie really really wishes not to go."

We looked at her. Jay burst into howls again, but I couldn't bring myself to join him.

"It's OK, Olls," I said. "If you don't want to go, you don't have to."

# Chapter 4

### Imaginary Lecture: Letter to Ollie

*Well, Ollie. I keep thinking that there will be a time when you'll ask for an explanation of me: Mom the Scientist. And what would they tell you, if I was gone, prematurely carcinogenic from random hyper-zaps of radioactivity? Daddy doesn't know exactly what I do. "She worked with blots," he'd say. "She blew up little cells and counted their chromosomes."*

*That's true, of course. But it's—like I said—the Black Madonna, the absence, the* intention *in science that defines us. What we intend to do is what we are. A great deal of my work centered on microstructures—but I didn't just want to play dollhouse, tinker with tiny worlds using molecular tweezers. At one time, I thought I saw lessons at the cellular level; I thought I could rewrite a whole section of biochemical history, based on the germ cell. Under the flag of genetic engineering, I'd influence the species' capacity to spell out its own future. This is arrogance, there's no doubt about it, Ollie, and yet I have to tell you I never knelt at that altar without reminding myself that it was* an altar *and and that I was a worshiper—privileged to lower my knees to its biotech prie-dieu: the bench.*

*For a long time now, whenever I want to make sense of my life, I go to the lab. I clear some counter space, like now—and I begin to write the story of my professional life for you, kiddo. I write on graph paper, I write with a Bic pen. Coffee spills on the page, and, every once in a while, acrylamide or acetone. But I keep writing.*

*You should have seen me when I was growing up; I looked like the cliché of the kid scientist, buck-toothed and myopic. But I was not like other juvenile experimentalists in style. I was messy, disorganized, attention-deficient. I liked to think about a lot of stuff at once. I did not employ the much admired Scientific Method: step-by-step logical analysis, deductive, inductive.*

*My speculative thinking would run in several directions. I'd grow crystals from bluing near the laundry tub, then try to "mutate" the crystals, adding chemicals from my set. I routinely put food or household objects on wheels (to determine what shape traveled through space fastest). I included a wire whisk in this experiment, as well as a cheese grater, a loaf of bread, and a Coke bottle. I launched these items on a downhill driveway course. Or I tested them for aerodynamic ability—from the roof. I took my dad's Gillette blades and floated them in a sinkful of water, showing how surface tension works.*

*For a high school Science Fair project I tried to show how alcohol affects physical reactions and decision making—I kept notes on my teetotaling white mice. They ran the maze, sober, in two minutes, forty seconds.*

*Then I ripped off a tumbler of Scotch from my dad's liquor cabinet, filled an eyedropper with it, and squirted it on the backs of the mice. I knew they'd boycott drinking straight alcohol from their plastic water bottle, but they would lick it off their own fur. It worked. They got blotto. They lurched around the maze, bumping into walls. My experiment clearly demonstrated how alcohol was first a stimulant, then a depressant. A mouse newly buzzed on Scotch could hoof through the maze in half the time, but later, soused, would stumble along—taking up to fifteen minutes.*

My study was disqualified by the judges, because of the liquor. I sipped a little myself on Fair Day and ended up telling Science Jokes ("What's a quark?" "An underwater fart in a bathtub!") to the small but appreciative crowd around my exhibit. What an awful child I was! The judges said that while my research was "inventive" I hadn't followed project rules and I was "making fun" of Science Fair ideals. One pulled me aside and hissed, "Where are your parents?"

That spring I built a DNA model in my basement. I used Ping-Pong balls and pipe cleaners. It was perfect, just like Watson and Crick's, and I sat and looked at it a long time. It was beautiful, aleatory. It was a flight of stairs: two paired furry pipe-cleaner rails winding around each other in a spiral. An inanimate molecule, I thought, but the structure allowed for replication; its storytelling was built in.

It had been called the biochemical discovery of the twentieth century, the Secret of Life, they said, God's Code, the Shape of the Universe (since the helix recurs throughout nature). Then it became some sort of Genesis model—as if it were alive, as if it could generate life.

It came to me at that moment, a kid experimenter, that science, though it seemed not to be, was really about metaphor—about saying something was like something else. Which is good, though it depends on who owns the metaphors. Metaphor teaches us how to make the unknown thinkable, but metaphors can eat up the world.

I'd been reading Descartes, who said that the universe was like a clock—then somehow the world assumed it was a clock! Suddenly we lived in a clockwork universe, now we discovered a spiral staircase, now a magic bullet, now a black hole. We could only comprehend facts shaped like our own thought. Unless, I thought, twisting the *pipe cleaners, science could come up with metaphors so new, so unthought-of, they could actually change the way we took in the world. Perception itself could change the physical world. I was reading a book called* Flatland, *written by Edwin A. Abbott in the nineteenth century: a parable of geometry. It was the story of the inhabitants of a two-dimensional world called Flatland, and what happens when a circle (who cannot really be "seen" in two-dimensional space) comes on the scene. We are trapped in three-dimensional Euclidean geometry like the 2-D Flatlanders: it was clear to me.*

*I have always been interested in theory, which means that like you, Ollie, I describe the world oddly. I lay in my rumpled sleeping bag on the basement linoleum, shining my flashlight up at the hand-drawn map of the universe I'd taped to the ceiling. Which way was left? Or north? And how could you explain that to somebody not standing on earth, but somewhere in space?*

*What if a Volkswagen crashed into a collapsing star? Was shape always a concept imposed by the observer's eye? Who killed Schrödinger's cat? It was 1961. There was DNA to think about, and dimensions beyond the* third, *and then there was physics. A physicist named Murray Gell-Mann discovered a new elementary particle which he called a* quark *(from James Joyce's* Finnegans Wake) *and then they labeled its variations* up, down, strange, *and* charm. *And I was weird? I mooned around and shot my flashlight beam in and around the constellations among the branching heating shafts and wondered, What would happen if you shot DNA into space? Cloned and carefully adopted it to another atmosphere? You'd get school-teachers, parents, science-club presidents, I thought. Nobody seemed to think like me. Or* want *to think like me.*

*Everything was better when I was at Harvard. Does that sound like the punch line to a bad WASP joke? But it is the embarrassing truth that the high point of my career hit when I wandered the Yard in a ponytail and stained white coat, a syringe in my back pocket, a bracelet of rubber bands around my wrist: a grunt, a slavey, a research mole in the funded vineyards of a high-profile prof, assisting his Nobel-level work in the lab.*

*OK, I was never really a mole—I was a protégée, a star pupil of Professor Kendall Quandahl, whom everyone called, affectionately, Q—or, (not so affectionately) Spock. He liked me; our personalities meshed. And nothing more. Just that simple: straight regard, like a shot of strong whiskey between us. Man to man, had we been equals. I certainly idealized him, and he, in return, saw in me an intelligent, loyal acolyte. I don't think he ever saw me as a woman.*

*First of all, I learned early on, in my undergrad days, there are not that many women in chemistry, and none in Organic. Operating on a behavioral premise I'd acquired as a little girl (that if men could do it, I could improve on it), I threw myself recklessly into this masculine preserve. Then I took Q's courses, Q became my mentor, guiding my research, which became, in biochemistry (then molecular biology) meticulous, inspired. I substantiated his theories, theories of molecular biology that focused on synthetic enzymes. We modified proteins, intent on discovering what enzymatic defects were responsible for certain genetic diseases. When he went on to gene cloning (single-gene-deficiency diseases) I followed.*

*Well, Ollie. The more I work on this, the more I see: no life ever organized itself expressly for a writer. But I have a scientist's perilous illusion of control. And doesn't life, after all,* appear *to organize itself for the scientist? Well, up to a point. And then, lab life doesn't* disappear, *it simply alters form. And your bio-chem biography and mine can be spelled out quite simply: A-T-C-G. That's adenine, thymine, cytosine, and guanine: the nucleotide bases, in specific sequence in each strand of DNA, that encode the genetic information that* is *us. (So the Biotech Bible story tells us!) One human cell contains enough*

*DNA to ignite the synthesis of thousands upon thousands of proteins. Opening its base-pair locked strands, DNA gives birth to its daughter-messenger RNA, and presto! The command is given for an aquiline nose, a tendency to gain weight, a tendency to be a moody sot . . . or the command is given for you, Ollie, you. The problem now is we have some control over these commands. So what instructions will be given—what kind of kids will we build? And will we select death right out of the gene pool?*

*Yes, said distinguished Professor Q, part of the new Shook-Up Biology at Harvard (the department of biochemistry and molecular biology, which broke away from the old department, when the DNA-magus, Mr. James Watson, arrived on the scene, presenting himself like the sphere to Flatlanders). Q liked my sexy dissertation ("Genetic and Chemical Engineering of Enzymatic Active Sites in Monoclonal Antibodies"). Q, with his single social bias: a preference for obsessive assistants, female or male. He moved about the lab in his characteristic high wind—all gestures, snorting, wheezing, unfinished sentences, pushing his glasses up and down his nose, scratching his bald spot. Breathing heavily through his nose like a great engine of asthma,* his genetic curse.

*He had big ears, did I say that? I see them as bat-winged babies, but I am finding lately, as I sit up till the wee hours, sneaking a cigarette occasionally, that memory has exaggerated his physical presence in all ways. He wasn't that tall, for example. And I think he was called Spock as much for his alien-seeming nature and his conflicted manner as for the ears. He curled into himself, with a chemist's hunched posture. Not the carriage of defeat, but of curiosity—the result of years of bending over microscopes, sinks, boiling points: close-up inspection of life's clues to itself.*

*I worked the usual postdoc schedule: sometimes up to ninety hours a week in the lab, finishing up my three-year sentence, which included a one-year lab at the Cambridge Medical School, the Harmon-Tannen*

*Cancer Institute, Genetic Diseases. The cancer institute was a hospital but also a research facility, an academic preserve. Physically, it was an architectural anomaly, a layer cake: There were two floors of research labs, followed by three floors of patients in beds, followed by two floors of research and so on. Every lab had medical fellows working in it—they worked in research as part of clinic training. Brushing shoulders with physicians will quickly teach a scientist what a clinician's opinion of an academic researcher is. Those docs took their research knowledge and applied it righteously to the ill. And the physical setup of the hospital ensured that we would never be too far away from ailing human beings—the final focus, the docs said, of all our work. We were, of course (by their definition), elitist—Ph.D.'s talking about "elegant" theories and they stuck together in a practical bullying sensibility. Some academics were intimidated by this—it was easy for them to "cross over," into the land of medical biotechnology, especially when encouraged by the NIH.*

*I felt like many other academic scientists—caught between the two poles. I cared very much about the people in beds above and below us, but I also cared about the simple precision of a procedure—and how the results of that procedure might affirm or change our view of nature, the "models" for the natural world. And I didn't care about money. We all know doctors have traditionally loved their bucks— and now, genetic research was an* industry, *everybody concerned could make a fortune. It seemed to me everyone was playing high-tech Monopoly.*

*One morning I came into the biochemistry lab after a trip down memory lane. I'd been to see my friends at the old organic lab. I had a glass distillation apparatus from the lab glass-blower in my pocket, and I rubbed my fingers over and over its cool smooth contours. I discovered Q slumped on the stained and burned couch in the corner, crumpled up, breathing violently through his nose, talking to himself. He was poring over photographs of clinical presentations borrowed from the medical-school lab: children with a variety of genetic diseases.*

*He flipped a sheaf of photos at me without speaking. (I admit that I have trouble with medical-textbook photographs. The subjects look manipulated, terrified. I find the clinical "framing" of the disease and its victim intrusive.) The first photo I looked at was of an albino child, who wore her unpigmented skin like a hair shirt. Under the photographer's harsh overhead lights, she looked bald and wounded, invaded by the camera: a pure-white chubby girl in a Care Bears T-shirt, her colorless brows knitted together above her pale red-glinted eyes. She was trying to look fierce, since emotion can give color; she squinted angrily, she shot furious red darts at what I imagined to be the cameraman's stupid ruddy glow, his gleaming black hair and mustache, the treacherous rainbow caught in his lens.*

*Q had worked, off and on, for a long time on the problems of albinism, trying to determine at a molecular level whether the genetic defect that led to pigment degeneration affected an entire chromosome or a single gene. The idea, of course, was that if one narrowed the field, one could develop an* in utero *screening test. Q knew this test was just around the corner.*

*I wondered what kind of reaction he wanted from me now, scientific or emotional. He looked at me foggily, breathing thunderously, his eyes twitching behind his wayward glasses. He was wearing a horrible tie, I remember there were pink parrots sewn into its sky-blue weave. I really hoped that he wasn't going to get sappy on me. He did this type of thing occasionally, making me feel manipulated. His wife was dead, he had no children, but he slipped, every once in a while, into an avuncular sentimentality so gross and powerful it was like drink; he wept and slurred words, he swayed at my shoulder, urging tragedy on me like a late-hour cocktail.*

*"Look at this," he gasped, then peered over his glasses at me. "When I look at these faces, I tell you, Esme, I get back on the track.*

*I remind myself that we are not isolated here. We're not a bunch of theoretical chemists, computer jocks!"*

*He coughed, a lengthy, stagy, wheezing bark. This cough had become famous among graduate students and fellows, who imitated it both in and out of the lab—it had a certain self-conscious bass quaver to it, as if he were about to break into a Ray Charles imitation. I'd gotten to know a medical student who could do a perfect reproduction of it—this guy reduced me to tears late one night in a campus bar by coughing, Q-style, several bars of "Georgia on My Mind." Now, however, I put these thoughts out of my mind and waited demurely for him to finish.*

*"We're* bench *chemists, wet chemists." He blew air through his nostrils. "We're in the* trenches, returning *fire."*

*He spat a little on me. I was embarrassed enough to be cruel.*

*"Save it for the grants committee," I said, without looking up at him.*

*I was finding it hard to tear my eyes away, flipping through the black-and-white documentation of nature's out-of-the-park foul balls: Down's syndrome, Tay-Sachs, sickle-cell anemia, beta-thalassemia, PKU, Gaucher's disease, Alpha$_1$ Antitrypsin Deficiency. This last disease, this horror, had been my own obsession. Colleagues of mine pursued immunological questions—AIDS being a primary focus—or tracked malfunctions in cellular growth, that is to say, cancer. I've always been intrigued by single-gene deficiencies, not just because they supposedly offer more promise of cloning and reintroduction of a doctored gene back into the body: I was just after this one. I stared at a photo of a young man, barely twenty (I could guess by his childlike facial expression) who'd developed the premature emphysema that characterized $a_1AT$. His chest was sunken, iron-ribbed from the terrible exertion of drawing breath after breath. His body looked fifty years old. I saw that he would be dead in a year or two, if he made it that far. The emphysema usually doesn't hit till the twenties, but* might *show up before then. To parents who had a kid who looked and seemed healthy, every cold, every sore throat was a potential nightmare, the beginning of the end. My father died of emphysema, but that's not why I identify with it so strongly. I reacted calmly to* $a_1AT$; *I felt outraged by it—but* focused. *I thought I knew how to pursue it. I knew its habits. But, at the same time, I knew we had no real cure rate.*

*I threw the photos back at Q.*

*"Horror movies," I remember saying. I looked at my nails and yawned.*

*He laughed. "Did it ever occur to you," he said, "that your feigned indifference is much more dramatic than pitched hysteria? You* should *speak to the grants committee."*

*I recall smiling stiffly.*

*"Glad I entertain you."*

*I tried to be cool. I got up and rotated my elbow, which had been bothering me in the lab, stiffening up on me, in a series of rapid, bone-popping circles.*

*He kept watching me. "What are you doing?" he asked finally. "Exercising the chip on your shoulder?"*

*I froze. "What chip?" I blushed. "What chip?"*

*He gave me that big limpid gaze over his glasses.*

*"You are naturally gifted in this field. I admire you, Esme. Nevertheless, nonacademic science might be too volatile for you. Did you ever think about that? You seem afraid to get emotionally involved, to* care."

*It was hard for me to absorb that comment. I was his right arm. I'd come to believe that I knew everything he thought about our work together, I thought I knew everything he thought about me. Unlike other professors, he was there. He had made himself available to me; we'd become friends.*

*To my horror, I turned girlish, making a little face at him, mur-
muring something about how I hoped that he really didn't believe
that.*

*He punched me on the shoulder, slid the photographs in a file, and
suggested we go to work. But I sat there for a while after he went to
wash up. I took out the glass apparatus and held it up to the tube
lamp. It exploded into prismatic light fractures, jumpy neon-white
right angles, spangling the walls and ceiling.*

*It doesn't worry me, Ollie. It doesn't worry me that you go to your
nursery school and sit by yourself and that you don't talk to the other
kids and that you sing a little song over and over to yourself. I know
you are not unhappy. I know what you're thinking. I was like that.
I remember being like that. You talk only to me, sometimes to Jay
or to your stuffed dragon. I understand. Language, the language we
speak out here in the world, is treacherous, ambiguous. You have to
figure the world out by observation, by experiment, before you can
enter the code.*

*That spring I invited my mother, Millie Charbonneau, to a department
party. It was ironic that she lived right in Cambridge, where I was,
and yet we hardly saw each other: My lab schedule was that demanding and her job as a Filene's buyer kept her on the run. But I
wanted to see her suddenly. I wanted, I wasn't sure why, to sit down
and talk to her about what I'd been like as a kid. I couldn't remember
much before five or so—and she'd always been closemouthed about
that stuff when I asked her questions. Was I a brat? Did I cry a lot?
Was I toilet-trained early? When did I speak? Walk? Was I a kid who
laughed?*

*Mom was delighted to come to the party. She wore a dark pink
suit, pearls. Her skin—it's so lovely—absolutely glowed. You know,
it's so strange: Since my father died, she'd been growing more and*

*more beautiful. At sixty, she looked youthful, her hair swinging in a kind of shiny salt-and-pepper bob. She laughed like a little kid—her whole body moved around.*

*I introduced her to Q and spent the rest of the party watching them fall in love. I was mesmerized. It was like watching a movie. Millie laughed her great laugh; Q pushed his glasses up the bridge of his nose with his index finger, closing his eyes, leaning in to make an animated point. Then they toasted each other, clinking their glasses together in front of the cheery fire leaping in its stone grotto.*

*"What an amazing man!" Millie cried in the car on the way home. I was driving, a little drunk—I remember being so hunched over my chin almost rested on the wheel. It was a cold starry April night. Everything outside looked eager—the black march of the lampposts, the first electrified shocks of green green grass, waiting to be frozen out or sweetly engaged with the season: stunned to the roots by spring.*

*"I see now why you think so highly of him," she said. She leaned over and touched my wrist. "And sweetheart, he thinks the world of you."*

*So I got to see it, like a formula, a balanced equation—two people I loved fell in love. I could relive a little history of human chemistry. I was permitted to see my mother young again, laughing, swinging a pocketbook. I got to see Q controlling a kind of joyful goofiness. He pursed his lips at odd moments and reddened, as if he was compressing a huge burst of laughter. He took off his glasses and rubbed his eyes, as if he didn't believe what he saw before him. Then he'd go dutifully back to work—and quit early! To take my mother to a Pops concert!*

*I started applying for jobs—it was time. I wanted to go to Southern California because it was unlike anything I could imagine. It might as well have been the moon. I wanted to get away from my mother, Q, Cambridge, the familiar labs. I wanted a life that belonged entirely to me. Once I had wanted an academic reputation; now I simply wanted out.*

*When I was hired by the University of Greater California, UGC, I was a little stunned. Now I'd done it. UGC is big, but its chemistry and biochemistry faculties are highly inbred. In fact, in my area of biochemical research, the department was made up entirely of men. But I didn't care if I'd been picked to fill a demographic requirement. I cobbled together a most peculiar situation at UGC. Though I was trained as a biochemist, with advanced work in molecular biology, I asked, as a special request, to teach undergraduate Organic. I wanted to prove to myself (and Q) that I could hug the earth and theorize. I wanted (I thought) to inspire the young with some kind of politics or rather, (god help me!) some sense of* honor *in a scientific age that goes without. At the same time, I didn't want to just transmit the politics I'd contracted from Q.*

*What I really needed was time to* think—*and fortunately there was some time for that built in. The one thing I did right was to insist that I not be involved in grant-seeking or fund-raising—from the government or the private sector. Some professional, hired by the university, could advertise my work to potential backers. I wanted to walk in my lab* and work, *walk in my classroom* and teach—*not hustle for bucks.*

*One night before I left Cambridge, my mother telephoned.*

*"I can't talk long, Mom—I've got a lot of writing to do on this manuscript. And I really haven't analyzed my data."*

*Mom was feeling terrible. She said she felt awkward bringing it up, but she'd been thinking about my "friendship" with Q and she wanted me to know that if her relationship with him caused me any anxiety, she'd end it.*

*I asked her if she was suggesting that I had a thing going with him.*

*"I'm not implying anything, Esme. He seems to think you might be feeling a little displaced."*

*This pissed me off. I remember throwing down the novel I'd been*

*reading instead of rewriting my manuscript for my last publication*
*as a postdoc. It was Charles Baxter's* First Light, *one of my all-time*
*favorites, and it pissed me off even more that the book lost pages as*
*it slid across the floor.*

*"Well, that's certainly fucking arrogant."*

*"Esme . . ."*

*"Mom. There's nothing between Q and me, except scholarly re-*
*spect. All on my part, of course. To him, I'm just a grunt, a slavey.*
*If you're attracted to him, that's great. I've never been, I swear. I*
*don't know, Mom, have you looked really closely at his ears?"*

*So then I had to face him, had to go in to his office and have it out*
*with him. All this time, I'd been avoiding him, making excuses, exiting*
*the lab when he arrived.*

*I knocked at his door, then pushed it open. He was startled to see*
*me, and he struggled to get up from his overstuffed chair. He began*
*wheezing and barking, rearing way back—he had a lot to say, it*
*seemed.*

*I held up my hand. "I am not in love with you."*

*I shrugged out of my knapsack, filled as usual with about forty*
*pounds of Xeroxed journal papers, and I dropped it with a big thud*
*on the floor. I went over to the window and looked out at the sunny*
*quad. I'd rehearsed everything that I was going to say and I didn't*
*want to screw it up. I turned around and faced him.*

*"I am not in love with you, but I am* suffering *because of you.*
*I couldn't say why for a long time, and now I've finally figured it*
*out. It's not you and my mother, I find all that kind of charming.*
*I figured out that what's really disturbing me is the way you*
*think."*

*Q sat absolutely still, for once unblinking, unwheezing.*

*"Go on, please," he said. His phone buzzed; he reached over and*
*clicked a button that held all his calls.*

*"Not long ago you told me that this work may be too emotional for me. I didn't understand what you meant. Now I do. I've always believed that science requires its practitioners be in a state of despair, informed despair. The problem with you is . . ."*

*What energy one derives from defiance! It fueled my speech, it filled my body, till I felt I was taller, stronger. He watched me, growing before his eyes.*

*"Look, Q, the problem is—you are too fake-hopeful—that's what screwed me up. You are full of this* crap, *this Romanticism of Science. We're not just investigating the nature of matter, but saving people as well. Affecting culture, determining the Good. How did all this social enlightenment creep into the lab? That's what I want to know. Did it come in with the big grant money, when molecular biology got so sexy?"*

*Q stood up, a little shakily, pushing at his glasses. He had a very long, fine-lipped mouth. He opened it, then closed it again.*

*Some students went by in the hall outside, laughing raucously, calling out to each other. For a second, the sun went behind a cloud, the room darkened, and all you could hear was their voices, calling. "Erik? Jackson! Erik? Come on, let's go!"*

*I found this a good moment to pick up my knapsack.*

*"I just want to be able to* think. *You know, maybe I'm not made for this bench work after all. Maybe I'm not such an egalitarian grunt; I don't believe I can save everybody in the fucking world. I want them saved but* I *can't do it—can you? MS, cystic fibrosis, AIDS . . . can you? Why are you pretending you can?"*

*Q sat down again. He looked more in control, though he let go a wheeze that sounded like a loose fitting on a radiator valve.*

*"You need to feel like this," he said. The desk phone buzzed again. "It's OK, Esme."*

*"Thank you for being my teacher, Professor Quandahl. But please don't patronize me ever again."*

*I paused in the doorway.*

*"You know what else I think, Prof Quandahl? I think the DNA industry is* hype. *DNA can't catalyze reactions on its own; why is everybody pretending it* can? *It's like Prof Lewontin says, we've made it into a* map—*of this holy genomic kingdom of the future. The whole Human Genome Project smells of* myth: We'll fix everyone's genes, we'll never die! *You brag about being a* bench *scientist, but you insist on seeing genetics as* design, *intellectual insight as superior to physical—you don't like the biological working class, the cell assembly line." I stopped for breath. I was shaking.*

*"All of you guys, every molecular biologist in our acquaintance," I continued, "has some sort of financial investment in biotechnology. Everybody's cleaning up on the Genome Myth!" He opened his mouth, then closed it again and shook his head, dazed.*

*"You're not going to let me talk at all, are you?"*

*I told him that I'd been listening to him for years. "It's my turn now," I said. "I'm entitled."*

*"One last thing," I said, over my shoulder. "I don't want to hear this conversation played back from my mother's lips."*

*He found his voice.*

*"Conversation?"*

*"Well, monologue then."*

*"I'll do whatever you wish, Esme."*

*I turned around again. I just couldn't seem to get out the door.*

*"You do make a great couple. I wanted to be the first to tell you that."*

*He smiled, then his secretary buzzed through the Hold. He inclined his head toward the speaker and it gave me some satisfaction knowing that when he looked up, I'd be gone.*

*Q was not the only one I said good-bye to. There was Jesse Falbo. Jesse was my roommate; he wanted to be my buddy—but he did best* as my lover. He was my lover during a time when a lover seemed an unnecessary complication, during the height of my lab research. But in fact, most of the time his presence soothed me, he made my life easier for me.

He was the one who did the imitation of Q's cough. More than anything, I think, I must have needed someone who could put Q in perspective for me. Jesse was the guy. He was completely irreverent. Harvard Med School had only made him more of what he was coming in: a tough Italian guy from Worcester, a jock, a deadpan joker, anarchist, son of a milkman, summer-upper, lover of solutions— occasional bar brawler when all other solutions failed. He was one of the med fellows at the institute and he'd discovered it delighted him to give me trouble—but I didn't mind. Unlike Q's criticism, Jesse's seemed like ragging from a sibling. Jesse I could handle, I thought.

We said good-bye in a Thai restaurant. Our drinks came with hibiscus blossoms floating in them. I put my blossom in my hair and immediately sneezed.

Jesse looked down at his shirt. "Amazing aim," he said. "You got snot all over me."

"Don't wash. It's the last time you'll get any of my bodily fluids on you." I was leaving, driving to California in the morning. I thought I couldn't wait.

"Last?" He raised his eyebrows. "The very last?" I looked at him, then at his hand resting on the table. It leaped into a focus of terrible anatomical clarity: bones and blood vessels beneath the skin: a clear throbbing map.

"Listen, Jesse, I'm getting sick. I keep sneezing. Or I'm allergic to this."

I stabbed with my chopstick at the hibiscus, which had landed in my plate, then speared it and waved it in his face.

"Watch out with that thing. It's pollinating. I've noticed a dis-

*turbing tendency in you toward hypochondria this last month or two. You say you're sick all the time; you actually skipped lab five or six times. Does it have anything to do with your mother and Spock?"*

I didn't say anything. A waitress brought our appetizer: chicken and pork saté with peanut sauce.

"I am sick. I've been getting migraines and I have a terrible pain in my heart."

"Yeah. Don't we all."

I did feel sick, but I picked up a chicken saté, dismantled it, and ate it, thinking irritably that he was right about the hypochondria. I'd had all my symptoms checked out and felt disappointed to learn that there was nothing wrong with me. But I couldn't seem to ever feel good these days; I'd get up and fall back into bed, exhausted, unfocused.

The waitress scurried around, bowing, lighting little candles in translucent lotus cups. Jesse leaned into the glow as he ate, and his features took on an eeriness, like a kid's face above a flashlight.

"Listen, Esme."

His underlit face and the deadpan tone made me perk up as I chewed.

"OK." He took a deep breath. "There's a feeling *in the air here. You feel it as well as I do. It's not that you're leaving, it's how you're leaving. This . . .*" He waved his hand back and forth between us. "*. . . doesn't get it. You're just gonna* disappear? *Huh? Hey,* talk to me about it, that's all."

His face moved out of the candle power and he noticed that I was laughing. I couldn't help myself. I put my head down and shook. The whole table shook. It had taken him a while to notice; had he thought I was weeping? The image of Jesse as ministering angel somehow made me giddy. But not because it was so farfetched. Because it was true. When I slept next to him, I felt safe.

*The waitress came with more food, covered the table with steaming platters. Jesse sat across from me, looking astonished. When I look back, I can call up the expression on his face; he must have known that I was faking him out. I sat, wiping my eyes, trying to control my laughter, which sounded phony now, even to me.*

*"I'm sorry," I said. "I don't feel that* bad. *Just* peculiar."

*There was a long silence. Jesse put down his chopsticks and picked up the hibiscus I'd thrown down earlier. It had furled itself into a tight cocoon, which he unrolled now carefully, pressing it flat with his fingers. I've always thought fallen hibiscus blossoms look like tiny shrouds, little dead babies littering the ground. This thought nearly sent me off into panicky, morbid laughter again, but I overcame it. We both stared at the blossom in his hand—unwrapped, gently wrinkled as human skin. His fingers traced the inward spiraling center around the stamen. This embarrassed me even more. His hands were deft, he was going to be a surgeon. They were always scrubbed clean, I noticed, unlike my own, hopelessly stained with lab muck.*

*I started to apologize again, but he touched my hand to stop me. "Forget it," he said. "Let's just leave it alone for a minute."*

*I sat there thinking about him and how, right from the beginning, I'd found myself infatuated with him. He'd come stealing into my heavily guarded thoughts; walking home from the lab one cool night, my mind immersed in contemplation of immunodetection of tyrosine phosphorylation on protein 70K, I rounded a corner and there he was. I'd seen him before at seminars or occasionally in a bar—we knew each other just a little.*

*He was playing basketball on a playground with some other guys. Under the arc lights, he leaped and turned, sweating, a baseball cap bill-back on his head. There was the staccato thump of the ball against asphalt, panting, cursing, the small brutal sound of rubber soles braking, squealing over cement. The whole thing looked choreographed: each player jumping, guarding, hollering, bobbing, flapping arms as if he could fly. Someone rising straight up in the middle like a jack-rabbit, lobbing the ball toward the hoop. I stood watching for a while. He pleased me, Jesse—watching him move, his dark-stained T-shirt pleased me, the sweaty rag hanging out of his back pocket pleased me, and his hair falling down over one eye. The sudden smile he threw over one shoulder, the rocketing ball beneath his hand as he pounded around the court. And I thought, What is this? Pleasure? Actual pleasure? I put my hand out, dazed, in back of me, like someone feeling for a familiar weapon, trying to locate the irony so readily, comically implicit in the situation, but somehow I couldn't put my hand on it. Desire: I admit that I was humbled by its power over me. When was the last time I'd leaned against a chain-link fence for so long that the diamond pattern stayed pressed hard into my cheek, when was the last time my heart pounded hard and a gold stream of warmth poured down the back of my neck like honey?*

*"I'm pretty sure I've been living inside my brain too long," was the first thing I said to him as he came around the fence after the game, panting and grinning.*

*So what had happened? What would the book of gene folklore tell us about our separate chemistries, why they'd reacted simultaneously? What genes had predestined us to feel delight in each other's presence, to lean into each other with lust and curiosity, to feel affectionate, languorous, vertiginous with desire? All that rush and tremor, I thought, for what? Good-bye in a Thai restaurant.*

*There was a pause. I sighed.*

*"Tell me what you're thinking about, Esme."*

*"DNA."*

*"What else?"*

*"Death."*

*"You know, Ez, after dinner with you I kinda look forward to autopsy lab."*

"*Don't be mad at me, Jesse,*" *I said through my teeth, which had suddenly begun chattering.* "*I'm doing my best. It's not Q and it's not hypochondria and it's not you and me. It's like a horror movie about chemical degeneration. I look at people and I watch them fall apart, fast forward. I think I can see what they'll die of.*"

*I put my head down. I really wasn't feeling very well. What I'd said was true but there was more. I was having nightmares, not just about everyone's DNA, a* dead *inert molecule, after all—so dead that you could thaw out a mastodon and still read its genetic info like a report card, but about all of us, all the sad people like me who never had the language, the words to ease fate. And I* had *come to believe that some of Nature's mistakes, the slipups, were fate. But that made my destiny and my inability to describe it all the more ghastly. I couldn't even be* funny *about it. Man, I was really going crazy, I thought. I had to get out of Cambridge.*

"*C'mon,*" *he said,* "*look at me, tell the Nobel Committee, what do you see?*"

"*Well, Jesus, I'm not going to tell you what I think you're going to die of, Jesse.*"

"*No. Just tell me, what do you see?*"

"*A guy.*" *I smiled.* "*A nice guy I'll never see again.*"

"*And what do you think I'll die of, a broken heart?*"

*I looked up and laughed.* "*No. No, of course not.*"

"*Well, maybe I will. Maybe I won't.*"

*I sat back in my chair and stared at him.* "*You won't.*"

"*You* know *what I like about medicine? What* every *decent doc likes. Being right there in the swamp: the emergency room, triage. No, really, don't laugh, I do. I'm in the ball game. You people, you blender jockeys, sit around splicing and snipping and staining slides, looking at squiggles in microscopes and deducing profundities. Looking for St. Germ. Saving St. Germ. Some tiny little organism, some protein sequence that's going to change the quality of human life, but only intellectually, only as a model for* thought."

"*Only as a model for understanding.*"

"*Understanding* it, *not* people."

"*Jesse? I'm sorry, really. I've got to go home and* pack."

*He nodded at me, then signaled the waitress, who tiptoed over to whisper that there was absolutely no MSG in our food tonight. We thanked her. After she'd collected some plates and disappeared, Jesse covered my hand with his.*

"*I want to thank God for what little chemistry there is left that you don't know about.*"

"*In that case, thank you, God, for Jesse,*" *I said, and raised my glass with my other hand. But even as I looked at him, then shyly away, certain we'd sleep together one last time before I got into my car the next morning and drove west—I felt the sense of stasis, the torpor certain expectations of intimacy evoke. His hand on mine implied that there had been something more than heat between us. I wanted to believe it had just been heat. I had to. However, I'd have to collaborate, at least for tonight, in this revised version of our history. I winked and put the hibiscus back in my hair. I smiled. I drank my drink.*

*Then the bill came and I watched him pay, thinking about nothing at all except starting my car, turning the corner for the last time, thinking about what the light would look like in the early morning. In my mind, I saw the shadows part; then I drove into them. They stretched, then covered my car like black, moving water.*

## Chapter 5

My afternoon lab students were at work on the Grignard Effect (named for the illustrious chemist Victor Grignard)—trying to make it happen in the lab. It was a synthetic reaction requiring some sophistication of technique; the task was to make a large molecule out of two smaller ones. The difficulty was always the same: getting the thing started. The reaction is very sensitive to moisture; traces of water in the flask or solvent will stop it cold. I looked around the lab; light filtered in from above and there was this insistent green *ringing* sound: fifty glass rods beating inside fifty glass tubes, mixing up the reagents.

I love Organic lab, I love coming down the hall, past the ice makers, the balance room with its computerized scales, the heavy solid melting-point apparatus—and waltzing into the lab, wearing the clear goggles everyone wears to protect the eyes from corrosive vapors, chemical splashes. The air stinks gently of sulfur and acetone and a hundred other chemicals, a sweet rotten smell circulating around and through the ducts, up to the roof and out. Even the make-up air system, pumped through the air-conditioning and heating ducts, can't get rid of that musty odor. Each work space under its fume hood looks like some kind of kitchen altar, with its bright silver fittings for steam and cold water, each with a vacuum line, thermal well, heating mantle, Claisen reactor, rack of tubes, microscope. I love enumerating the lab's infinitely patient, self-contained components: the centrifuge, the big cupboards filled with large brown bottles of butanol, chloroform, chlorobenzene, nitrophenol, the sink with its gallon jugs of acetone for cleaning hands and glass fittings, the flameproof vacuum-storage cabinet, the safety shower. I would never compare entering the lab to entering a church, yet the lab glows with an unmistakable aura of prefigurement and awe—the ducts and tall flasks stand like holy effigies, the distillation apparatus and rubber tubing swing from hooks like ornate censers; it is a sealed-off world touched by grace. A place of reverse miracles—miracles happening in a controlled state.

I paused under the fume hood of Albert Chang, one of my best students. He had completed the experiment and documented the reaction with remarkable speed. There before our goggled eyes was a round-bottomed flask in which ether boiled below the core temperature of the human body at ninety-five degrees Fahrenheit. We stood staring at the murky low-level bubbling and I patted Albert on the shoulder. He smiled at me shyly, one side of his mouth turned up.

"Nice work, Albert."

I looked at his carefully handwritten notes next to the flask. Under the headings PURPOSE, REACTION, APPARATUS, PROCEDURE, OBSERVATION, and DATA, he'd written exactly what he'd caused to happen. And how. I pulled off my goggles and read the notations with interest: not a wasted word.

There was a loud glassy crash across the lab. I put down Albert's lab book and hurried toward the noise. Here was another one of my students, Donald Brandeman, who'd come up to me after class recently and told me that I was "wasting precious time" by airing my political views in class. Donald was a tall, handsome, blank-faced boy with sculpted, metallic hair and an irritatingly expansive manner. When I tried to talk to him privately, he always insisted on drawing others, his pals, into the conversation. He was a frat boy, a competitive swimmer; he wanted to be a successful scientist employed by a large corporation with government contracts and he wanted an end to my "unnecessary digressions," as he put it. I found clichéd behavior amusing, because I always *assume* the presence of irony, but after a while, it occurred to me that Donald Brandeman was very earnest.

I was used to getting along with my students. It surprised me that he disliked me so intensely and, though I'd never have admitted it, it hurt my feelings. I had overheard him telling his friends in the hallway just outside my office that UGC was sorry they'd hired me, but they "had to have a woman" for Affirmative Action reasons and now they were stuck with me. "She doesn't *produce*," I heard him say, "not like the male professors."

I was sensitive on the subject of my career at UGC. I was a hotshot from the East when they hired me, a demon gene-splicer, on the synthetic-protein trail; since I'd married Jay and given birth to Ollie, my research had moved to the back burner, my reading and lab time dwindled. I'd sat in my office for a long time after taking in the boy's comments, which I knew had been destined for my ears. I sat there until it got dark.

As I approached him, Donald Brandeman looked coy. There was shattered glass at his feet, but he made no move to pick up. Three of his ever-present companions, coughing into their hands and shrugging, backed away as I came up. One of them snapped the straps of his goggles like a rubber band.

"What happened here, Donald?"

"Aaaah, Prof Charbonneau, I don't know." He hung his head and glanced sideways at his pals. "I broke a standard taper joint, I guess. It leaped right out of my hand."

"How?"

"How? Umm, well . . . hmmm, good question." There were muffled snorts of laughter behind him. "Yeah, good question. Well, I was having some trouble getting the . . . male and female fittings together, you know." The laughter grew. "And I was trying to stick the male into the . . . female and it wasn't, you know, sliding right in . . . so I got some, whaddayacallit, stopcock joint grease here and it just got me so slippery, Prof, you know, the stopcock grease lubricant and the glass fitting shot right out of my hand like a . . . well, um, I don't know what . . ." The pals were rocking with laughter now.

"Shut up," I said calmly. "Not one of you goons is going to pass this semester, so how 'bout hauling ass back to your hoods and boiling some water. Maybe you'll be able to keep house when you flunk out of college. I'm talking to *Brandeman* here, not you guys."

The pals shuffled apart; there was a mumble or two, then quiet as they returned to their places.

"What you were doing here," I said, "had nothing to do with Grignard, did it?"

"Well, Prof . . ."

"You guys were just having a little fun, right?"

Donald Brandeman looked back at me with an absolutely contemptuous face. His skin had a filmy sheen to it, I noticed, wondering if his rigorous daily immersion in chlorine had given him a permanent subcutaneous gloss. His hair gleamed mutedly, slick and swirled as batter.

"Prof, I have to ask you something. Do you think you swear a lot—I mean, for a woman?"

"I *do*, Donald. I do swear a lot, it's true. So often I forget I'm around sensitive ears like yours."

I smiled at him; the look of hatred on his face was riveting.

"Wait a minute, Donald—now don't be coy! Have you actually *found me out*? I mean, my thing for *testosterone*. So I take a little in a vein every now and again, so *what*, huh?"

His eyes narrowed. "Is this supposed to be one of your famous jokes?"

"Donald, Donald, Donald. You really need to develop a sense of humor. As a matter of fact, that's exactly why I added the synthetic estrogens to the stopcock joint grease you ended up smearing all over the taper joint! I just had a feeling you'd end up . . . coating yourself. You don't have to worry, Donald. The changes you'll notice at first will be *small*—subtle tapering, developing curves, trill in the voice, that sort of . . ."

He cursed under his breath.

"*What,* Donald? Now don't get *upset,* sweetie. If you need help from one of the *guys* cleaning this up, let me know!"

I smiled and turned away. There was a great deal of banging and crashing as he swept up the glass. When he'd finished, he tore his goggles off and hurled himself through the lab's double doors and out into the hall.

"My, my," I said, looking up. "Grignard seems to have gotten everybody *wild* today."

Later that day I was called into the department chairman's office. I'd been expecting this summons: One of my students had reported back to me that Donald Brandeman had "gone to the top" about my conversation with him in the lab.

The chairman was on the phone as I came in, and he indicated a chair. I faced him across the large, littered expanse of his desk. At the edge of the desk was a cluster of tiny glass beakers filled with synthetic flowers. I liked this touch. There were photographs of children, framed degrees, an Escher print, an African mask, a photo of Heinz Pagels shaking someone's hand. I looked at each wall hanging three times as his phone conversation droned on. It was getting late. I had to be at the nursery school at four-thirty to pick up Ollie. I glanced at my watch and shifted in my chair.

He signaled to me that he would be just another second and I smiled stiffly at him. His name was Walter Faber and he headed a department that he described, at faculty meetings, as a "department for the millennium." Teaching and research went hand in hand, he said. Publication and research went hand in hand, and grants and research also went hand in hand. I began to wonder if research was an octopus—how many hands did Chairman Faber think it had?

He hung up the phone and nodded at me. Then he opened a drawer and pulled a cigarette from a leather pack, which he held out to me.

"No thanks," I said, though I would have liked one. I didn't want to relax too much here. The old nervous pain in my chest was back anyway, and if I looked too long in Chairman Faber's eyes, especially his left, wandering eye, I began chemically deconstructing the whole ocular structure. No, it was better that I didn't smoke.

"I hope you don't mind if I *do*," he said. "The wife goes crazy if I smoke at home, so I indulge myself once in a while here."

"Please go ahead."

I found myself staring involuntarily at his eye. It was clearly a neuro-muscular problem. Maybe the nerves controlling his ocular muscles had been wired all wrong in a developmental screwup. I pictured Faber as an embryo with a huge bulging eye, sealed shut. Then his developing neurons extended, pale tendrils from the nascent brain tissue, feeling around for the bits of protoplasm needed to form ocular muscle. I noticed that the glycosylated road maps drawn glittering through the lobe (cells migrate along the sugar trails!) looked a bit askew; one or two neurons weren't going to connect right! A microscopic mistake in the map—and here was Faber with his spinning eye.

He lit the cigarette, popped the match in an ashtray, and in a constricted voice, as smoke rippled up, masking his face and seeping into my nostrils, he asked me what was going on between me and Donald Brandeman.

"What's going on between us? I don't understand."

"Well, I certainly don't either, Esme. I don't know why the hell this boy would charge in here this morning all upset and ranting on about politics in your lectures, high jinks in your lab, and something about you having a sex-change operation and accusing him of being gay?"

I laughed and Walter Faber laughed too, never taking his eye off my face.

"The sex-change operation doesn't look like it *took* to me," he said. We continued laughing.

"Well," I said, "where to begin. A lot of charges there."

"Serious ones, too," he said. His tone changed suddenly, all humor gone from his face, which was long with a neat but full dark beard. He actually looked a little like Abraham Lincoln, but a mildly psychotic Lincoln. His eye rolled like a security camera scanning the premises.

"Serious?"

"He's complaining about *politics* in your lectures; he feels you're proselytizing or something. Can you explain what's upset him so much?"

"Occasionally, I introduce . . . moral considerations into my lectures. I've been thinking a lot about this lately. I'm not sure myself what form ethical inquiry should take but I feel that I have to say something about responsibility in science: personal, social. These kids have never been exposed to that idea, *no one* has been talking to them about this."

"And?"

"And . . . that's it."

"Esme. I would have to do more investigating to determine exactly what we're talking about here, but my first impulse, being candid, is to agree with Donald Brandeman. You were not hired as an ethics specialist, a philosopher, if you will. You were hired as a professor of biochemistry and molecular biology, who desired to teach organic chemistry. Period. These students pay tuition to take courses from you in Organic or Biochemistry—not Sociology or Philosophy."

The pain in my chest was increasing. I took a deep breath. "I know that."

"Then we agree?"

"No. I don't expect we do. I think we have a disagreement here. My problem is I'm supposed to pick up my little girl at nursery school at four-thirty and it's three-forty-five now. Could we continue this discussion tomorrow?"

He looked annoyed.

"I'm booked solid tomorrow. No appointments open. I suppose I can *summarize* my concerns quickly here. The university has never been in favor of professors preaching special interests in our class-rooms. Look, Esme. I *know* a lot of this is lighthearted. You're a funny person, I *get* it! I appreciate a joke as much as the next guy. You're being provocative, outrageous, but I have to request that you stop. We have a tradition to uphold here."

"I would like to talk more about this. If not tomorrow, some other time. I'll make an appointment with your secretary. I'm only asking that my students *think* about a few things. Just for discussion's sake. I don't want them to just mouth politically correct positions, be-lieve me."

"Esme, are you aware that there are university courses, in other departments, that speak to current questions about the environment? 'Science and Modern Values,' in Soc, for example. . . . You have a set syllabus, with a lot of material to cover in a semester and no time for woolgathering."

"I've got to go," I said desperately. I stood up and turned toward the door.

He called after me. "One other thing, Esme . . . please don't change your sex on us."

I turned around, waiting for the inevitable.

"Don't do it. We have a hell of a time from Affirmative Action as it is. We don't want to start all over again!"

I looked back at the peripatetic eye, rolling behind a cloud of new-blown smoke. "Thanks," I said. "I like feeling needed."

I checked my watch as I ran out to the parking lot. I was going to be late picking up Ollie. The teacher would be standing at the door, Ollie beside her, holding the Princess She-Ra lunchbox her grandmother had given her, talking to herself. The teacher would be furious, she had her own kids to get home to, she had to face the traffic too, but she would not show this anger. I would apologize, over and over, and the teacher, Sasha, would say it was OK. But it wasn't, I could see it now. This was not OK.

## Chapter 6

It was late morning and I was watching Ollie dance in the living room. Ollie moved from side to side, wearing her painted TV box on her head. Abruptly she took it off and set it down, patting it like a dog. Then she barked at it a couple of times. Then she began to whirl in earnest, at first turning stiffly, then picking up speed. She circled near the floor fan and her little plaid shorts and top filled with air. She kept up a soft, running commentary on her actions as she spun around: "Ollie turning Ollie turning Ollie turning Ollie turning Ollie turning Ollie tired Ollie tired sitting down Ollie sitting down Ollie up Ollie up!" She spun herself around again, then circled toward the front door, opened the screen door, went outside on the steps, and sat down. She was motionless in the bright sun, staring out at the street. For the moment, still.

I put down my coffee cup and crossed the room, pulling aside the thin muslin curtain at the porch window. Her profile was as pale and stoical as a small household deity. Her eyes and her full lips were closed, dreamy. Then the angle of light changed; she turned reddish-gold, almost *pink,* her skin and hair acquired a neon quality. More cars went by. Outside it was quiet, but filled with L.A.'s silent sound, a contained momentousness, like a concert orchestra, bows raised, about to play. A pom-pom of dried palm fronds fell with a rustle. She began talking to herself again. The sprinklers had left a small leaf-filled puddle on the walk; Ollie got up and moved toward it. She picked up a stick and lifted a dollop of bird shit from the grass and dropped it into the puddle. She dropped the stick and knelt down to watch the glossy green and white guano spiral apart in the dim water. Then she returned to her seat on the porch steps.

I dropped the thin curtain, opened the door softly, stood quietly behind her on the steps, in her shadow. Then I sat down beside her. The beagle from next door came halfway up the walk and stood staring at us uncomfortably. He always looked to me like a tiny man trapped in a dog costume.

Ollie looked at him but continued mumbling: "Cat comes gold cat gold cat no car two cars two cars come swim trees swim leaves up side of trees gold cat cat cookie dead cookie . . . Mamma, this cookie died?"

She turned to me; her face struggled for an expression. She looked down and I followed her gaze. Someone had dropped a partially eaten chocolate chip cookie on the sidewalk. It was covered with ants.

"No, honey, it's not dead. It's just turning into breakfast for these ants."

Ollie stood up, placed herself in front of me, staring straight into her eyes, her small strong hands gripping my shoulders. I felt surprised, as I did almost every time I looked into Ollie's eyes. How unfamiliar her expressions were, yet instantly recognizable: the real physical embodiment of thinking, a consciousness at work on its surroundings. A face that reflected thought was always mobile, rarely organized itself into expression, I thought, and Ollie's face flickered, flickered and burned before me.

"But where are the *wheels* of the cookie? And the bad ones who shoot bees and snow?"

"The wheels?" But she was off again, a *new* question.

"Mom, the air stops? It goes up to the blue and stops?"

"No. Air and sky are the same, Ollie. Air just goes up high and is sky. It gets thinner as it goes up."

"No, Mom. This air in my hand, in this minute, is not blue."

"The sky looks blue to us because of light, the way our eyes see light."

Ollie stared at me, her eyes impatient, then patient, trying to understand. She continued holding my shoulders; she twitched a little.

"I see light in you."

I felt her wholeness—nothing moved away from me, irretrievable, in Ollie, knew Ollie shored herself up against me, Ollie rose and swelled in the rhythm of my breath. Yet Ollie could fly, could leap suddenly and reappear light-years away, on a branch over a ravine, and I could not cry out, or run to her, extend a hand—I had to wait, breathing quietly, for her to return intact. I waited, asking myself how I dared to know what I knew about Ollie—that she was sound, odd but sound. My own certainty about this somehow made me doubt myself: maybe *I* was bad, a bad mother, visiting my own failures on my child? Maybe I was lying to myself. But how was it possible that Ollie could have been hurt without me knowing it—or that I might have hurt her myself, without intending to? It was not possible, I knew this. Then how had nature touched Ollie, marked her? How had nature intended that I see Ollie's strangeness, in what context? Gifted genetically, wounded genetically, transfigured by the mind or devoured by it? I felt tears suddenly on my face, and began to cry softly as Ollie stood, facing me, her hands on my shoulders. Then I bent forward, Ollie murmuring; she climbed into my lap and we rocked, rocked slowly together for a long time on the step, Ollie humming her little song, me crying as if the tears, once they'd started, would blot out everything—a flood that sprang up from the beginning of my life.

———

Jay came home early that day and we all piled in the car and took off for the beach. It was one of those slow-building hot days, patch-smoggy but mostly hazy. A smell of dry herbs, rosemary and sage, filled the air.

Jay wore cutoffs and a Dodgers baseball cap. He drank a Bud as he drove, the can warming between his hairy thighs.

"N-nice day, huh?"

He smiled at me warily. I nodded.

"H-how about I try out a routine on you as we drive?"

I reached over and touched his leg.

"Jay. It's a beautiful day."

He looked abashed, then philosophical.

"H-how you doin', Ollie?" he asked softly, his eyes in the dashboard mirror.

"Two dreams. Three dreams."

"Way to g-*go*."

The jeep tooled along—we didn't speed. The Santa Monica Freeway wasn't full, just a few cars, and the ocean appeared on our left in record time—that breathtaking curve of horizon and sea.

"Look, Ollie, look. The sea!"

She put her nose to the glass and smiled. She liked the ocean.

"It is never too hot to be the sea."

"Huh?"

"Wait, Jay. What do you mean, Pickle?"

"It is never too hot. So Ollie is hot."

"Is Ollie hot?"

"I am very hot, I am talking in the red language."

"The red language?" Jay sat up straighter, worried. "Sweetheart, can you tell Daddy what you m-mean by the red l-language?"

"All the very hot words."

"Oh. What's a *hot* word?"

"*Hot.* And wind-without-corners. A red bite which grows and grows over your tummy. When I cry bird that's very hot too. I fell down."

There was another silence.

I poked Jay again, smiling.

"Nice view of that old not-so-hot sea, huh?"

He shook his head and we turned into a parking area.

We carried blankets to the flat sand by the waves, along with a cooler and the beach bag loaded with suntan oil, zinc oxide, sunglasses, Handi Wipes, vitamin C, spray-on Evian, Matchbox cars, pop-up books, and Ollie's dragon. Jay set up the big striped umbrella and we all lay down, half in and half out of the shade, and listened to the tide coming in, the big thundering rolls. They didn't quite reach us, but every once in a while, cool spray settled on us. Ollie would scream and jump up and run away to dig in the sand for a while.

Jay was lying on his stomach, half asleep. After a while he rolled over and stared at me.

"Do you understand her when she talks?"

I shrugged. "Not always."

He shut his eyes.

"I almost n-*never* understand her when she talks."

I waited.

"Last week she told me she couldn't eat her food because it was *tired*."

Again I waited, expecting the stand-up shoefall, but Jay wasn't, for once, being funny.

"I asked her what she meant and she just kept repeating that it was t-tired, tired food. Finally I said, trying to get into the spirit of this, should we put the l-lamb chop to bed? And she looked at me like I was nuts and basically said, 'Dad, it's a lamb chop, why would you p-put it in a *bed*?' "

I laughed. He didn't. He sat up, opened the cooler, and took out another Bud. He popped it, then rolled up a beach towel behind his head and lay back.

"Why can't she talk the way the rest of the world does? *Why* doesn't she say 'Hi, Daddy' or 'I want *a cookie*'?"

"Is that the way you *want* her to talk?"

He shot me a look. I noticed that he was tired. Daytime tech directing and stand-up nights were wearing him down. His Oxford-undergraduate look had given way to a wan, strained expression about the mouth and eyes. He pursed his lips as he looked at me, the unconscious pout of a man older than he, a prim, orderly man.

"Yes, I'd like it if I c-could understand my own daughter. A simple declarative sentence with a normal insight or t-two—'The sky's up, the earth's down'—would be a relief. I admit it."

I watched Ollie, who'd dropped her orange sand shovel and was following a huge seagull on scavenger duty—and sighed. As always, she whispered, a running account, in the third person, of what she was doing. "Ollie dig. Ollie dig. Ollie run. Bird going up. Ollie is big." She picked up handfuls of sand and piled them up, smoothed them. "Core," she said. "Mantle."

"I don't want anyone to hurt her," I said.

"Who's hurting her?"

"Nobody. I didn't mean that anyone is hurting her. I mean I think ahead to . . . possible situations in her life and I . . . just don't want them forcing her into some *pattern*."

"Esme, is she retarded?"

"Jesus, Jay. How can you ask that? Listen to the questions she asks. She's *thinking* all the time!"

"But her thoughts don't m-make sense! Ever!"

"Her thoughts make sense to *her*."

"Well, that's as g-good a definition of 'nuts' as I've ever heard."

"But look. She thinks along unexpected lines. She's escaped somehow a lot of the patterns that are imposed so early on kids. I mean, we never taught her accepted responses to things . . ."

"We never t-taught her anything."

"*I've* taught her things."

"What things?"

"I teach her some science. Some things about gravity, the planets. I show her when we water the plants how osmosis works, I explain the vacuum . . ."

"No wonder she's like this. I wish you'd just let her develop n-normally."

"You mean watch TV all the time?"

"I would prefer that to a weirdo who b-builds a TV and lives inside it."

We turned away from each other, avoiding a fight.

Ollie shuffled up, covered with sand, and I handed her a fruit-juice packet. Together we worked at inserting the straw and getting it to draw up the juice.

When the juice was functioning, Ollie rubbed her nose and then began to rock a little on her heels. Back and forth. She sang a song about the bird she'd been following. Jay sat up.

"Hey Ollie. Wanna take a walk with Daddy?"

"Daddy legs are dark and away."

"What?"

I laughed. The umbrella shade had cut off his legs at the thighs. His lower body was lost in darkness. I pointed to the shadow. Jay nodded, relieved.

"Let's g-go, Ollie."

He picked her up and she sat solemnly on his shoulders, bobbing a little as he plodded along through the sand. I lay back, letting the sun seep through me, watching the two-tiered person grow smaller and smaller as it headed up the beach.

There were a few people around. Nearby a young couple on a Ninja

Turtles towel tended a huge radio, a ghetto blaster. The radio generated a steady bass that reverberated for a while dizzyingly in the air, but the regularity of its beat made it inaudible finally—it erased itself. There was an occasional sharp noise: a car horn. Children arguing over a pail. Gull cries. I started to drift off.

Jay shook me gently awake. The sun was low and I felt a chill.

"You know what Ollie said to me?"

"What?" I sat woozily up and brushed sand from my legs.

"We were just *drifting* up the b-beach, wading, picking up shells —and I started trying out a few *very* very basic routines on her . . ."

"*Jay.*"

"Come *on.* You know I tried one of my . . . I don't know what to c-call them exactly—my weird Kiddie Stories? You know how I do the one about Santa Claus wearing fur, smoking, being overweight, b-breaking and entering . . ."

"Yes, yes . . ."

"Well, I started the one about Cinderella and her extended family and she *stopped* me. I was sitting down on the sand and she came up and put her hand over my mouth and she said, 'You know, Daddy, that's very nice, but I'm just not *happy* enough for all this.' "

Late that night, at home in bed, Jay asked me if I had coached her to say that. Of course not, I said. I asked him why he would doubt that Ollie came up with it on her own.

"Well, gee, h-have you noticed that she never says anything nearly that sophisticated?"

"Yes she does. Occasionally, she says something really amazing, profound. But only when she feels like it."

"That *is* amazing."

My head was partially buried under a pillow and Jay lifted the pillow and began to kiss my neck. I rolled over on my back and looked at him.

"I'm sorry," I said. "I'm just not happy enough for all this." He laughed. Then we were very quiet for a while; then Jay went to sleep. I got up, sat in the living room in the dark, and thought about Ollie, then about my mother, Q, and Walter Faber, in that order. I smoked some cigarettes and then it was dawn. I thought about how infinity was *tangible*. I was very tired, but I sat still as the furniture became visible and morning traffic noises started up in the street. The things I thought about, before I went to sleep sitting up in my chair, were times when I could slow my life down, go into a kind of trance; this made me—if not rapturous—close to *restored*. If I thought about slowing down, I paradoxically thought about running a race as a kid, I could feel that long-ago morning's air on my skin, I could feel the expectant surface of my skin and the miraculous engine of my nine-year-old body, in a steady pumping *cessation* of movement, moving fast but *suspended*, in my green hightop Keds; then I thought about a poem in French I'd learned in fifth grade: *"À Verdun, à Verdun, / mon petit cheval brun"*; I saw a woman's hands (my mother's?) working a lump of dough for half-moon cookies. We painted one half with white icing and the other with chocolate; I loved that line down the center: symmetry! Then I reconstructed a particular afternoon in the lab with Q when we'd made a discovery about a certain protein's phosphorylation—I'd gone jigging out into the hall, throwing my goggles up. Q was wheezing like a teakettle, laughing and coughing his famous cough. The final bit of euphoria had to do with Jesse: his face, the way it looked to me once when we were making love and I was on top. His hair was in his eyes and he was unshaven: it was early morning. The way he looked as he began to come: I remembered putting my mouth on his, I remembered a certain way he moved and how my body, surprised, responded—one long shudder, a sound, and then, very slowly, we came together.

# Chapter 7

I sat on the baby swings with the public-school kindergarten teacher. As we talked, we would swing a little, put a foot out, stop, swing a little, dragging the toes of our shoes in the dirt.

I liked this teacher. Her name was Gloria Walther and she taught kindergarten at the Sixth Street School of the L.A. Unified School District, where Ollie would be going next fall. We'd been talking for a while, me trying to explain Ollie, Gloria Walther trying to explain her kindergarten: the thirty-four children in each classroom, the lack of resources. She'd been working without an aide, without enough paper, textbooks, audiovisual aids, since Governor Reagan and Proposition 13 had gutted the California public-school system. There were many Korean and Spanish children in the school who could not speak English. Gloria Walther said she had bilingual parents to assist her in the classroom. Gloria herself had learned these languages.

I had visited her classroom and watched her in action, her eyes traveling everywhere in the room—reading group to coloring group to math manipulatives group to computer group, at work on the single, slightly rundown Apple.

I watched Gloria now as she talked, a solid, pretty black woman with cornrows, bright hazel eyes, a startling smile. As she talked to me, she checked out the playground—a little boy climbing the jungle gym, two girls on the seesaw. I saw her adding up, taking away: Who was where? Who stayed in, who came out? It was after school, but some parents hadn't collected their offspring yet. It was a mild autumn afternoon, with the sort of champagney breezes and clear air, the falling red leaf or two, that made me love L.A.—L.A. without smog, without gridlock traffic. A good day to drive fast 'round the curves on Mulholland; better yet, a good day to sit in a schoolyard on a too-small swing, reducing one's expectations. Letting things get smaller instead of larger, not thinking about any chemistry but the sweet chlorophyllation process of the tired and toxic trees of Los Angeles, $O_2$ rising from the leaves. I stared at a solitary small desk sitting by itself on the asphalt: An extra seat for Ollie? Or a sad little misfit? I brushed my hand over my eyes and listened to children calling to each other, Gloria Walther answering another teacher's shout, the seesaw complaining quietly, *sleep-night, night-sleep,* and the sound of a tennis ball pock-pocking against a wall in the adjacent yard.

Gloria Walther had been teaching for a long time. She was not put off by what I had to say about Ollie; she wanted to meet her. She and I shook hands; the chains of the baby swings rattled as we reached out to each other, then rattled again as we stood up.

"Everyone tells me Ollie should be in a private school," I said. "But the ones I've seen terrify me, their values seem so screwed up. At one of these schools, Ross Rossner is a parent. So, because he's president of a studio, he treats the kids to first-run adventure films, he throws parties for them at the studio. OK, *great,* but someone told me that he opens the door of the school in the fall—and that drives me crazy. If Marie Curie or Einstein opened the door of the school, or Freud, or Margaret Mead . . . *that would be appropriate*—but here's this guy representing education who's known for nothing but making a lot of money from big-market films and he opens the door of the *school?* What does this tell us about Los Angeles?"

Gloria Walther put her head back and laughed heartily.

"That it's a company town? Calm down, Esme. It will be OK. Ollie will be OK. Sixth Street will be her school and we'll love her here. And *I* open the door of my classroom."

I shook her hand and left, smiling, breathing deeply the freshened air.

I hadn't mentioned it to Gloria Walther but I'd actually taken Ollie and checked out a school for "highly gifted" children. It was called Ariston and prospective students had to score 148 or higher on the Stanford-Binet intelligence test to qualify for admission. Tests were given all year round, I assumed because so few children actually qualified to enter. I hadn't thought about the Stanford-Binet for a while, not since IQ tests started getting a bad rep for being monocultural and skewed to little middle-class minds. I remembered it vaguely as slightly outmoded—and wasn't it only yesterday that 135 or so was considered near-genius? I paged through the clunky prose of the Ariston brochure, numbing my distaste. Well, *somebody* was raising brainy tots. Ariston had acquired quite a sizable little population of whiz kids, including the offspring of some famous movie stars.

Ollie had a cold, but she was very restless around the house and when I asked her if she'd like to take a little test at a school, she said, "Think this is wind, guess and test. Coming fruit in the tree, Mom."

The avocado tree had bloomed again: we stood looking up at the dark-green glossy pears, pendulous and perfect, the sun leisurely fingering through the fat leaf-blades. Ollie smiled happily. "Light light," she said. "Trees test and test and fruit comes."

By some miracle there was no traffic and it happened that we entered the Ariston School's large high-ceilinged drafty lobby a few minutes early—we sat waiting on a leather couch as the pinched-faced receptionist typed and sighed, rustling papers. Ollie sniffled, breathing noisily through her nose, humming a little. I looked around. Trophies and plaques: speech contests, interscholastic science competitions, drama statuettes. Signs that said WE WON: WE'RE NUMBER ONE. I shivered, I felt like I was catching Ollie's cold and shakily fastened the top button of my pea jacket. I searched the walls: not a single child's drawing, random and miraculous—only some framed things in a glass case on a far wall labeled Prizewinning Student Art, all of it palely derivative of Great Masters, pre–twentieth century. A bird and jug, *nature morte*, ballerina, Quixote figure. All roughly the same. No dropped toys, no music, no spilled candy. I sneezed. Ollie smiled at me and burped loudly. The receptionist looked up, disapproving.

"Miss Oplesch says you may go in now."

A door in the near wall opened on cue as she spoke and a dowdily girlish person in a gold-and-brown plaid skirt, wide face, wide glasses, wide mouth, and a shellacked helmet of hair crooked her finger at us.

She waved Ollie into the room, then stepped in front of me. She was squat as a fire hydrant; I almost ran her down, just managing to swerve at the last second. The word *bouncer* swam before my eyes. I stared down into the brown roots of her gold hair.

"Oh, no, Mamma," she said. "We don't need you to help take a test."

I put my hand on the doorjamb. "Oh, no, of course not. But Ollie is—I just thought I'd get her settled . . ."

"No, Mamma," she repeated. "We don't need any help settling in. If Olivia tests in, she tests in. That's it."

I nodded as she closed the door in my face.

After half an hour (I was now feverishly sneezing and blowing my nose), the door opened again and Ollie ran crookedly out, zigzagging, then turning and leaping into my lap, burying her head in my jeans.

Miss Oplesch stood in her office doorway, looking attentive, as if she was hearing a sound in a higher register, like an animal. She crooked her finger at us again and when I pointed to myself, she nodded.

Inside her office I looked again for kid drawings and here, at last, there were some real primitive beauties: big heads, elongated houses, and turtle cars—but I couldn't shake the feeling that they were displayed as some sort of *evidence*. Miss Oplesch's master's degree in psychology was prominently mounted as was a baccalaureate degree from a well-known Catholic college.

Ollie sat on my lap, bouncing a little. I peered around her, suppressing a sneeze.

"Well," said Miss Oplesch. "We have a very unusual case here."

"I'm not surprised you say that. You see, I was going to explain about Oll . . ."

"I require no explanation. I simply *test*, Mrs. Tallich. And what these tests reveal about Olivia is quite . . . singular."

Silence. I was damned if I was going to say anything.

"Ariston gives the California Aptitude Test as well as the Stanford-Binet. The first only tells us what a child has been taught, the latter actually reveals intelligence quotient."

"Forgive me, I thought that IQ tests were only capable of measuring ten to fifteen percent of intellectual ability . . . so I wonder how you . . ."

Her look stopped me. "Your information is incorrect, Mrs. Tallich. It yields complete IQ information. And in Olivia's case, the CAT reveals that she has very little clearly organized knowledge—I mean this is a child who could not identify the shape of a teapot but recognized the word *electricity* as well as the word *number* and several others including *test*. When did you teach her to read?"

"I didn't. It's new to me."

Miss Olpesch narrowed her eyes at me; was I lying? I sneezed, fishing in Ollie's pocket for a tissue. She frowned and continued. Then

Ollie sneezed. Miss Oplesch flattened her flat figure against her chair-back, avoiding germs.

"At any rate, her Stanford-Binet *seemed* very high, higher than our minimum admission score. I say *seemed* because while her spatial aptitude looked high, her *verbal* is impossible to interpret exactly. This is a child who cannot recognize a teapot and put sentences together in any comprehensible fashion. Is she *acting* like this? She has absolutely no ability to *speak!*"

"I don't know the answers to these questions. I guess that's why I'm here with her. And she's never seen a teapot, because I usually brew my tea in the cup."

Ollie and I snuffled together. Miss Oplesch got up and stood at the door, shutting her eyes and offering her flat naked-looking face, covered with tiny pimples. It hurt to look at her, the way it pained one to behold the stippled, goose-bumped flesh of a starfish, torn untimely from a tidepool. She kept her eyes shut, quivering, as if she expected me to kiss her.

"Before any child is approved for entry into Ariston, an interview with Dr. and Mrs. Fleenarch is required." Her eyes were still closed, but her hand pointed toward a hallway. We moved in that direction, sneezing.

I pretended to sneeze again as we entered the offices of Dr. and Mrs. Fleenarch—in fact, I was suppressing a gasp. If Dickens had joined us at the millennium and cheerfully updated a few characters, I couldn't have imagined a more perfect re-creation of Mr. and Mrs. Squeers than the one before my eyes. Of course, each had been air-brushed, coiffed, and recolored in contemporary tints. Dr. Fleenarch was Squeers after a lot of dental work: caps and crowns, a jolly brisk tweeze of the nose hairs, a pat or two of men's pressed powder and some serious tweedy tailoring. But Mrs. Fleenarch was Mrs. Squeers behind the thinnest veil, peering out of her beady little shrike's eyes under Halloween eyebrows. She had made an attempt to make herself up in the mirror, reaching toward some dim, inaccessible cosmetic ideal, some half-grasped combination of glamorous and good, as if someone had tried to vigorously sketch, say, Kim Novak's features over Torquemada's in repose.

What child would ever climb on these laps, smile into these cold, depthless eyes?

Ollie cowered behind me. Miss Oplesch introduced everyone and I pulled Ollie into a chair before the huge desk. Dr. and Mrs. Fleenarch sat up straighter across from us and Miss Oplesch, after a brief whispered consultation with them, disappeared.

Dr. Fleenarch turned to me. His wife sat forward and stared at me, glanced briefly at Ollie, then stood up and vanished into an adjoining office, where I could make out her shadow and part of her profile in the doorway as she hovered, eavesdropping. Ollie sneezed and started to hum. Dr. Fleenarch ignored both of us for a while, he seemed intent on reading the front page of the L.A. *Times*. At last he looked up and asked me if I had any questions about Ariston School.

"Well," I said, "what sort of education do you provide for these children?"

He knit his brows. "They get a leg up," he said, "a leg up on Harvard or Yale. That I can tell you."

I couldn't think of another question.

"Now," he said. "I'd like to address my questions to . . . *Olivia* here, if you don't mind."

I said I didn't. My nose was running copiously. I asked if there was a rest room nearby and I patted Ollie's hand.

"Be right back, I promise."

She actually stayed in her chair, looking after me with huge questioning eyes. Dr. Fleenarch leaned forward.

"Now tell me, Olivia, how do you spell your name?"

"Your face makes a start and it hurts."

I listened to the silence as I fled. I heard him mumble something, then repeat his question. I turned quickly down a corridor, wandered a bit, gave up on the rest room, then retraced my steps past a classroom. I glanced inside. The teacher was occupied in the back of the room, bending over a student. I stared at the walls. Twenty-five versions of the same theme, all printed extremely neatly with the same beginning sentence: "The White House is the residence of our President." The kids appeared to be working on math problems in workbooks. There were *workbooks* everywhere: English, Math, Social Studies, Reading: but no *books*, no sets of encyclopedias, battered with page-turning, no hardcovers, no storybooks, no slim volumes of poetry. Drawings on a bulletin board, all the same, a computer-generated pattern, colored in, no crayon marks outside the lines. I spied a box of pop-up tissues, winked at a chubby little girl in the front row who was staring at me, and snagged a few. She looked shocked. I turned to leave, noticed that the teacher had misspelled the word *murmur* as "mermer" on a posted word list, WORDS TO USE INSTEAD OF SAID. I felt a rough tug on my sleeve. It was Mrs. Fleenarch.

"This way," she growled, and pointed me back toward the offices.

"I'm so sorry," I croaked, "I just wanted to find a . . ."—but she poked her index finger in my spine like a pistol and hurried me along.

"This way," she said again. "Visitors are not allowed in the classrooms."

When I came back, Ollie and Dr. Fleenarch were both staring at the wall. Mrs. Fleenarch vanished again.

Dr. Fleenarch looked up as I entered.

"This child," he said, jerking his head toward Ollie, "is English her *first* language?"

I nodded.

"I cannot follow this child. I asked her several times how she was and she spoke in a foreign language. I could not follow a word of what this child said."

I took Ollie's hand and we went to the door. I bowed at Dr. Fleenarch.

"It's Estonian," I said. "She speaks Estonian, but with a slight Honduran accent."

He blinked slowly.

"I see."

"Good-bye, Mrs. Fleenarch," I called to the shadow behind the door. Her profile jerked back, out of eyeshot.

Ollie and I ran to the parking lot, sneezing. At the car, I patted Ollie's head.

"You're a smart kid," I said. "Stick around and I'll show you what a teapot is."

She sneezed.


I drove home, where my favorite student, Rocky Salinas, was minding Ollie. When I came in, I found them in the kitchen, dyeing sand with food coloring. I'd been teaching Ollie the layers inside the earth; we'd taken an old empty aquarium and started from the inside out. We dyed the first layer of sand red and poured it into the aquarium as the core—then dyed succeeding layers yellow, green, and purple, stacking them one on top of the other. Rocky and Ollie were continuing work on this project. Through the aquarium glass, the earth—inner and outer core, mantle and crust—resembled nothing more than a runny cross-section of rainbow lasagna.

"You look tired," said Rocky as I came in, slipping a little on the sandy floor.

"You look bored." I knelt down and accepted the pink and green handful of sand Ollie offered me. There was sand in her hair and around her mouth.

"No, no, man—I *love* this. Maybe I could try it in lab, since I bombed out on every other procedure."

Rocky was having trouble lately in Organic; her grades had fallen and she couldn't seem to get anything to work for her. She set a pie tin of sand aside, looking preoccupied. She had so much curly dark hair that her face seemed overshadowed, a tiny planet surrounded by flames.

I didn't want to pry. I watched Rocky pick up her Walkman and her red bookbag; I stuffed some bills in her leather jacket pocket.

"Thanks, Rocky."

"Sure. Anytime." Rocky bent down and kissed Ollie, who was still at work, pouring orange food coloring from a large bowl to a small one. Ollie reached up quickly and touched Rocky's nose. Rocky laughed and smeared the orange dye all over her face. She was so pretty, I thought, tall and thin, coltish.

"Better than blush-on, right?"

"Rocky, you want a tissue? What's the matter?"

Rocky stood looking straight at me and made a strange noise, a muted cry. Her face was full of panic.

"I'm going to flunk out, I know it. I can feel it happening to me in this kinda *slow motion*. I just can't hack Organic, Prof."

"You know, Rocky? You shouldn't start thinking this way! This is what happens to women in Organic—they start out—"

"Please don't give me no big lecture, OK? I'm not all the women who ever took Organic. I'm *me* and I'm selectively fucked up."

I put my arms around Rocky. Her thin shoulders shook. "Would you like to stay to dinner, Rock? I don't know if Jay's going to make it, and it's only stew on the menu, but you're very welcome."

Ollie stood up, poured green dye over her head, and walked out. I indicated her with an extended hand. "And the *company*!"

Rocky hung her head. "I'm supposed to meet this *guy*."

"Selectively fucked up, huh?"

"Yeah, it's always *somebody*. But I don't feel *nothing*—I'm gettin' laid, that's it."

"There's a test tomorrow. Column work. But you know that."

"Oh yeah. I know that. I'm going to try and get in *real* early tonight." We looked at each other and laughed.

"Rocky. Please don't flunk out," I said. I felt close to tears myself. "I know you don't want to hear this, but you're gonna be a goddam depressing *statistic* if you do. I can help you, we can work a little extra in the lab, what do you think?"

"What I think is that I have to go give Lance a blow job. I mean *Troy*. Man, these *Anglo names*! This guy should be called Ski Mask."

She put her hand on my shoulder. "I'm going to try not to flunk out. But the thing is, I'm not as good as a lot of other ones in that class. I see it. Real clear. Maybe I should admit it, you know?"

"No. I don't think so. You just need a little tutoring."

"Good night, Prof."

I watched her drive off. Rocky had a little Austin, dented and rusted, but it gave her an aura of freedom, her radio blasting Bonnie Raitt. I envied that freedom for a split second, staring out the window, till I remembered the clichéd ending Rocky was probably headed toward. I closed the window. It was cold. When had it gotten so cold?

"Come on, Ollie," I called. "Let's get washed up. Time for dinner."

## Chapter 8

Imaginary Lecture:
Ab Initio—Earthquakes

*Ollie dear, listen to me. It's late at night, I stare at a buzzing, blinking tube light on the lab ceiling. Driving over here to work, I realized that I hardly even notice my surroundings anymore. But the day I arrived in Los Angeles I saw into its heart.*

*I was more than a little out-of-it from gunning through the last leg of my cross-country trek. I'd driven through Needles and Barstow— having crossed the Mojave—where it was still ninety-seven degrees at four in the afternoon.*

*I hit Los Angeles at rush hour. All the freeways were jammed, then on the 10 West, I watched as one of the many hot and exhausted motorists, lurching toward his exit across four lanes, cut in front of a young man on a car phone who'd been trying to whipsaw diagonally across to the fast lane. The cars jackknifed over each other: a Porsche and a Toyota Camry: snared and yoked at the jowls. No one was hurt, but traffic in three lanes stopped and the left lane slowed to a crawl, as the drivers got out to argue.*

*I'd been on cruise control for some hours—images flying past the windshield with the depthless vibrancy of travelogue film. I'd seen desert, mountains, oil refineries, miles of fast food and motel clutter, military bases, and I'd driven for some minutes in the folksy shadow of the Goodyear blimp. But for the last few miles, as we neared the suburban sprawl of Los Angeles, I'd noticed an odd phenomenon. Alongside the streamlined, late-model, fabulously expensive cars were wrecks-on-wheels: old trucks, ramshackle trucks. Old pickups and broken-down dumpers with rust rot and crunched fenders and flatbeds loaded with people: up to eight or ten Hispanic men and boys, filthy and exhausted, crushed together, sweaty bandannas wound around their skulls, torn dirty shirts. They rode squatting on their heels or leaning on the wheel bulkheads, bouncing, facing backward into on-coming traffic. They shared their space with gardening equipment, blowers and rakes, or construction equipment, sledgehammers and picks and—most extraordinary—they stared with a single collective gaze into the eyes of the drivers following behind. It was not a stare of accusation, I thought, but straightforward acknowledgment. This was El Norte. This was the City of Angels, city of high wages and steady work that so many of them had risked their lives to see.*

*I sat waiting for the Lexus in front of me to move, exhausted, my chin on the wheel, watching the profile of a blond lacquered woman in the silver Mercedes in the lane next to mine. A ragged band in the wreck in front of her sat gazing into her eyes. She stood it for a while, then flipped down an overhead mirror, applied lipstick, bared her teeth at the mirror, checked her nails. She tapped a finger on the wheel in time with her favorite CD. She looked at me, bored, then away. The men continued to stare solemnly across a fantastically bright chasm of sunlight and after a while, the woman in the Mercedes just glared back, her profile jutting belligerently, as if there were nothing before her but the rear end of a truck—and the men, whose faces had been occasionally animated, now faced her hungrily, transfixed.*

*I watched. The traffic moved slightly. A police car and a fire depart-
ment vehicle tried to fight their way through traffic to the smashed
cars. She stared, the men stared. We moved forward inch by inch.*

*Nevertheless, Los Angeles is not a bad city for a scientist. Those
gardeners riding backward into the future reminded me of an early
theory of Stephen Hawking's, since rejected. This theory, predicated
on the Big Bang (and everything expanding away from that initial
explosion), said that certain high-density regions stop expanding and
collapse to form galaxies, stars, and us. But what if the universe itself
stopped expanding and decided to contract? We might notice, Hawking said, as the universe shrank back on itself, broken cups gathering
themselves together on the floor and jumping back on the table. And
people's "psychological arrow" of time would be backward. In other
words, they would remember events in the future and not remember
events in their past. When the cup was shattered, they'd remember it
being on the table, but when it was on the table, they wouldn't
remember it being on the floor.*

*I can't think of a better scientific analogy for my town—a town
that remembers the future, but not the past. L.A.'s psychological
arrow of time, with all those past lives and New Age channelers and
conveniently amnesiac agents skewered on the shaft, is shooting forward into the past, into a perfection of forgetfulness, effect preceding
cause. Isn't that relaxing when you think about it? Causeless effect:
no history, no accountability—but backwards order. Results before
action. Answers, then questions. No self to speak of, but nostalgia
for the future. Pure desert under policed water, reconstructive surgery,
MTV, freeway exit signs that you forget as you exit the entryway.
Miss Orange County's tears fly back into her eyes, as the crown is
lifted from her head and held in the hands of the former queen . . . as
the new queen opens her mouth to scream, as her name is announced.*

*And after all, I came here to forget. I wanted to lose my past, whistle off toward dawn with my boon companions—the thermo-dynamic and the cosmological arrows, and, naturally, the psycholog-ical arrow of time, which informs us (yes!) that if disorder is increasing, then we* must *be on the right planet. And the universe must not be contracting.*

*Though the* earth *does funny things out here.*

*I came to think of earthquakes as the perfect disaster for Southern California. Terra firma: the illusion. There was an earthquake during my third week in Los Angeles. The day of the earthquake, a docu-mentary TV crew was shooting on the UGC campus. The documen-tary was about students who had chosen a career in science. I was asked by the biochemistry department chairman, Professor Walter Faber himself, if I would agree to be interviewed for a segment of it, called, unhappily, "The Female Element in Science." The department had decided (rather shamelessly, I thought) to get immediate mileage from its new girl colleague.*

*I was wearing a red-and-white-striped T-shirt and a short white skirt with white high-top Reeboks—an unfortunate early notion of an L.A. look—and I was being videotaped walking here and there in the high-noon sun, on a tree-lined campus walk. Beside me, a man with dreadlocks was kneeling on the seat of a wheelchair, rolling down the narrow paved walkway with a video camera in front of his face. The wheelchair had been explained to me as a steadying tech-nique for the moving camera. I'd been speaking loudly, in what sounded to me like a painfully false voice. Every so often, someone would signal to me to pump up the volume.*

*My interviewer, full of uninspired, surly questions about women in science, was a chubby fellow with a nose ring, dressed in what appeared to be a black scuba diving suit, with small round espresso-black glasses.*

*As we stood in the center of a grassy expanse, I felt something like*

*the uptown IRT under my feet. My mind stuck on the word "subway"
and I watched an arc lamp across the walkway shudder and sway,
its metal shade swinging wildly. Then a student lifted off her skate-
board and stepped into thin air as if she were being assumed bodily
up into heaven; she staggered and fell and the board rocketed away.
Underfoot, the ground shook and shook, then stopped. The air rippled
like a frame of film stuck in a projector. I got the feeling of something
missing at my side; then I remembered: Just before the earthquake
hit, my interviewer had asked a brilliantly stupid question: "In what
style do you dress in the laboratory?" Then he'd dropped to the
ground and rolled up in a tight ball. I stepped back and nearly fell
over him. I noticed his spiked hair standing up like a porcupine ridge.*

*Afterward, I invented a couple of giddy responses to his question.
"Well, I tend to wear clothing that shakes things up" was one, followed by: "Why yes, I do have my crotchless red lace panties on
today!" Terrible jokes, but for days afterward, I loved laughing at
the earthquake. It reaffirmed my sense of L.A.'s passive extremity.
But the thing really scared me.*

*As soon as the ground stopped moving, I turned to the cameraman,
swaying in his wheelchair. I was looking for reassurance. "What was
it?" I asked, knowing full well what it had been, but knowing also
that it was important for me just to hear somebody say the word.*

*When he did, I smiled conspiratorially at him, as if the documentary
team had somehow staged this temblor as a test of my mettle. I wanted
to appear brave, unflappable, a pioneer:* First Woman Faculty Member in Biochemistry at UGC Unruffled by Major Quake.

*At the time, I was confused—how did people act after earthquakes?
I stood still in the enormous silence, watching people gather in small
groups, shaking their heads. A blast of static came through the earphones the cameraman had pulled away from his head. The interviewer, who'd gotten himself sheepishly back on his feet, glared at*

*me. "You're supposed to fall down and protect your head if there's a quake," he said peevishly, as if I'd committed a faux pas at a cocktail party.*

*I winked at him, but then I noticed that I was staggering a little. I felt drunk. An ambulance siren rose, came closer and closer. There was a bullhorn announcement, indecipherable. Then another. I felt sweat moving down my back. Then a hand on my shoulder.*

*There stood a tall ponytailed guy wearing a wine-colored corduroy jacket and blue jeans, bending solicitously toward me. He wore earphones pushed back on his head; then he slid them off so they settled around his collarbone as he spoke. His face was lean and tan, and it wore a fairly continuous look of pleasant incredulity, as if he'd just surfaced from a punt overturned on the sunny Cam, still holding his glass of hock.*

*Was I OK? he asked.*

*I nodded, then I found myself, to my shock, leaning against him.*

*"I'm fine," I said, "but what the hell am I doing?"*

*He laughed. Feeling his laugh rise up in his chest and ripple outward reassured my body. I straightened up again. We stared at each other. His eyes were very pale, blue-grey, with laugh lines around them. I liked this laconic person.*

*"It's so weird," I said. "So unlike anything else. The earth is supposed to hold still."*

*He put out his hand. "Jay Tallich. I'm the d-director of Science: The Fit Survivors. I apologize for not introducing myself sooner. I was in Burbank. I've b-been tied up by our shoestring budget for the last couple days. If you'll excuse the pun."*

*"Well, yeah, I guess you know what my name is, then." I grinned stupidly at him. I wondered, idly, if his slight speech impediment was a temporary result of the quake.*

*Abruptly, we were surrounded by people: the documentary crew, students, everyone speculating loudly on the quake's Richter rating.*

"A 5.1," someone yelled. "No way, we're talking at least a 6.5, I bet." There was a much repeated report of damage to a campus parking structure. A concrete overhang had buckled and broken into massive, sliding chunks. Someone else said that a student had been injured by a piece of concrete. Power was out. Yet the atmosphere was relaxed, even festive.

I turned back to Jay. I could hear crackling voices in the earphones around his neck. I was pleased that he didn't answer the tiny interrogating voices and that he still stood near me.

"I think," he said, "we might j-just as well wrap for today. We've already got a lot of good stuff on you. In your office, sitting by the fountain. We can f-finish tomorrow when the power's back and we've looked at exactly what we've got."

"Too bad," I said, "that you can't keep the earthquake on the tape. It must be all there, right? The sound, the shaking, people's fear and everything?"

He just looked at me.

"You s-sure are new to this town," he said.

We began seeing each other. First as friends, then as lovers. At first, we seemed so much alike. Jay's mind was technical, like mine. He could explain how television used space and time, should anyone care to know this. He could have been a scientist, had he wished. When he began doing technical directing he invited me to run-throughs, blockings, tapings.

I came to know his other side. Like many people in the television and movie business in L.A., he was patriotically sentimental about Hollywood: its history, its stars, its gossip. I myself had very different heroes. I decided that I needed to broaden my definitions of entertainment. And I quickly found out about Jay's secret life as a stand-up. For some reason, I liked this alter-ego Jay, unstuttering, brazenly bad in performance. Still, I let him down, I had no Hollywood I.Q.

*One night, before a movie, he showed me some of the famous footprints and handprints in the cement in front of Mann's Chinese Theater.*

*"Peter Lorre," I murmured, staring at a pair of cement feet. "Was he one of the guys in* The Magnificent Seven?" *It happened that this was the only movie title I could remember from my childhood.*

*Jay looked sad. " 'L-Lor-ree.' Peter Lor-ree. Not 'Lor.' I don't see how it's p-possible not to know who he is. You're kidding, right?"*

*"OK, so he's not the one who can't talk and plays the harp, right?"*

*Jay stared at me. "I hope you're kidding. I find this really d-disturbing, Esme." He kept staring at me as I put my feet in Mr. Lor-ree's. "It's genuinely pathetic," he said.*

*"Do you know M-Marilyn Monroe's real name?" he asked, after a second or two. Then: "Esme, it's kind of a-anthropologically startling, like f-finding a tribe in West Guinea or someplace who've never seen an airplane."*

*I took my feet out of Mr. Lee Marvin's feet and looked up at the real stars in the murky L.A. night heavens. As if Jay had ordered it from Props, a small plane whined overhead.*

*"Do you know who Lavoisier was? Or let's just take women— Madame Wu? You don't know? She did the definitive experiments that disproved the Conservation of Parity in the Weak Force. Do you know who Arda Green was? She's my personal favorite, by the way. She discovered what a firefly's light is made up of—a* luciferin, *isn't that a great word? It took a century to figure out that little blinking light—or Gertrude Elion, she won the Nobel in 1988, or Barbara McClintock?"*

*Jay squinted hard at me as if I had just dropped in from the rain forest, carrying my stone tools.*

*"Esme, why would anyone c-compare the two? Nobody knows anything about science. Nobody has ever kn-known anything about*

*science—it's too d-difficult for civilians. People want to be enter-*
*tained, Esme, they want to relax and have fun."*

"People want to be brain-dead, have you ever noticed?"

*We squared off and faced each other. Jay's lips were moving, he*
*was trying to stay calm by repeating what he wanted to say next to*
*himself—if the emotion got control of him, his stuttering worsened*
*dramatically. The plane droned off and away.*

"J-just one m-more question. R-really."

"Shoot."

"I know you'll g-get this one. H-Hedy Lamarr!"

"Of course I know Hedy Lamarr."

"Well, w-what do you know?"

"She was a legend."

"So what are your f-favorite films of hers? You like Ecstasy?"

"Ecstasy? What's that? Hedy Lamarr was a great scientist—she
invented an anti-jamming device to block Nazi radar during World
War II. You didn't know that? Her real name was, honest to God,
Hedwig Keisler Markey. She never got credit though. The War Department, the dumb jerks, turned down her offer and eventually
her patent on this thing ran out. Now Sylvania or somebody has
adapted it and it runs satellite communications all around the
globe."

*Jay stared at me, put back his head, and started to laugh.*

"Y-you mean to t-tell me that Hedy Lamarr isn't kn-known to you
as a movie star, you know her as a . . . what?"

"Scientist, inventor, whatever."

"I have to go s-sit down somewhere and h-have a b-beer. I'm l-
losing it."

*So we tried to compromise. I actually visited film museums and read*
*ghostwritten or "as told to" biographies; he came to my lab. But I*

*couldn't help it, I had little natural interest in the subculture and it was hard to pretend that I did. I mean, sometimes I walked into the kitchen seeing bubble universes twisting themselves free like glassine blossoms, I saw great vibrating strings twisting helically, I saw and heard four-dimensional harps playing Mozart. I was a heretic, a dinosaur: television and film both struck me as tedious mediums— paradoxically, because they moved so fast. Their speed and flattened dimension reduced them to banality, plus I had trouble with L.A. movie audiences. In what other town did people sit grimly through the long roll of end credits, commenting on names of friends or foes—in the fields of Lighting, Makeup, A.D.-ing? In what other movie theaters in the world would you overhear a breakdown, sotto voce, of every camera angle, or a bitchy discourse on casting? And why was it that despite the fact that I can break down Heisenberg's Uncertainty Principle for you, I am incapable of grasping what it is that a producer actually does?*

*All of this made Jay defensive about his enthusiasms, this made me exasperated, but oddly willing to continue being with him. In the past, I'd have left him without a qualm. But there was something still on my conscience about Jesse, something bothering me about myself and how I screwed up when I loved people. And it was undeniable, in some way, that Jay and I were oddly suited—his stutter was the physical embodiment of my emotional reluctance. We were to each other (had we only noticed) a reminder of the necessity of perseverance in love. I stayed with Jay, I tried hard with Jay, and slowly acquired a life with him. It was no longer exhilarating, because we'd doubted each other so early on, but we kept staying. One night, then the next, then the next. We stayed, we got used to each other. Ollie, listen. We learned to love each other.*

*At UGC, I ended up in an odd position. I began taking it slow, for the first time. I was spending time seeing Jay's Los Angeles, learning*

*Jay's Los Angeles. Perhaps that was it. If I couldn't learn to love the movie culture, I learned to appreciate the city, its rhythms. But there was something else. I met my classes, put in my hours in the lab, but this fire I've always stoked inside me was burning low. I was setting up a lab—funding was going to come through from Derridex, a sci-tech corporation, for my work on Alpha$_1$ Antitrypsin—and I was asked to lecture to the biochemistry and molecular-biology faculties, but sometimes I caught myself sitting still at the bench, in the lab, dreaming. I sorted through my days with Q, I called up my mother's face as she looked first at Q, then at me. I conjured Jesse: I watched him from above as he bounded up the narrow steps of our brownstone toward me, his jacket and hair covered with snow, a scraggly pine tree cradled in his arms like an adopted stray, shedding needles all the way. "Some guy selling pot on the corner offered me* this *instead of a lid! We can* smoke *it or string lights on it!" He stopped on the fifth step from the top, leaning back, looking up at me, snow in his eyelashes. "You tell me, Ez," he said. "You tell me."*

*"I w-watch TV because it comforts me," Jay said once. I hadn't asked him a question, we hadn't been speaking, just sitting quietly in his living room. He was slouched in a lounger, wearing only Jockey shorts and red socks, and I was actually trying to sew something: a loose button on my lab coat. It was taking me a while, but it lent a kind of cheery pseudo-domesticity to our scene.*

*I looked over at him.*

*"When I was a kid and I came home from school, my parents were never around. I loved the fact that I could turn on the tube and the same people would always be there to greet me. The folks on* Gilligan's Island, *the* Star Trek *crew. My family, if you know what I mean." He turned back to an HBO movie starring a dog that could fly.*

*I stared at him. He was not stuttering at all.*

*There was a silence. The dog landed on Mars.*

"My mother drank a lot," Jay said. "And she was very loud. I was embarrassed by her. I loved the mothers on television."

"How's your mom now?"

"She still drinks, she's still loud. And I'm still in love with TV families."

"And now you drink, too."

Jay turned to look at me.

"I kn-know why I love TV families so m-much. But e-exactly."

My father watched television at the end. I remember him sitting in front of it, smoking, smoking and coughing. I associate those sounds with certain sitcom theme music, the oceanic murmur of baseball games. The sound of disappearing, the sound of never coming back.

Jay and I stood at the top of Mulholland Drive, looking down on Los Angeles. My hair was blowing in my eyes. "Eighty-one languages spoken in this city!" Jay cried, pointing down excitedly. "C-can you imagine it?"

I tried to imagine a Babel of tongues rising up to us, where we stood ankle-deep in the brownish iceplant. Jay said something else.

"What?" I cried. "I can't hear you!"

He kissed me. I kissed him back.

We made love. It was wonderful.

Then Jay asked me a question. "D-did you c-come?"

We started to laugh. We c-couldn't s-stop.

Ollie, I rented a small house in Hollywood, our house. It had an avocado tree in the backyard that actually bore fruit. I bought it with a low-interest loan from the university. I was overwhelmed by the ease and swiftness with which all this happened.

I spent time wandering around my little house in the early-morning hours, wearing nothing but a pair of Jay's boxer shorts and a halter, *eating a peanut-butter sandwich, humming. I'd made my peace with Los Angeles. Every once in a while, I would sit on a hassock or lean on a gleaming blond butcher-block island and think: I have a place to live. I have a job. I have a sweetheart. I looked at myself in the hallway mirror. Red red hair, fiery topknot. Strong nose and chin. Big yellow-green cat's eyes. Looking back, it seems I was under a spell. I wasn't thinking about science during that whole time, I wasn't thinking about anything but recovering some part of myself. Certainly I relied on my skepticism; it had always come in handy before, why give it up now? But I still walked from room to room in my new house early in the morning, singing little off-key songs to myself.*

*When I got the letter announcing Q's and my mother's engagement, I felt relief. Some nights later I sat in my office at school, waiting, listening to two after-hours researchers bang locker doors and call goodbyes. Then I took my lab keys, opened the door, and went to the bench. I lit a Bunsen, pulled a clean tube from the rack. I opened my bag and took out a vial filled with my own urine. Then I put the tube in the spinner, the centrifuge, watched it separate into a colloidal suspension. Then I hung the tube in the rack. I had a wait ahead of me.*

*I wandered into another section of the laboratory, where a colleague of mine kept Drosophila flies in bottles for a study of the male accessory gland. She watched them mate, then kept a check on this gland, which lost one third of its protein after copulation. She watched to see how the gland made RNase and remade protein. The postcoital male flies were put in a bottle labeled "Exhausted Males." The females, tragically, ended up in the Morgue. There were bottles called Monasteries, where celibate males were placed, and a Motel, where the slow-going sex between the flies went on. Then there was a Dim Bulb Division, where mutants, slow-learner flies, bumbled about, bumping into the bottle walls. There was a "hot" area, where she injected the males, after mating, with radioactive isotopes—zapped them, lit them up, then sliced out a cross section to see what was inside. The idea was to mimic in vitro—that is to say, outside of the body—what went on after copulation.*

*At three in the morning, nodding with sleep, I went back, held my tube up to the light, and saw the newly formed agglutinate, the antibody clumping reaction in the bottom of the tube, which testified to the presence in my blood of the hormone HCG, human chorionic gonadotropin. The clear conclusion, as I stood there, the tube trembling in my hand in the harsh overhead light, was that conception had taken place. Think of this, Ollie. I saw firsthand, I held in my hand, the chemical message that you had arrived.*

*I washed out the glass beaker and tubes, cleared away some notes, checked the burners and other equipment, took my keys, and left. I got into my car and drove out to the beach. It was close to dawn. As I pulled off the Pacific Coast Highway into Temescal Canyon Beach parking lot, the sky was lighting up. I found a jacket in the trunk, shrugged into it, and walked across the flat terraces of sand to the breakers. There was no one else on the beach. The roar of the breaking surf was tremendous and my jeans got soaked when I walked too close to the waves. I walked for miles. At around seven A.M., I noticed a food trailer parking. I bought a cup of black coffee and found a pay phone. I placed two long-distance calls. The first was to my mother. The second, a much longer call by far, was to Q.*

UGC was not happy about the maternity leave, but they'd already become somewhat philosophical about me. The six-month leave really only applied to tenured professors, but they agreed to interpret the policy broadly. They were still edgy about bad publicity, and I sat sphinxlike in the chairman's office, wearing a BABY INSIDE T-shirt and twirling my hair. No one in the department had a clue as to what I was about, and I didn't mind keeping it that way. I frightened them to a man, I thought.

*I told Jay that he didn't have to marry me—and I meant it. We sat in my backyard at a little wooden table under the avocado tree, drinking lemonade. His glass had gin in it.*

*Jay was laughing at my refusal to marry him. From the day of the earthquake, I'd loved his laugh. I rode it over and over in my mind like a surfer shooting the curl.*

*"C-come on, Ez," he said. "Look. We met. The earth m-moved."*

*"We don't share a sense of humor," I said.*

*"So? M-marry me and I'll acquire your scientific sense of the absurd, I promise."*

*"I'd say that my sense of the absurd has almost peaked in this town. Sometimes I long for a little humorlessness: I want a quiet person, say, a Presbyterian."*

*"But," Jay said, "I'm your j-jujube, tootsie—I'm transparent and I have staying power."*

*He told me that he knew I thought I didn't love him. "B-but you do," he said. "You j-just think you d-don't."*

*We argued for a long time about marriage, but Jujube was inexhaustible and Tootsie was not. I gave in. We flew to Las Vegas, to the Chapel of Ceaseless Trickling, and flew back to L.A. one night later, husband and wife.*

*We stayed in my little house. We continued living there after you, Olivia—Jay's name, for some movie star I can never remember— were born. You were a very easy delivery and very healthy. You cried a lot, though, and wanted to be held all the time. Jay began to say that I was spoiling you, because I always held you, always picked you up when you cried in the night. We began to fight about how to handle you. Then we began to fight about how to organize our lives, now that we had a child. We were tired all the time, and irritable, and we could not calm you sometimes. When my six-month leave was over, the fights got worse, because we needed sitters for you and we could never agree on whom to hire.*

*We both began to notice that you were unusual, Ollie. Wonderful, but just not following the so-called normal patterns of development. A doctor agreed with Jay that you might need therapy—or drugs. I thought they were both wrong. You and I always communicated very well.*

*Jay was gone all the time. His technical-directing work started early and ran late. And then he had his stand-up gigs. The industry: It eats up your life. I hired sitter after sitter, rushed home from UGC.*

*Then, one day, amazingly, it all changed. The theory came back to me. All the excitement I used to feel working with Q suddenly returned to me. I was standing in the hall outside the biochemistry lab at UGC at eight A.M. with my second cup of coffee in my hand, and I felt— just like that—that I was ready now to start over again. I wanted to change my research plans; I'd been rethinking my theories. This is not to say that I was born again. I was exhausted, dazed; I was wounded.*

*But I was going to do real work again. If I was falling apart, well, then, maybe I could use the information I gathered, falling. Maybe I could use the exhaustion, the stand-up, the late nights, the arguments with Jay, money problems, broken promises, the hopeless sitters, Jay's bottles in the trash. I could use them like the elements of the periodic table dancing before me. Ollie, I got a little ethereal: I could put them in the mind's centrifuge and fly them around into suspension. I could alter them, name their new names as they combined and recombined in the burning alchemical blaze: like poetry, I thought. I felt cleansed now, I could drink my coffee up, then walk into the lab, for the first time since I'd come to the University of Greater California, as if it were mine, as if I belonged there.*

# P a r t   T w o

*Today I was reading about Marie Curie:*
*. . .*
*She died      a famous woman      denying*
*her wounds*
*denying*
*her wounds      came      from the same source as*
*her power*

—Adrienne Rich
"Power"

# Chapter 9

I rather liked the lab I'd been given at UGC, in which I was to pursue my gene-splicing *and* (it was clear) do something flashy, fund-attracting—find a cure for a congenital disease, invent an artificial gene for genius, analyze a dead president's DNA. But as time passed, I grew reflective; I sat in my laboratory lost in thought. I hunched over in my chair, twirling my hair—in those well-equipped rooms in the one-story prefab building (OBERMAN HALL) next to the Physics Lecture Hall Building. Maybe theory was in the air. What was I thinking about? Electromagnetic particles, the sidereal shifts of stars. One step, two steps: out into the universe. I lusted after a TOE, what scientists call a Theory of Everything. I herded my chiral molecules shyly, like chicks, into the huge incubating light of this desire.

I found some extra funds to hire Rocky as my assistant. She and I had a long talk about women and science. Then we talked about men. "I've broken up with Troy," she said, and smiled her beautiful, untrustworthy smile. "I'm not promising nothing, Prof, except, you know, a real crack at change. This is *it*, man. I'm taking a very tough look here at my self-destructive behavior." She shook her hair into her eyes, peering out at me through the dark seductive tangle: an absolutely irresistible and completely unconscious liar.

"Put a lab coat on," I said, "and would you mind sparing me the bullshit?" I was looking at a crayon drawing Ollie had done on graph paper while sprawled on the lab floor. She was spending time with me at work now—Jay was around less than ever. Because of certain chemical-splash risks and low-grade radiation levels in the lab, she was restricted to the entry area, where there was more circulating air and less cookery. She'd been slowly drawing everything she observed. Her drawings were quite realistic except for sudden distractions urgently sketched in: a great winged blue monkey, arms crossed, slowly spinning atop a centrifuge—or a shower of watching eyes poured from a suspended pitcher into a rack of Eppendorf tubes. And who's to say these visions weren't scientific? Didn't Einstein imagine elevators free-falling in deep space, people traveling in trains at the speed of light? He looked people straight in the eye and told them that if you moved a clock through space, it lost time. And it was true. *Why did Einstein throw a clock out the window?* Somebody saw angels spinning the planets with puffs of air from their beating wings; they saw the universe mounted on the back of a giant tortoise; they saw black holes, baby universes, bubble worlds, big bangs, superstrings, event horizons, and oh yes, microwave background radiation from the glowing of the hot early universe, red-shifted . . . *He wanted to see time fly.* Ollie pulled at my lab coat and gently took back her drawing of the centrifuge with the giant blue monkey on top. "Mom, I'm going to put in the ambulance birthday cake," she said gravely. "At this minute, not the next minute."

"Man, I hate these lab coats." Rocky shook back her hair, bent down, and tweaked Ollie's nose, then smiled up at me again. "Those slits they got instead of like, *real pockets?* They keep getting caught on doors and hooks and stuff. They're *dangerous!*"

"We're going to be working with some organic solvents and hot tracers later—*that's* dangerous. Put on a lab coat." Ollie looked up at me and Rocky frowned a little—I was feeling pressured and my tone was annoyed.

"Just *try* it," I added in a gentler voice. Rocky saluted and went off to find a coat. Earlier, she'd been fitted with a "hot" badge and a ring. These were protective devices; they recorded radioactivity levels in the human body. When the bit of film got developed in the badge or the crystal structure altered in the ring, it was time for Time Out: You were getting a little too cooked. The lab levels weren't high compared to, say, working in a nuclear reactor, but I was weirdly proud of the fact that I, like my lab peers, could stutter a Geiger counter to life with a wave of my hand.

Being hot didn't bother Rocky much either, no joke intended. Not much bothered Rocky; she was blessed with an even temperament. It was easy to teach her the ropes; in a biochem lab that's rope enough to hang a novice. But Rocky was also smart. She had a quick, curious mind and she was tireless. She learned fast—dideoxynucleotide sequencing of DNA, for example:—I showed her once and she had it. Considering that dideoxy sequencing isn't exactly on the level of jotting down Troy's car-phone number, it was an impressive acquisition of technique. The stuff involves both manual and intellectual dexterity. I reminded her that there were four components of DNA: A, T, C, and G, arranged like a string, one long sentence describing maybe everything there is to know about you or me. We'd commandeered the enzyme machinery used by bacterial cells and forced it to "read" and replicate DNA for us in a tube. Millions of these little robotlike enzymes would read this long long sentence, making a duplicate strand—an "echo" sentence—then stop randomly at any given letter, so we'd have sentences ending at each of the letters.

Rocky got the hang of moving this reaction quickly; handling pipettes, a stopwatch, and lots of slightly radioactive tubes in a body-temperature water bath—with flawless timing. She told me it was like a game show (*Password*?) and I was the host, challenging her, Rocky, a prize-winning contestant. I promised her that the next step ("What's behind the curtain?") would be more challenging. We'd have to analyze reactions on an acrylamide gel, which she'd create by slowly and steadily pouring a liquid between two big glass slabs set only 0.2mm apart; no bubbles allowed. It all had to be completed in (hands down!) *five minutes,* before it gelled.

She got the gel poured on her third try. We loaded the tubes of replicated DNA strings onto one end of this gel and zapped them with two thousand volts of electricity—coaxing these charged little strands through. The longer strands would have a harder time moving through the gel's mesh; the shorter ones zipped along. The different-length molecules would line up, making a "ladder"—one size above the other, each a single letter longer than the last.

At the end, Rocky and I put the gel against film, where the radio-active tracer in each separated strand burned the ladder pattern into the film.

"So we can read them one letter at a time up the ladder!" She beamed. "I win whatever's behind this life!"

Rocky, I swear, could see *through* things. She saw the little enzyme machines as they crawled along the original long template DNA strand, dutifully copying each letter in the long statement, like so many microscopic Byzantine monks. She saw the "Bible" of human words standing in illuminated-manuscript splendor. She noted how each of the DNA molecules was driven through the gel by the lash of two thousand volts—"like a line of slaves," she murmured. She answered my questions before I could ask them. It turned out that when Rocky concentrated, when her attention was truly engaged, she was a surefire lab technician. *And* how naturally the metaphors fell from our lips as we discussed our procedures!

She was a natural, humming away, a flask in her hand, sweating a little, the fluorescent lighting altering her features so that she looked elongated, El Greco–ish. Suited up in the old stained lab coat I'd found for her, she moved about like a canny shadow, deftly lifting one end of the glass slab off the black bench top, coolly popping her gum. With a sure hand, she poured that steady stream of liquid acrylamide onto the lip of the glass, where it soaked up slowly between the two glass plates. A little stream of acrylamide spilled from the edge of the plate, puddled on the bench, and dripped to the floor, but Rocky kept her cool. The gum cracked; she poured steadily, so that there was perfectly aligned seepage between the slabs. Totally absorbed in her work, she made little satisfied noises in her throat. She'd brought her tape player to the lab: James Taylor wailed and the backup percussion throbbed, "I'm a steam roller, baby, I'm a napalm bomb."

We were growing and processing some bacterial cells in a cloning procedure. "Did it ever occur to you," she asked, staring at the dissolving dot-candy-like colonies which only moments earlier had been cheerfully growing on a white paper disk, topping a nice moist nutrient agar, "did it ever like, *occur* to you that this amazing thing, this genetic-engineering stuff, looks like some two-year-old's *spit-up* bib?"

The colonies were now turning into gooey little brown blobs after the lye hit their cell walls.

She winked at me. "Or *worse*?" She grinned apologetically. "I mean it's exciting, don't get me wrong. It's awesome, Prof. But most people would scrape this shit off their *shoes* if they found it there."

Well, it's true. You cook up a solution and then to analyze genes, you stare at blots, pieces of paper smeared with dyed genes. Blots, blots, and more blots. We even give them directional tags: Northern Blot, Southern Blot, Western Blot.

I pulled a cup of coffee from the machine and disappeared for a while. It happened that Rocky's comments depressed me. I could feel myself losing the natural joy I used to feel in the lab. Even the simplest procedures used to charge me up. For example, we grew lots of animal cells in tissue culture, and those guys had to eat—I used to look forward to feeding time at the zoo. What the cells snacked on was a serum of calf's blood, bicarbonate of soda, vitamins, and hormones. We poured it over them in a warm rain. Little Shop of Horrors. Ollie, in particular, was fascinated by this flesh gardening. Then we'd provide new housing for the colonies of multiplying cells. I even liked *that*. Dishes had to be split: The cells kept replicating to maximum density. I hustled to accommodate the overspill. Some were sucked off into oblivion, into flasks filled with antiseptic iodine to kill all living cells. Others had their contents immortalized for posterity in gels. We filled our notebooks with photographs and dried remnants of these gels, stained fluorescent pink for DNA and RNA, purple for proteins.

"What's up, Prof?" Later Rocky leaned in under the fume hood, where I was fiddling with a beaker. Ollie wandered up behind her and they both stood, looking at me.

"You know," said Rocky, "today's the day I'm supposed to learn how to extract DNA—maybe you forgot?"

I hadn't exactly forgotten. Still, amazing though it seems, it was a common enough procedure in the lab that it could be put on a back burner, literally. Amazing, because what we were talking about here was nothing less than the isolation of deoxyribonucleic acid from a solution—you could actually pull it out and handle it with a glass rod, whip it around like a string cheese.

I looked at Ollie. "Would you like to see an interesting experiment?"

Ollie shook her head. "Ollie do it."

"You can help, sweetheart. You can watch."

"Look." Ollie offered me another drawing. This one showed very tiny people growing from petri dishes; the dishes were set on the floor of the forest and were surrounded by huge dark Christmas trees. A human-faced star looked down on the scene.

Rocky, looking over my shoulder, snorted.

"Kinda ruins the Smurfs for ya, no?"

I folded up the drawing and put it in my lab-coat pocket.

"Hey guys," I said. "Let's make some human taffy."

Rocky and I went to the incubator, where a couple of days earlier she'd placed some human foreskin fibroblasts. (Now you know what happens to all those little circumcision leftovers, guys!) We also carry human breast-cell lines, from mammary biopsies. *Tip or tit? Briss or breast?* the irreverent among us ask on our way to the fibroblast freezer.

In special media, in large plastic petri dishes, the cells had grown up and now crowded the bottom of the plate, clinging to the specially treated polymer surface. I showed Rocky how to suck the media off with a house-vacuum tube connected to a big Erlenmeyer flask, attached to another tube with a Pasteur pipette stuck on. The poor cells were now exposed, gasping. We scraped them off with a "rubber policeman," a kind of glass-handled rubber spatula, and rinsed them into a centrifuge tube. We spun the hapless cells into a heap at the bottom of the tube and sucked off the liquid above them again—this time replacing it with a nasty mix of detergent and RNA- as well as protein-degrading enzymes. The cells blew open with the application of detergent, exposing their proteins and RNase, soon to be chewed up by the enzymes. Without the proteins holding the scaffolding together, the chromosomes unraveled their neatly spooled DNA string. The strings sparkled modestly from a little distance. Close up, it all looked like a light slime in the tube.

"Is that it?"

"That's *it*. Look, Ollie."

"Holy shit! DNA!"

Rocky tried to lift some of the white fluff-slime on a glass rod and discovered that it was sticky, viscous, slippery. We watched it glitter and swing on the end of the rod for a second, then drop back into the tube.

"I can't believe this. This is fucking DNA."

"DNA, Ollie, this is magic stuff. It makes people."

"Candy people? Talking candy?"

"Not exactly, Ollie."

"Is it a thought from my head that grew?"

"You wanna answer that one, Rocky?"

Rocky looked up from playing with the malleable strand.

"Man, I can't believe *this*," she said again. Her face was all lit up.

"I know, isn't it something?" Going through the steps to fetch DNA with Rocky sent me back to my pre-postdoc days; I felt an involuntary shiver of wonder. "You know, this is what some people call the Word, Rocky. This is what they call God's Code!"

Rocky grinned at me again. She looked ecstatic.

"Yeah, and who would ever have imagined *this*? This goddam DNA looks, fuckin' deoxyribonucleic acid looks and feels just like *snot*!"

Ollie tugged at my sleeve again.

"Is it from my nose?"

"Jesus," I said. "Let's put this in the spinner. It's almost six o'clock."

"I just can't believe it. *Snot!*"


Sometimes, when I could get a sitter, Rocky and I worked nights in the lab, wandering in and out of temperature-controlled rooms, talking to ourselves. More and more, I'd begun to feel like one of the cell cultures I routinely isolated: With the overhead lights in the domed ceiling shining down on my feeling of smallness, my murmuring multiple selves, with the unfresh air recycling, I felt like a worker phage, stuck tight to the agar, reproducing myself. I wanted my own TOE.

A single theory that would unite all the others, so I worked on the computer now; I spent hours writing out equations.

But the lab: In the lab, it all continued in the same way. We went on working, we focused on certain reactions and focused again, repeating them. We immortalized cells, strains of cancer, other diseases. Sometimes we went chromosome-walking; I taught Rocky how. We moved out, gene by gene, looking for the faulty one, the screw-up: thousands of possibilities, in some cases, stretching from here to Morocco and back; but we stepped out, little by little, into the gene universe.

You could find us sometimes in the Warm Room, where it's raunchy and overheated, like a public sauna, or the Cold Room, which is airlocked at four degrees centigrade, where RNA can survive. And sometimes we wrapped ourselves up in plastic to handle recombinant viruses capable of infecting humans.

But even though I went through the motions of all the routine tasks of the laboratory, my body performed them pretty much on its own. In my head, I was walking out into space, where my real lab was.

---------------

# Chapter 10

It was late afternoon. I was winding up an informal lab review with some of the newer grad students. Step by step we enlarged our knowledge of Alpha$_1$ Antitrypsin (a$_1$AT) Deficiency, a genetic plasma protein disorder—a condition created when a plasma protein stops or blocks the action of a protein-splitting enzyme, trypsin.

We have here at UGC, I explained to them, one of only a dozen or so laboratories across the country studying a$_1$AT, because the present typing system is technically difficult, time-consuming, and (I smiled at them) a boring, back-breaking job. Our reference labs *do* Pi (protease inhibitor) typing here, the genotype characteristic related to a$_1$AT, which is unusual. Many labs do not measure Pi types directly but guess them from chemical values, which are often misleading.

I talked on about the chemistry of the disease, about how a$_1$AT was an inborn error of metabolism, an autosomal hereditary disorder manifesting low serum and lung levels of Alpha$_1$. I described how it destroyed tissue, led to emphysema. I told them about the Swedish scientists who discovered it, by using electrophoresis, a process of subjecting blood plasma to the force of an electric field—their technique for characterizing plasma proteins. After doing that, they noticed that about half a dozen blood samples out of thousands lacked the alpha$_1$ globulin, then found that three or four of these six patients had developed emphysema as young adults, and bingo! The wires touched. Now the clinical manifestations of the disease have been fully published; the troublemaker gene cloned; the molecular bases of the major deficiency states have been defined; techniques for workup have been used for prenatal diagnosis. Liver disease (childhood liver disease, that is to say, another gift of a$_1$AT) is still an enigma, and that problem is one we work on in this lab. Among other things, I thought.

They looked carefully at the protein, the structure of alpha$_1$ (a single chain of 394 amino acids) and its natural substrate, neutrophil elastase. I talked a little about advances in gene replacement, or the implantation into the lungs of victims of a healthy gene that can produce Alpha$_1$. This has been done with animals, I said. We've planted a human gene in monkey lungs—and it worked. No one had tried it with humans.

The wall phone rang. One of the grad students, Shelly Sullivan, answered it and nodded to me. I snaked through the aisles and the impromptu gatherings of student research groups and plucked the receiver from her hand. She waved to someone across the room and hurried off.

"Professor Charbonneau."

"It's Jesse."

I heard myself asking him where he was in a neutral voice, forgetting to greet him or ask how he was doing. It was as if I'd expected him, as if he'd been on his way toward me—for some time.

"I'm over at everybody's rival institution, UCLA. I'm here for a conference, but things came up back in Boston and I have to get back tomorrow. I called your department and they rang me over to your lab. Are you busy? Can you come out for a quick drink?"

I glanced at the wall clock. It was nearly four. Jay was due home early and, of course, had plans to go out later for a stand-up audition—but I could call him, tell him I had to work late, and ask him to give Ollie dinner and a bath just this once, put her to bed. Then I stopped musing. *If I go,* I thought, *something will happen.*

"Esme?"

"Yeah. I'm just thinking. My husband's home tonight, so he could maybe take care of my little girl—"

"I *heard* you had a kid! I'm going to see a lot of pictures, right?"

"If you want to see them."

"As long as you don't tell me labor and birth stories."

"I see you've got the same great bedside manner."

"You oughta *remember.*"

"Tell me where you want to meet, Jesse. I'll be there."

Jay put up a halfhearted argument, for form's sake, when I made my suggestion. I told him that I had to work late. (It did not occur to me to wonder why I didn't just tell him the truth: I was meeting an old friend, so what?) I was afraid that he'd fall asleep on the couch before he tucked Ollie in, but I couldn't express that concern or he'd explode: Why was I *criticizing* him? So I said nothing. And I said nothing about when he should expect me. He forgot to ask.

I hung up and stood for a minute, staring into space. I was thinking about making love with Jesse, and I stood there smiling idiotically till one of my grad students came up and raised and lowered his hand in front of my eyes.

"She's not blinking!" he yelled to the others. "We stunned her with our questions!"

"No, it's just lack of stimulus," I said. "Come on, let's go make a stink bomb."

I saw him across the room in the fancy bar on Burton Way, and I understood, with the force of a blow, part of what had been missing in my life. *Love of the body:* but not L.A.'s human statue love, no. Love of the way someone crossed a room, stood up to greet you, put weight on one leg, cocked his head, put an arm around you, held you tight. Love of a *face*, a collection of expressions, a set of reactions, a familiar sidelong eye-flicker.

He stood up as I neared and we shook hands, then kissed each other lightly on the cheek.

"You look great," he said. "Your hair is long."

"So is yours—God, it's almost shoulder-length!"

"I put it in a ponytail for surgery."

He looked a little different, I thought: darker, more intense, more serious in his jacket and tie. The attraction I'd always felt for him leaped up full-blown and presented itself to me, and I tamped it down grimly. I hadn't quite remembered how everything about him seemed connected to his *ease,* his being-at-home in his body, a relaxed sexuality. It shocked me, close up. There was the leisurely landscape of his manner: an amused, unshakable gaze combined with his habit of dropping an ironic take on everything around him, his quizzical dead-pan look. I reminded myself of his faults: No doubt he was still an interrupter, hot-tempered, arrogant, inflexible (a failing of most medical docs); no doubt he thought *I* still had the hots for *him.*

I sat down and we smiled at each other.

"You look great," he said for the second time. Was *he* nervous? Then he added: "Maybe it's being a *mom,* do you think?"

"You mean, *hormones* made me what I am?"

"No," he answered seriously. "Really *loving* somebody. Your little . . . it's a *girl,* right?"

"Right. Olivia. *Ollie* for short."

We smiled again, stupidly.

The tuxedoed waitress brought our drinks as he admired the fan of Ollie photographs I spread across the table, a kind of protective shield between us.

"She looks like you," he said, "burning with that fever—it's in her eyes. And she's got your red hair and that . . . You know, that talking-out-the-side-of-your-mouth look of yours."

"Everyone seems to think she's screwed up but me."

"Well? Who knows her best—you or *them*?"

We talked briefly about Ollie, and in the course of that conversation, I felt relaxed again about her, about myself, about her behavior. The tensions of the last months dissolved into a new shiny substance that ran brightly, seductively, in my veins: I was a good mother after all, I was brave, everything would be all right. It shocked me, the extent to which I needed this reassurance—needed to know that *someone* thought I was doing all right. My pathetic manner made me smile, and Jesse smiled back at me.

"Remember the last time we met like this?"

"Sure. Gold Moon Thai. You raised your glass to say good-bye to me."

"And here we are again."

He nodded emphatically. We sipped our drinks, sizing each other up. Then he looked down at his hands.

"My father died a few months ago."

"Jesus, Jess, I'm sorry."

He held his glass up, looked intently at the contents, then put it down.

"I had gotten a lot closer to him these last couple years. He never talked to me much when I was a kid, and suddenly he'd reached a point in his life when he wanted to just . . . unload some stuff about himself. We'd go out to a bar or just sit next to each other on a bench at the park, watching a pickup ball game. He'd tell me all about his childhood, about meeting my mom. Amazing. After years of silence."

"How did he die?"

"Heart attack. Classic myocardial infarct. Boom. Just like that."

"No history of heart disease?"

"He was overweight, didn't exercise. I was always after him—but he'd had an EKG a month before in a routine checkup and there wasn't a sign of trouble. Nothing. Like an echocardiogram of a kid."

He lifted his glass and drank. Then he looked at me, that inquiring calm look.

"I had a dream about him a little while after he died. But it didn't *feel* like a dream. You know that preconscious state you're in before waking? I was right there sleeping in my bed, but awake in some way. He came and sat beside my bed and put his hands on my chest and pressed down. I started to wake up and he kept pressing gently on my chest, saying it's OK, everything's OK."

"He was pressing on your chest?"

"Yeah, well, I'm a little slow. It took me a while to realize that he was telling me that he was OK, he was all right, yes, which was what I needed to know—but also that *my* heart was OK. He was reassuring me that I wasn't going to die of a heart attack too."

"You?"

"Shit yes. Well. I didn't realize at the time just how afraid to die I was." He looked at me, a self-deprecating glance. "I mean, I'm a *doc*. But then, maybe I was more terrified because I *am* a physician. I'd been doing all this bullshit death-defying stuff, hang gliding, bungee jumping, after his death just to prove that I was brave, ready to face the Zero. But of course, I wasn't facing it at all. He knew that about me. There isn't a day that goes by that I don't think about him. He knew all this about me, he came back to release me. He blessed me with his hands."

We smiled slowly at each other again. Then his smile turned dangerous. "Not to ruin the mood, but there was *another* manifestation of my need for release, but absolutely *real*."

I held my breath. I knew Jesse; I knew what was coming.

"Yeah?"

"Well." He looked around, shaking his head. "It was *weird*. I was on a plane flying to a conference in Florida right after my father's death. I mean, it was *right* after the funeral, a *day,* maybe, and I was still in shock. I was sitting on the plane; we'd been in the air for a while. I had an aisle seat for leg room, and this girl, this young Asian woman, very pretty, was suddenly leaning over me, asking if she could take the empty window seat next to me."

He looked at me anxiously. I sipped my drink.

"She sat down and immediately covered herself from the waist down with an airline blanket. She looked over at me: beautiful eyes and skin; perfume; wearing a flimsy kind of blouse."

I started to laugh.

"No, *listen,* Esme. I mean it's *what* you think, but it also is *not* that. I'd been sitting there shocked, almost drugged feeling, and I returned to this state after she sat down. Then she spoke to me. She said, 'You look really sad, are you OK?' I mumbled something and she stared at me and said, 'Here, give me your hand, I can help you,' and she took my hand and put it between her legs—she had taken off her underwear."

"Jesus, *Jesse.*"

"*Listen.* OK, so there I am, thirty-seven thousand feet above sea level, with my index finger on this young woman's *clitoris,* and it's *not what you think*! I mean yes, yes, it was deeply erotic, of course, but further, it was, it was . . ."

"Spiritual."

"Esme, listen. Don't judge. Just then the pilot announced our gradual descent into Miami International and we started to bank and lose altitude. I'm massaging her, and I'm inside her, but it was not just *sexual,* it was this slow intense dreamy release. Then we descended, down, down through the cloud layers, and she started to come. Christ, it was overheated in the cabin; the sun poured through the windows as we banked, we had our heads together and she was making those *sounds.* We landed all at once, we dropped out of the clouds and I could *feel* this long long orgasm happening in my hand, coming up into my *fingers,* through my hand, my arm."

"Sounds like you helped *her* instead of the other way around."

"No, no. I'm telling you, it was like being *born.* Falling through the clouds, connected to the power at the *center* of this woman."

"Then she unbuckled her seat belt, pulled up her pants, got her overhead baggage down, and split?"

He laughed. "Yeah. She walked a little funny, though."

"God, you're horrible, Jesse. Why do I like you?"

"Is it because I tell you the unvarnished truth? Or is it because I tell it funny?"

"It's because you don't have to *try.*" I paused. "Either way."

There was another pause.

"Is it OK if I ask about *you?*"

I drank deeply of my margarita, then put it down, tasting salt.

"About me is simple. I'm not particularly happy in my life right now and I'm vulnerable to . . . you know." I looked around, flustered, shrugged. "Losing *altitude.*"

He nodded gravely.

I leaned toward him.

"I'm *drawn* to allegory, Jesse. You always did tell good stories." Another long pause. "But if you talk about . . . *blessing,* you know, that's the whole point. I think that in this fucking state of entropy we live in, the power to bless is the only real power for good that we have. That's what *I* think."

He stared back at me, then covered my outstretched hand with his: warm, light.

"Let's go somewhere, Esme. Let's go now."

We checked into that hotel on Sunset, famous as a celebrity get-away; this afternoon there were neither celebrities nor the people they were trying to get away from. I looked up at the Regency ceilings;

the lobby of dignified shadows made me feel more sober and mature, less impulsive—as if I'd weighed this decision for years instead of minutes.

We stood side by side on the elevator, saying nothing, staring straight ahead.

"I like your shoes," Jesse offered finally, lamely; we stared in silence at my black suede pumps.

After room service had brought a bottle of chilled chardonnay and a silver bowl of delicately perspiring grapes, pears, and plums, and after the heavy walnut door had closed with finality, Jesse poured a glass of wine for me and one for himself. I sat down in a chintz-covered chair near the window, overlooking a courtyard full of blue-blooming jacaranda trees and a bluer pool. Jesse stood awkwardly near the desk. Neither one of us looked at the bed.

"I'm not going to say 'I can't believe I'm here,' nothing disingenuous," I said after a few minutes. "I do believe that this is real, that I'm here. I *want* to be here."

He smiled from across the room.

I sipped my wine. Suddenly he was kneeling at my feet. He lifted the wineglass out of my fingers and set it aside.

We began kissing and moving—caught up in some sort of underwater motion that beached us finally on the bed, him on top of me. I was laughing, thinking, No more good-bye in a Thai restaurant; he was laughing too. He kissed exactly the way I remembered—his whole mouth over mine, like Ollie sucking on an orange half. It was mildly disconcerting at first, then completely absorbing.

I sat up suddenly, pulling back from him.

"OK. OK, so I'm disingenuous—this *is* really happening, right?"

He'd wrenched free his tie and his shirt was half open, revealing his dark chest hair and the beautiful olive sheen of his skin. He sat up next to me, touching my half-unbuttoned blouse. He cupped my face in his hands.

"This is really happening," he said.

I turned away from him again and he turned my head back to face him straight-on. His eyes were direct and inquiring—a bar of lamp-light clarified his expression, as if he were just under the surface of an element slightly more viscous than water, a colloidal suspension, clear. His face shimmered, then stilled.

"Don't go off in your mind, Esme," he said. "Stay *here.*"

"I'm *here!*" I snapped. "*OK?*" Then, to my shock, I began to cry. Tears slipped out of my eyes and down my face, flowing over his hands and over my own hands, cupped over his.

"Christ." I squeezed my eyes shut and breathed deeply, but the tears kept welling up and ran over. So I abandoned myself to it: I didn't sob, but made a series of lengthy inaudible statements that collected themselves, finally, into sounds of grief.

Jesse held me in his arms and rocked slowly, kissing my hair. How long had it been, I thought, since someone held me like this? Exactly the way I hold Ollie?

"Shhh, shhh, Esme."

After a long while, I got my breath, and the tears fought to the surface one last time, then ebbed.

"Well," I said, dabbing at my eyes with a bedside tissue. "*That* was fun! Did *you* come?"

He covered my lips with a finger.

"Shh. Esme. Whatever you do right now, don't be *funny.*"

So I wasn't. I wasn't funny at all, I didn't sneer, no wisecracks, as we lay back down and slowly moved together through the ancient portals of that ludicrous, profound cliché of human passion. We touched each other with immense wonder, there was no laughter or even an abstract smile when he slid his tongue over my breasts, between my legs, as I sucked his cock. There was a hint of levity, but it was the *other* levity, meaning *lightness,* that quality or state of being light in weight, unfettered, even defiant of gravitation—we *floated* through each other like subatomic particles. . . . No. I'll say it right: We stayed exultant in our own flesh, our own blessed bodies; there were no subatomic plots, no cloud cover: Jesse and Esme fucking each other. Jesse pushing suddenly deep inside me, me shouting something as he entered, him lifting me up so that I sat on his thighs; we faced each other as he moved, both of us gasping with pleasure. Then we were turning over and over again, as if we'd been spun up from under water into a breaker line; I was adrift on my back, my stomach; he was over me, under me. We kissed frantically, our bodies soaked with sweat; he clutched my hair, pulling my head back, and groaned, moving faster inside me, then triggered a lengthening spark at the center—a long moment—slow levels of ascension, one by one—then I came, then he came, we came talking into each other's mouths, sliding rung by rung back down the humming spiral. And only then did I make a sound—*then* I laughed, I laughed helplessly, my hand shielding my eyes from the glare, for a very long time.

I parked the car at the curb instead of pulling into the driveway. But the living room lights were on and I could see Jay inside, getting up to peer out the window. I opened the door. Behind him, the TV blared. I walked over and snapped Letterman off. There were a few, not too many, Bud cans on the floor.

He came up behind me and I turned and looked into his eyes. He was still pretty sober.

"Hi, Jay."

"Hello, Esme. D-do you want to tell me where you've been?"

I glanced at the wall clock. It was almost one. I dropped my bag and briefcase on the floor and sank into a chair.

"You were with s-someone, weren't you? You didn't work late, did you?"

"No," I said. "I had a drink with someone I used to know. I just forgot about the time."

He sat down directly across from me.

"Wh-who was it?"

"It doesn't matter, Jay. You don't know him."

"It m-matters to me."

"Jay, I'm sorry. I can't tell you."

I was still in a daze. Jesse and I had made love a second time, more slowly and less explosively but with a languorous, vertiginous *detail* that stayed in my blood, walked in the door with me. My body felt utterly calm, but my mind struggled to understand, to make sense of what the flesh so readily absorbed—pleasure, joy, terror.

I looked at Jay, dazed, guilty.

He got up, shaking his head at me. He began to pace around the room. "I s-stayed up, Esme. I had a funny feeling where you'd gone and I wanted to be . . . awake to see you when you came in, to hear what you had to say. *Now* I n-need a drink."

He stomped off to the kitchen, then turned and came back.

"I want to know, Esme. Did you sleep with this person?"

"Jay, please. Let's drop this now."

"What do you expect me to do? *Ch-cheer* when you come in in the middle of the night, looking like . . . l-looking goddam *happy*. What the fuck am I supposed to say?"

I stood up, angry. "You're supposed to say, 'What's wrong?' What's wrong with my marriage if my wife goes out to have a drink and comes back looking *happier* than when she left? What's wrong with my marriage if my wife and I can't *talk* to each other? What's wrong if my wife *feels free* when she leaves me?"

"You felt *free*? You *did* sleep with the guy! Am I r-right?"

"Jesus!" I cried. "So what? Yeah! I slept with him."

Jay reached out suddenly and pushed me, hard, with the flat of his hand. I stumbled backward, holding my arm where he'd slammed it.

"Get away from me. I can't look at you!"

"Oh? This is all about *you*, just you?"

"Tell me something!" he shouted, pointing his finger in my face. "Are you going to see this guy again?"

I swallowed. Jesse and I had had a talk, each of us shaky, absolutely stunned by the implications of what we'd done. It was simple, impossible. Anyway, I knew Jesse. He always had another plane to catch.

"No," I said. "I am not going to see him again. We talked. I have a child who means everything to me and I don't want to shake up her world and make life any harder for her than it already is right now."

I stared off into space.

"Anyway," I said, "he's leaving tomorrow." I smiled involuntarily. "Flying back to the East Coast."

Relief broke across Jay's face, became quickly distorted into an odd resolve.

"You th-think I'm going to forget this, Esme—don't you?"

"Jay, I'm sorry. I didn't do this to hurt you. I did it for myself. One time. I needed this one time. I needed to make something clear."

He laughed bitterly. "Make something c-clear. You're always *making things clear* to yourself, aren't you? Just this one time: *y-your* theory, *y-your* universe. *Meanwhile,* you're a goddam failure as a wife. Did I ever tell you that?"

"Jay."

He started for the kitchen again, then turned back again. He threw the words at me like stones.

"You're *p-pathetic* in bed, *unreachable.* I hope this guy you were with didn't have to work as hard as I have t-to. . . ."

"Jay, come *on*. Stop now."

"See you later, Esme. *I'm* going out now for a while. Maybe I'll make a f-few things clear to myself too."

"Be my guest," I said, but I muttered it under my breath and I'm sure he didn't hear me. He was out in the kitchen then, banging things, and I was suddenly very tired. I left my briefcase on the floor and went to bed, turning in my exhaustion to the remaining broken gold fragments: Jesse's face, lamplight, our cries, familiar and lost, coming down through the clouds.

## Chapter 11

The day everything changed was the day I got a letter from my mother describing her marriage to Q: "We drove up to Portsmouth, New Hampshire, Kendall's birthplace, as you know, Esme—and were married in a little chapel in Strawberry Bank, in pouring rain. A brief honeymoon in Bar Harbor, then back to Boston. How's my precious Ollie?"

I loved the "as you know, Esme"; I laughed out loud when I read it. As a matter of fact, I had no idea where Q was born, to me it was if he'd sprung full-grown, like one of Ollie's drawings, a homunculus from a petri dish in a sacred grove, under the gaze of a human-faced star.

I took the letter and sat down in my favorite chair and stared at the "Kittery, ME" postmark on the envelope of my mother's letter for a while, sipping a cup of nearly cold blackberry tea. Then I glanced at the other mail. There was an official-looking communication from the Los Angeles Unified School District, addressed to Mr. and Mrs. J. Tallich. It was a report on Ollie's progress in kindergarten. She was being recommended for a special-ed program for attention-deficient children. A personal note from her teacher at the bottom explained that some testing had been done and though it was too early to tell, it looked like Ollie needed help. It said that she was not hyperactive; it had been determined that she did not "yet" need behavior-modifying drugs like Ritalin, but she had a great deal of trouble concentrating for more than a few seconds on anything. There was a second letter from the Los Angeles Unified School District. It said that Ollie was a potential candidate for the Magnet program for gifted children and that I should fill out an application form to get her name on the list now.

I was looking at these two letters when Jay came in. He glanced at me quizzically and I flipped them in his direction. He put down his gym bag, frowning at me, and slumped against the wall to read.

When he finished the second letter, he frowned harder at me.

"OK. I don't g-get it. How can she need special ed at the same time as she's gifted?"

"You know, I wish I could answer that one. But I've been sitting here for the last half hour, stumped."

He threw the letters down on a side table, heading out to the kitchen for a beer.

"She needs a p-private school, I told you this, Esme. But did you listen? D-does anybody?"

He was opening the refrigerator door; I raised my voice.

"You think paying a lot of money provides your kid with people who have insight, are aware of her needs? Or care more? Think again." I was touchy here—I know schools didn't matter, *teachers* mattered, and Gloria Walther had been transferred (for some obscure bureaucratic reason) at the last minute to another district. Ollie's teacher now was an elderly woman who turned off her hearing aid when the kids got noisy.

I heard the refrigerator door shut and the sound of a metal cap hitting the wastebasket. Then silence as he drank.

"Think again," I repeated.

The bottle followed the cap into the basket and I heard him opening the refrigerator again.

"Please don't," I added softly, but he didn't hear me. He came out of the kitchen with the second beer in his hand; he brushed by me on the way to the TV. He clicked it on with the remote channel selector and then, as a picture of dancing cartoon bears flashed, flipped it off.

"You look tired," he said, but his voice sounded accusing, instead of solicitous.

"I am."

"How was l-lab?"

"Routine. How was work?"

He laughed softly. "Ah, come on, Esme. You d-don't really want to know about my w-work, do you?"

"I asked, didn't I?"

He shook his head slowly and downed his beer. A thin high whine filled our ears. It sounded like a human mosquito.

"W-what the hell is *that*?"

"That's Ollie humming. It's a new habit. She sings songs and hums."

He raised his eyebrows at me—then backed out of the room still staring at me. At the hallway intersection he inclined his head.

"Ollie! S-stop that noise *now*!"

"You don't have to yell at her."

"Yeah, I do. I *have* to yell at her. I c-can't s-stand all this unearthly shit anymore."

"Maybe it seems worse than it is 'cause you're drinking."

"Maybe I'm drinking because it's w-worse than it seems."

He smirked at me and moved toward the kitchen, defiant.

"Wait," I said. "Are you telling me that Ollie is the reason that you're drinking so much?"

"God. Esme. You f-figured that out just like *that*."

I followed him out to the kitchen, watched him open the refrigerator. The possibility of conflict, even this spiritless argument, in the wake of our recent numbness toward each other seemed appealing to me. Since my night with Jesse, we'd spoken in strained but neutral tones. I felt sparks moving in the air.

"I don't think Ollie should be blamed for what you choose to do of your own free will."

His shoulders hunched, then he straightened up again.

"You know, Esme, I've been th-thinking. Ollie seems like a living symptom of what's wrong with our . . . with *us*. She can't t-talk, or won't talk, she turns till she's d-dizzy. We have a difference of opinion. You say she's . . . p-preoccupied. I say she's *sick*." He closed the refrigerator door, holding the sweating beer bottle upright till he fished up the silver opener swinging on its rusted wall chain, prying the cap off with a soft pop. I noticed, idly, burying deep inside a reaction to what he'd said, that he operated on my "wrong" side as I watched him; he was left-handed. He let the opener on its chain fall heavily against the wall.

"I don't know. I k-keep asking you if you love me, Esme. You say yes, but I think m-maybe you're incapable of loving me. Believe me, I've been through all the possibilities. *I'm* the one on the outside."

He set the bottle down on the counter. Then put his head in his hands.

"It's not even about your f-fucking someone else. D-do you have any idea of w-what it's like living with you t-two? You're like some mother-daughter *act*—the weird duo: Mom has her head in the stars and the kid acts like she's from Mars."

He looked up at me, then down again.

"You turn from me in bed because you're thinking about *Ollie*. She sleeps between us."

He was drunk now—I'd watch his face flush and fill slowly with rancor, red annoyance—but now he looked so broken, so defeated, that I reached out instinctively to touch his hair. But as my fingers grazed his head, a storm of chemical dissolution blew in. The molecules of the fibers of his hair, his scalp, the bones of the skull—all unmeshed and leaped out at me, and I pulled my hand back. Insects boiling out of a hive. I stared at his head, then abruptly, superimposed over the turbulent molecules, I saw a Jay, reaching forward again and again, opening a beer bottle with his left hand. Then I saw him putting a hand up suddenly to catch the phone receiver I'd thrown to him last week, reaching up to the shower caddy for soap.

"What about *me?*" I heard him cry, shaking his head. "What about *me?*"

Vertigo: I put my hand to my own head. It wasn't enough that I had to watch the world come apart, reducing itself to its particulate structure before my eyes—*now,* literally on top of *that,* I was conjuring phantom images. "Mars," he said, "stars"— Then, abruptly, it all stopped. Simultaneous to my pain and with the force of absolute certainty, I understood what was really happening: I saw that I was being given a gift; maybe a vision. Out of my store of domestic images, from the shards of chemical fragmentation, a door was forming, opening—the *hand* beckoned from inside, *Come, this is the way.*

"Jay," I murmured like someone in a trance. "Do that again."

He raised his chemically eroded head to stare at me. "D-do what?"

"Open another beer bottle."

He gawked at me. "You're *asking* me to d-drink another beer?"

"Go ahead." I laughed. "Just do it."

"Esme, l-let me get this straight. You *want* me to drink another beer right now? Before I'm even f-finished with this one?"

I smiled dreamily at him. "I didn't say *drink* another beer. I said would you please *open* another beer."

"You mean *you* w-want one?"

"No."

He opened his mouth to speak, apparently thought better of it, then strode to the refrigerator. He pulled out the fourth bottle, his movements a little stiff and unsteady, transferred the bottle to his right hand, then picked up the opener in his left. He looked over his shoulder, smiling a little, uncertain, as if we were playing a little game. What was this leading to?

I laughed. "Bingo," I said to myself softly.

The sound of Ollie's tuneless humming grew louder as she approached.

Jay dropped the opener and whirled around, suddenly furious.

"OK, wait a minute. This is a Scientific Moment, right?" He came closer, glowering at me, I could smell the beer on his breath, and another, subtler smell, which I couldn't place. Then I got it: aftershave, a woodsy lime-y smell.

"Here is a m-man, some poor j-jerk trying to talk to his wife about how their marriage is f-falling apart and his *wife,* his wife is . . ." His face twisted. "I'd like to know. Where are you?"

"Where am I? I'm right here. I'm listening to you. I'm listening to what you're saying, but it happens that what you're saying hurts me. It's like Philip Glass music. It's *right* but it drives you nuts. I listen and I *don't* listen. I love you and I *don't* love you. And yes, I just saw something. I saw something . . . connected to everything, you know, that I've been thinking about."

Jay flipped the full, just-opened bottle in the trash. "And whatever you do, Esme," he said grimly, "*stay* connected."

It was funny. I *saw* him go out the door. I heard what he was saying as he left, but it just didn't touch me. I was talking a little to myself. I sat looking at the refrigerator, the opener, a couple of things Jay had set up in the kitchen for his southpaw convenience: left-handed scissors on a string, reversed handles, an extra pencil on the left side of the grocery pad (where he wrote his work messages). I kept shaking my head and laughing to myself. And the whole time I heard her behind me, humming her tuneless song.

---------------

# Chapter 12

Imaginary Lecture: Theoretical Chemistry,
or A Bedtime Story for Ollie

*Let me tell you a little story—the plot's a familiar one. Only the
circumstances of the tale won't be readily recognizable.*

*Here's how it begins: Everyone in the world is right- or left-handed,
right? Well, amino acids in almost all living things on earth are made
of, though it seems odd to think of it this way,* left-handed *molecules.
How can an amino acid, or its molecules, be any kind of* handed?
*Well, to understand, you must think of a screw. You cannot twist a
right-handed screw into a left-handed nut, no matter how hard you
try. The building blocks of life have a "twist," almost as if some great
right hand had turned us, given us a spin into ourselves.*

*This twist I'm talking about is called* chirality, *from the Greek,
meaning "handedness," and the equations I'm writing out daily happen to be obsessed with chirality as a phenomenon in the universe.*

*If I told you some stories about chirality here on earth you'd be
intrigued. It happens that chemical compounds are chiral—in other
words, they have "handed" molecules and some of these molecules
have enantiomers, opposite twins. Think of a left-handed glove and*

*its right-handed mate. But the opposite "glove" can have completely different characteristics: For example, DARVON is a sedative, and its twin, NOVRAD is a cough medicine. The chemical compound carvone, $C_{10}H_{14}O$, has a left-handed twin that smells of spearmint; the right twin smells of caraway. Pharmacological researchers are out there locating the right-handed mirror-image twins of certain left-handed chemicals in order to produce drugs or perfumes or sugar substitutes that we will buy and take into our bodies to soothe headaches or smell good or help us sleep. You want to lose weight? It happens that the sugars used by the body are right-handed; left-handed sugars are indigestible. Is it surprising that someone is patenting a sweetener that is completely unfattening, made up of some left-handed sugars? So you can have your Frosted Flakes and zero calories too?*

*But this is not the story I want to tell. My story takes place in space, in deep space, where all direction becomes relative. And because the direction of a molecule's handedness determines the types of interactions it can have with another molecule, why not picture these particles turning around freely out there and then ask if they could react without direction? That is to say, in deep space they have only each other to lend orientation. These are lovers, each half of a set of twins—and my question is, has been for some time now, Would these chirals recognize their enantiomers deep in disoriented space? When I saw Jay repeating a series of left-handed tasks I saw a halo around him, as if his image had been lifted up and out of matter; that image raised over the churning molecules gave me new insight into my approach: Let the chirals float out into the universe, get them moving.*

*Francis Crick (you remember Watson and Crick, the DNA vaudeville team?) Crick, the Nobel Prize–winning physiologist, asked the question, but kept it earthbound: "Could we not have two distinct types of organisms, one the mirror image of the other, at least as far as its components are concerned? This is what is never found. There are not two separate kingdoms of nature, one having molecules of one hand and the other their mirror images. . . . The first great unifying principle of biochemistry is that the key molecules have the same hand in all organisms."* But, Dr. Crick, if we take biochemistry into space—what then?

*If I were rephrasing this for my TOE, my series of equations, I'd say something like:* Surprising as it may seem, *the asymmetric nature of tetrahedral carbon has been recognized for more than a century, and yet no attempt has been made to evaluate the interaction energy between two asymmetric tetrahedral molecules. Two tetrahedral asymmetric but chiral molecules whirling in space. With math, a series of equations, I define the coordinates in a Cartesian system. That is to say, I look at Nature and I try to reduce the infinitely complex questions to a model that is "solvable." Will these two come together out there?*

*Why should these two rather ordinary molecules popping around in space interest us—won't they just hum and click together when and if they bump up against each other? No, here's the thing: Chirality cannot be superimposed—you can't just push these two together and make them "fit." The molecules have atomic bonds which, even as they tumble over each other's surfaces in space, have to be matched, lined up exactly; if they are not, chiral "recognition" does not take place: The lovers do not rise, on fire, swaying toward each other, arms outstretched, on target.*

*So my experiment is this: I take my chiral tetrahedral molecules and I analyze them in the limit of free relative molecular rotation and thus I add another variable: a very very high temperature. Whew, it's hot!* When these lovers try to touch (molecules are attracted to each other, but they can get stuck on each other too soon) they require high energy, *which is high temperature to make them move fast. But it's not, by any means,* balmy *(palm trees, a beach in Aruba, coconut scent of suntan oil)—it's astro-hot, star-hot, which makes my mo-*

*lecular sweethearts spin and spin even faster, since heat increases velocity. And why, as author of this experiment here in the red-shifted Now, do I simulate such torchy circumstances—why do I create such unimaginable heat, heat we've never experienced on earth? Because, it's simple, it's elegant: I'm after the Origin, I'm trying to re-create conditions as close to the Bang as I can, as close to the beginning of the world or even the millisecond before the explosion, before matter and radiation flew outward in all directions, before hydrogen formed and mixed with dust and created protogalactic clouds, before ellipticals, spiral galaxies, before supernovas. I want the moment when it was all one, before God's chiral hand came down, spun us, asked the question—and blew us apart forever.*

*If I could reproduce that moment, in theory, the moment the cosmic soup thickened—say I got my chiral molecules to find each other and flip correctly, what do I prove? I don't know. Maybe the circumstances of chiral recognition will indicate how the four forces of the universe (electromagnetism, gravity, strong nuclear force, and weak nuclear force) influenced molecule formation; maybe I'll get a glimpse of the hierarchy of these forces. If it gets hot enough, the center will not hold, as Yeats said; the bonds will blow apart, the molecules blast off. You see, they touch, they kiss, then BOOM, the kernels pop. What is there before the moment of conception? The thought of conception?*

*Jay comes into the kitchen, Jay opens a beer, his brain calibrates exactly what infinitesimal adjustments are needed to guide his extremities. Pop the top, flip the cap in the trash, shift the bottle to the other hand to pass the beer to a right-handed receiver. Shake hands with a right-hander at a party, palm the bottle to the other hand, lift the fork from the left side of the plate to your mouth, turn to the right to tell a joke, flip the beer (a trick), drop it, watch it shatter. Turn to make a point over your shoulder to your wife, whirl around* to face her, furious, raise the left hand to point at her, shout, let the left hand make a fist, threaten, let it drop. Sit with the left hand over your eyes, slumped at a kitchen table. Crawl into bed later, touch her with your left hand, touch her left breast with your left hand, begin to talk to her in the strained tones of the wounded loyal. And stutter: *The synapse circuit closes, the neurons quiver, but the tongue resists slightly the cerebral command—this is not a misfire, this is an exquisite hesitation, pre-aural sabotage by the mind, which wants to say something else, something different, something it will never be able to say.*

*In space, my molecules keep turning. They have to fit together, and now my calculations are telling me they have to have three pairs of centers on the atoms where they touch—in other words, they can't just like each other, they have to attach surfaces, they have to have a lot in common. It wasn't enough that they made each other laugh, it wasn't enough that they had dynamite sex. They had to recognize each other, on some other level. They had to fit. So Ollie, they're still spinning Out There. And Daddy's gone now. I can't say if he'll be back. I don't think he will be. I'm the one who failed. His nature was, I suppose, kinder, till he realized I didn't believe in his kindness. The cruelty he invented to defend himself. Marriage allows you an unremitting gaze at the other person; even when you don't want to stare any longer, you can't stop looking. You have to know when to look away. Then you can move together again; your eyes search each other out again, abashed, humbled. I could not let him love me, I could not muster the attention forgiveness demands, because I lived in distraction. Now he is falling away through the space I am trying to reassemble in a theory. To understand—what? The origins of life, the order of the universe? Will I walk out into the cosmos? Giddily, gladly. But I won't follow him out the door, I won't stand by the car, arguing. I have no interest in human drama. Why don't they understand that the damage has already been done? Even Q misun-*

*derstood me there. I am in a despair so joyful only the elegant precision of your inward-turning face, Ollie, of your unconventional speech, expresses it exactly. The damage has been done to us. But I can choose the conditions of my defeat. And that's the end, Ollie. The End. Except they're still out there, whirling, turning around and around each other, stalking each other, in the vast, indifferent, storybook night.*

# Chapter 13

*You must obtain a laboratory coat and wear it in the laboratory. In addition, please be aware that some instruments are hazardous (for example, the ultraviolet light sources and the high-voltage power supplies) and that many of the chemicals and reagents may be harmful if ingested (for example, ethidium bromide) or dropped onto exposed skin (for example, phenol). Therefore, you must take care and wear appropriate apparel when necessary—for example, plastic goggles when using ultraviolet light, and gloves when using ethidium bromide and phenol. As far as is known, the biological materials—phages, bacteria, enzymes—are harmless; nonetheless, we will use weakened strains of* E. coli *to prevent any possible spread of recombinant DNA molecules out of the laboratory.*

The instructions were taped to the lab door. I stood reading and rereading them, not seeing them. Rocky was in there, I knew: I could hear the strains of Traffic. I couldn't bring myself to push open the pneumatic door; I couldn't bring myself to put on a public, cheerful face or even a private, suffering one. Jay had left me. He'd been gone for five days and I was edgy, sleepless.

I slumped down the hall to my office, let myself in, and turned on the harsh overhead light. My desk was covered with papers and graphs and spilled beakers and bent tubing. I moved to the bookshelves that lined the walls and ran my fingers along the dusty spines. I reached in my pocket for a crumpled pack of cigarettes and lit one, throwing the dead match at the wastebasket, just missing.

I smoked and stared at the titles: abstracts and biographies. There were occasional lives of women along the shoulder-to-shoulder stories of men in science. And what kind of lives were the lives of women scientists? Could they (should they?) be categorized as a *type* of life?

I crushed the cigarette in an old crusted beaker. It hadn't tasted good. On my way down the hall, I'd been consoling myself with certain self-serving daydreams: even if my husband *had* left me, I was going to be renowned in my field (and here I might light a smoke and swagger a little). OK, OK, *not a Nobel laureate,* but a theoretician in whose wake perceptions of reality exploded, re-formed? As if a scientist's life was in itself a neat vengeance!

I wrenched open a stuck window, sat down, and pulled my journal toward me. Papers fluttered a little; a photograph of Stonehenge I'd taped to the wall a year ago blew under a cupboard.

**Imaginary Lecture:**
**A Brief History of Women in Science**

After your father left me, I went on in the tradition of . . . whom? I glanced up at a little wall chart I've made for myself—a random litany of the lost names. *Aspasia,* physician; *Annie Jump Cannon,* astronomer; *Nettie Marie Stevens,* cytogeneticist; *Amalie Dietrich,* naturalist; *Jane Sharp,* midwife; *Hildegard of Bingen,* cosmologist; *Hypatia of Alexandria,* mathematician and philosopher; *Augusta Ada*

*Byron,* mathematician, inventor; *Caroline Lucretia Herschel,* astronomer.

All those lost *lives!* Of women who (like me) wanted only a little space, a little time to putter or theorize. Craved a little knowledge, dying to pursue an answer or two. I could hear the voices: a cry here, a comment there, bits of lives outside narrative, circling.

Late one night I made some notes, picking up volumes: personal memoirs, histories, biographies of men—extracting the odd offhand insight into the silent lives of sisters, mothers, wives, teachers, friends. The bits of lives flew to me like iron filings to a magnet.

Here's *The Compleat Midwives' Book* by Jane Sharp, a seventeenth-century British midwife. Jane stood at the childbeds of women who died, feverish and hemorrhaging—women who couldn't have read their own tombstones. There is no anger in Jane's voice, only resignation. Women, she says, are "denied knowledge," not "bred up" like men.

*Bred up,* an interesting phrase. Because represented here are *bred up* women, women bred within an inch of their lives, like Byron's daughter, Ada, Countess of Lovelace, a mathematician, a genius who, in the 1840s, helped Charles Babbage invent "the difference engine," a precursor of the computer. Her breeding got her essentially nowhere, except into a footnote in Babbage's biography. We do have an exasperated quote from her, a snap at old Babbage, who *would* fuss with her mechanical descriptions: "I cannot endure another person to meddle with my sentences!" One can almost recognize Father in these tones, except no one ever fussed with George Gordon's lines.

But even if I put together a narrative, where would it begin? Fourth century A.D.? Hypatia? *She* was torn apart by a mob of fellow Alexandrians, led to riot by a certain Bishop Cyril, who was jealous of "her wisdom exceeding all bounds, especially in the things concerning astronomy."

Well what the hell business did Hypatia have, anyway, knowing so much? Wasn't playing dumb the smart thing for a smart woman to do? I'm thinking now of Caroline Herschel, astronomer, sweeping the skies with her telescope, credited with discovering eighteen comets. She gave all the credit to her brother, William, who allowed her to work as his laboratory assistant. She called herself a "well-trained puppy dog."

Or Mary Fairfax Somerville, mathematician, experimentalist, talking about herself and *all* women:

I was conscious that I had never made a discovery myself, that I had no originality . . . no genius; that spark from heaven is not granted to the sex. We are of the earth.

So what do *I* have to complain about, Ollie? These voices betray suffering I don't bear. I'm alone now, but I'm my own woman. I have my own lab; I run it myself proudly. I *am* the only female in a department of men—but my work is respected, I am compensated. I am free to work.

But look, here's a publication on a bookshelf just a hand's reach up, as recent as 1982, that says I have *the wrong kind of brain* for scientific achievement! I page through the issue of *Science* magazine. Published inside is a famous study: results of tests that present seemingly definitive proof that the posterior end (the splenium) of the corpus callosum (the great bundle of nerves, commissural fibers) that connects the right and left hemispheres of the brain is *larger* in women than in men, thus making communication swifter and easier between the two halves of the female brain. From this fact, the test's authors drew an interesting conclusion. They said that this indicated the male brain is more specialized, giving rise to further conclusions such as, This is why more men are musical, mathematical, and scientific geniuses. In other words, the more *lateralized* your brain, the *smarter* you are. And where does that leave *women*—leaning over the neural picket fence and *talking* faster? *How* is it that what could be interpreted as a biological advantage (communication of short-term memory and learned tasks *faster* across the divide) becomes evidence of how male genius is made?

I picked up a framed black-and-white photograph of Jay (next to one of a just-born Ollie) on my desk. He was wearing his Dodgers cap, squinting into the sun at the beach. I'd always loved this picture of him. I opened my desk drawer and put the picture inside.

I watched myself start to slide to the floor, then sit up, ready to kick ass. (*Aspasia, Annie Jump Cannon . . .*) Instead of arguing that women have "less hemispheric specialization," why wouldn't it be *as valid* to say men could use more intercortical communication? I know common wisdom used to be that women couldn't *think;* men used to make fun of women for being—what? *Scatterbrained,* intuitive, emotional, incapable of focusing? Now, some people argue that this kind of multiburner thinking is a *power.* In fact, you could argue that what the male physicist—at the apex of cosmological theoretical speculation—is in essence trying to do is *to think like a woman.*

Trying to align his cognitive rhythms with spatial *flux:* soaping the baby's rib cage, counting parallel universes, *saying aaah,* tracking gluons as they pass through walls, fixing the wheels of the broken toy, soothing the high fever, talking to the high fever, noting infinities that plague calculation. Ollie, listen: To pursue the merely abstract is to overlook the nature of the brain *and* the universe. Thought is given to us in *metaphors,* which bridge worlds, *crossing over:* the corpus callosum itself a metaphor for that intersection.

Now, on my feet again, I ran my finger along the book backs and stopped on the biography of Madame Curie by her daughter, Eve. God, Madame Curie. Why was it whenever anybody anywhere was asked to name a woman scientist it was always Madame Curie? Well, she was indeed the chosen, the only one of us granted enormous recognition and prestige. In her spousal research team, she had the original ideas, did most of the cutting-edge experiments. After her husband's death, she finally did it all, but she is often listed second: his appendage.

Curie did what no man has ever done: She actually won *two* Nobel Prizes—in two different fields, physics and chemistry. She crossed right over those "specialty" boundaries a lot of scientists squawk about. The year she received her second Nobel was the same year the French Academy of Sciences refused to admit her because she was a woman. She was married, very happily; she didn't seem to be a witch or a dyke or a madwoman, she was approved by the patriarchal judges of professional character.

But she was never called by her name, Marie Curie; she was *Madame* Curie, Pierre's wife. Imagine the two of them: inseparable, together in the lab all day, every day. So close they barely had to speak. But poor Pierre was an absentminded fellow. One day he was crossing the rue Dauphine in Paris, his eyes turned inward on his radium-cure theories; he slipped on the wet pavement and fell under the wheels of a heavy wagon drawn by two horses. His head was crushed. It was a showery spring day, April 1906. Not long before this gruesome event, his wife had had a weird premonition. She'd come running to Pierre, her face wild, in tears, crying that if one of them disappeared the other could not go on, was that not right?

He'd looked at her, replied, "You are wrong. Whatever happens, even if one has to go on like a body without a soul, one must work just the same."

So now she worked on alone. She was the first woman given a position in higher education in France. Immediately after Pierre's death, she was named professor at the Sorbonne, given her husband's chair in physics. At the first meeting of her course, she began her lecture on the theory of ions in gases at the precise point where her husband had ended his final talk on the same subject. The day of this lecture, the auditorium was a circus; reporters and curiosity seekers shoved in beside the students. Curie received a standing ovation when she walked in. But she refused to acknowledge the waves of emotion—she gave her lecture in the coolest possible tones, then exited the lecture hall with dignity. Class, you say. Style, character.

But the same reporters who'd earlier questioned her ability to take over her husband's position now complained that she had no feelings, she was "cold." Was she a woman or not? What kind of woman *is* a scientist, anyway?

How could any man have imagined that this was the same Marie Curie who frightened her sister nearly out of her wits shortly before the Sorbonne lecture? Marie called her into the bedroom one evening, begging for help. Before her sister's eyes, Curie opened a parcel she'd been carrying next to her heart for days and days. The parcel contained Pierre's bloody clothes and the doctor's linens used to wrap his crushed head. She pulled out the clothes, stiff with blackened gore, crying that she could not let go these remnants of her husband. Her sister knelt beside her, trying to quell her hysterical weeping, then gently put a scissors in her hands, helped her cut the clothes to pieces, toss the pieces in the fire. From one of the last folds of cloth, fragments of brain matter fell free; Curie held them to her lips, hunching over like an animal, making inarticulate sounds; the sister dragged the clothing and the scissors away from her and cut the final pieces, stuffed them into the fire.

But Curie gave the lecture. She betrayed no emotion at all, she discussed ions and gases. She went back to the laboratory. She put her hands, her bare hands, on the radium, on its "cool light." She did the work, the work that killed her. I turned my back on the books, leaning against them, breathing hard. If my mood was melodramatic this morning, I'd indulge it, I'd go further into hell. I spun around again and stabbed with my finger, hitting Einstein, his *Collected Papers,* containing his early correspondence with his first wife, Mileva Maric.

Ah, Einstein. Harpo Marx–ish angelic face, Daddy of the Universe, everybody's favorite genius—licking a big cone of vanilla ice cream, his wise eyes alight beneath that great halo of wild white hair. How he spoke in Great Quotes! God does not shoot dice with the universe! Could anyone not adore this gently mischievous, dreamy old guy who refused to wear socks? I pulled his *Collected Papers* out of the shelves and turned pages.

In 1896, Albert met Mileva Maric at the Federal Technical Institute in Zurich. She was Serbian: striking—long dark hair and deep eyes in a wide cameo face—and as smart, it seems, as he. Intellectually compatible with Einstein, and three years older. She'd been a child prodigy in math and science, she was sent to the Institute as its only woman student. He fell in love with her for her beauty and her brains and her maturity, and she reciprocated, she loved him, though she was funny about it—my favorite thing. Mileva had a sense of humor. "I'm from a little country of bandits," she'd say to people, by way of introduction. And when Einstein complained to her, in a letter, about the world's blindness, she wrote back: "I do not believe that the human brain is to be blamed for the fact that man cannot grasp infinity." It was conditioning, she said. Infinity would be in man's grasp if "when he was learning to perceive, the little fellow had not been so cruelly confined to the earth . . . or among four walls, but instead was allowed to walk out a little into the universe."

They were both nonconformists. Einstein was a high school dropout—his Great Youthful Quote was "School is no place for inquiring minds," he found his teachers repressive and conventional-minded, and so did she. They were bohemians, meeting in the cafés, two young physicists who talked about the cosmos the way most people talk about their front yards. They formed a club, an "Athenaeum," a sort of esthetics-minded café gang that met to talk about music and art and philosophy.

When Mileva became pregnant, in May 1901, this idyllic, gently rebellious student world changed, at least for her. She went home to her parents in Serbia, and Albert went home too, to persuade his parents to bless the marriage. Einstein's mother disapproved of Mileva, the marriage, all of it. When she said no to the union, did Einstein fly to his lover, to be by her side for the birth of his daughter? No, Einstein stayed where he was, trying to persuade Mama to relent—but by then Lieserl had been born (without her father present). Lieserl had been "given up" (it seems she was sent to Serbian relatives, then put up for adoption), and because of the elder Einsteins' objections, and intervening wars, was lost to her parents forever. Mileva and Albert did finally marry, and had two sons, Hans Albert and Edouard, before they split up—but what happened to Lieserl? Mileva had wanted her baby to be a girl. She went through a long, difficult labor and then she held her daughter safe in her arms. And Einstein wrote that he had no wish "to part with her." Tell me, does God not play dice? Did their lost daughter ever read that quote? Neither a birth certificate nor a record of her death can be found.

I try again to imagine Mileva at school—the only woman at the physics institute, trying to keep her sense of herself intact, walking into the laboratory, where the scowling professors waited, smiling at everyone, cultivating a thoughtful anonymity, trying not to be called upon. But she was a scientist, after all—her courage came from her calculations, from her proofs. She could answer questions; she could find solutions. Forgetting herself, her sex, she'd rise to her feet sometimes, filled with a fervor to explain an unorthodox answer (for, like Einstein's, her mind worked in unconventional, metaphoric ways) and in the narrow aisle, she'd stumble a little, grasp the desk for support. Mileva limped slightly: a condition resulting from a childhood fever.

As a toddler, in Serbia, she'd been nicknamed La Petite Boiteuse, The Little Lame Girl. It was supposed to be a fond diminutive, but sounded cruel. She became even more self-conscious, having lost her balance now; her voice lost authority, but she went on speaking. Over in the corner of the classroom, Albert mugged at her, made a funny face at the professor's back. She laughed aloud at his antics ("Oh that Einstein fellow!")—and went on with her explanation.

So they fell in love. Often they hiked together in the Swiss mountains, and they took a trip to Lake Thun of a weekend. I can see her: At a café she sits next to him, surreptitiously pulls down her cotton lisle stocking and brown kid pump and feels for the yellowed callus on the sole of the foot of her shorter leg, a callus formed by the regular plunge and shock of her limp. She is wearing shoes that do not fit her correctly, worn for style, just once, rather than sensible support. She pulls up her stocking, shrugs, puts her hands behind her head. Her foxish face is sunburned, her grin lopsided. He is bold-eyed, inquisitive, bristling with energy, his tie and collar askew. Even his mustache looks off-center. Occasionally, he shivers a little, an involuntary twitch—stares into space then, laughs nervously. He takes an orange from her and nibbles on it, pretending to eat it all. They both burst into laughter. They are so young. What have they been talking about all afternoon, these two lovers on the beach, familiar as sweethearts painted on the lid of a taffy tin? Molecular motion, differential equations, double integrals, thermal motion. Parasols, prams, a man with a cart selling ices. The possibility of relative motion in the universe.

But Pauline Einstein threw herself down and sobbed like a child. "She is a *book* like you!"—Yes, Mileva was a *book*: an intellectual, and also she was a shiksa, a Serbian, of uncertain class; she was *forward* (competing with men!), she limped . . . And *more*—Pauline Einstein had guessed (though her son denied it vehemently) that the two were sexually intimate. Her son was sleeping with this shiksa

Serbian limping scientist. Mileva represented bohemianism, feminism, the demimonde—and Mother said to Albert, "If you get her with child, then you'll be in a pickle!"

Mileva worked on a scientific project with a colleague and signed her papers Einstein instead of Maric. Another friend asked *why*. Because we are *ein stein*, she said, we are *one stone*.

In Einstein's first papers on the special theory of relativity, Mileva signed as Maric, as co-author, according to the Russian physicist Abram Joffe, who saw all submissions to *The Annals of Physics*, where Einstein's breakthroughs were published. The papers were published under Albert's name only; the original manuscript somehow disappeared. After their divorce, when he won the Nobel Prize in 1921, he gave all the prize money to Mileva. He spent the rest of his time trying to create his doomed unified field theory, and she retired into obscurity. Let me ask you a question: Does God play dice with women's lives?

Well, that was a long time ago, Ollie. Beyond the usurpation of Curie and the tragic mystery of Mileva Maric Einstein must stand— who? A contemporary woman? That makes sense. And let's rig it even more—let's posit a scientist who's an unmarried woman, single and independent, tough-minded. None of this soap-opera, weeping-into-the-beakers stuff! Surely, for a woman scientist like *this*, life and work would be easier?

I turn again and slide my finger blindly till it stops at the famous team of Crick and Watson and immediately the name "Rosalind Franklin" leaps to my mind. It would not do so normally. The only reason it leaps to mine is because here in my hands is a biography of Rosalind Franklin by a woman named Anne Sayre, a friend of Rosalind's. OK, we are in a different, more contemporary time, the fifties—close to our own. We expect that women will be more accepted in the academy, in the laboratory, right? We expect that this accomplished

woman, educated at Cambridge, whose chosen milieu was biology—
or rather, what we would now call molecular biology (emphasis on
X-ray diffraction, with specialized work on subcrystalline materials)
—would have an easier road?

Rosalind Franklin, after all, had claimed her independence early.
She did not marry; she devoted her life to science, and when she went
from Cambridge to the prestigious Randall Laboratory at King's College, she had set her goal: to do research on DNA. Everybody who
knew Rosalind knew that she was tough, the stuff out of which great
scientists are made; hers was the illuminating research on DNA—
she, in fact, produced on an X ray the first image of the double helix.
Why, then, don't we all know her name, the way we know Crick's
and Watson's?

Because she did not discover DNA; they did. Or at least that's the
way it's gone down in the history books. Yet her research was central
to the discovery of DNA—what happened? What happened was this.
Anne Sayre sets it out carefully. Rosalind did not get along with her
Randall associate, Maurice Wilkins. Wilkins refused to view Rosalind
as anything other than his assistant, though she was brought into the
Randall lab to pursue her own research. To say that there was friction
between them would be like describing the *Titanic* as a minor boating
accident. Wilkins had enormous trouble accepting a woman as a
partner in science, particularly a woman of confrontational style with
no time to flatter the male ego.

Meanwhile, over at Cambridge, the team of Watson and Crick
decided to jump into the search for DNA, which Franklin and Wilkins
had begun at King's. Watson attended Franklin's seminars; the two
utilized her already completed research in their experiments. There is
nothing to indicate that Rosalind ever knew, ever noticed. Watson
got to know Wilkins and sympathized with him for having to put up
with such a shrew. Sayre's book says he commented that Wilkins was

being put through "emotional hell" by Rosalind's unorthodox temperament.

On February 6, 1953, Watson paid a visit to Maurice Wilkins at King's College and Wilkins allowed him to look at an X-ray photograph that belonged to Rosalind Franklin. The X ray showed a B-form diffraction pattern suggesting a helical pattern containing two, three, or four coaxial nucleic-acid chains per helical unit and having the phosphate groups, or the bases, in the center and the backbone on the outside of the structure. When I read this description (Rosalind's own, straight from Anne Sayre's book) I get the shivers. Rosalind was *right there*. She had it in her hands. We have Wilkins himself describing it:

I had this photograph and there was a helix right on the picture, you couldn't miss it. I showed it to Jim, and I said, "Look, there's the helix, and that damned woman just won't see it." He picked it up, of course.

Hey, he picked it up. Later, Wilkins said that he regretted having shown the photograph to Watson. He said that "perhaps" he should have asked Rosalind's permission. No shit. I have to admit, I'm looking at this series of events from the perspective of current attitudes on what we call scooping in up-to-the-minute science. Things *were* a little freer then—but showing someone's research to a competitor? Without asking permission? It's true that now scientists "edit" their conference seminars, only hinting at "hard" information, so as not to hand the competition one's edge. Submissions to technical scientific journals are logged in with a date and a time, and remain unopened until the last minute, to protect the authors from a scoop. Rivalry is fierce—research grants and fellowships, prize money, etc., are limited; it's ugly out there.

But Rosalind was working away, unaware of Wilkins's "tip" to Watson. If it had mattered to her, I can't imagine what form her protest would have taken: Her lab was enamored of regular "interim reports." In December of 1952, the head of the lab had published a report covering recent work done and included her findings. And even before Christmas the same year, Wilkins sent drawings of the "B" patterns in squid sperm to Crick. Wilkins was a real hot source. And, the biggest question in this biographical sleuthing: What became of an interim annual report written by Rosalind Franklin a full year before Wilkins showed Watson the X ray—in fact, interpreting the B-form diffraction pattern as a "helical structure." She *did* know. But why did she wait?

I think I know. But here's what happened in history. On February 5, 1953, Watson and Crick had nothing in mind to help them build a definitive model of DNA. But between February 6 and February 28 they learned enough to build the famous "Tinkertoy" model every schoolkid has seen, the one I built in my basement: the double spiral staircase. And you see, that's it, that's why Rosalind took longer. *They* were biologists—they loved to build atomic models: fast instructive visual aids. And this was a prefab Arthurian tale, with crusading knights, and a Holy Grail built like a twin helix. Rosalind Franklin was a crystallographer, a theoretician; she was interested in taking some time to demonstrate the structure of DNA on X rays, in crystal molecular formation. She was working on the integrity of each section of the canvas, like Cézanne painting: a scientist deep in her subject. And as far as a "race" goes, she had no notion at all that anyone outside Randall had access to her information.

In 1962, the Nobel Prize for Medicine and Physiology was shared by Francis Crick, James Watson, and Maurice Wilkins—in recognition of their work on DNA. Rosalind Franklin's name was missing. But then, Rosalind was missing in general. On April 16, 1958, Rosalind Franklin died of cancer. She was thirty-seven years old.

———

I let my hand drop, glancing up at the top shelves, where I know stands a biography of Barbara McClintock, whose research into "jumping genes," retrotransposons (using corn, plain old kernels of corn, as her model!) changed genetic inquiry. Her research led to high-resolution bonding techniques, but she was laughed at and ignored for years. Finally, in the sixties, her work was looked at objectively and, in 1983, she was awarded the Nobel Prize.

But I'm sick of this now. This glut of . . . what? Sexist Highlights of Science History? The SH of SH? At least my theory is *my theory.*

*I look up at the wall clock. Ten-thirty. Jay,* says a little tin voice. I shake myself. *Jay.* I think of the way his eyes close, in a trusting manner, just before he stutters. I hear his voice, its musical timbre. His laugh. Then I shake my head.

My *theory,* I think. I look at the clock again, then pick up my bag. I've made my decision. I'm going over to USC to talk to (another name for my litany!) Professor Lorraine Revent Atwater.

# Chapter 14

I found Professor Atwater's office with some difficulty. She was on mini-sabbatical from the USC chemistry department; she was at work on a new project and had squirreled herself and her computers away somewhere in the warren of small offices in an offshoot of the chem building.

I knocked hesitantly at the door, which was half open, and blinked into the shadowy interior, where two (no, three!) leaping computer screens sat stacked up like animated building blocks. She was at work, bent over a yellow legal pad lit by the spotlight of a gooseneck lamp—she didn't hear or see me.

I'd met L.R. (as she asked me to call her; "I've been 'L.R.' since grad school," she said) at a seminar-conference at UCLA when I'd first come to L.A., and we'd stayed in touch. We were interested in the same things. Months into my chirality theorizing, we'd run into each other at Radio Shack—and, as if there were a kind of theory-ESP in the universe, she began telling me what she was working on. It was amazing, remarkable: We were both at work on chirality and we were both on our way to the conclusion that testing the tetrahedral molecules' chirality in deep space was the place to begin.

There was no competition here. I liked L.R. and I was interested in what she'd come up with. I didn't want to be scooped, and I would never let myself be scooped in the way Rosalind Franklin was—but this was different: L.R. and I both believed that chirality was such an evolving model that we didn't worry too much about reproducing each other's results. Besides, I was the neophyte; I was newer than the newest kid on the block. She had superior age, knowledge, and experience. It was not a Q-type feeling that I had here, but a simple hard look at what was up. Plus she was a woman—never maternal, not even sisterly, but she offered me the reinforcement one gives a respected if younger colleague of the same gender.

When I first met her I felt renewed in my conviction that theory's elegance and abstraction needed just this kind of champion. Way back in the sixties, when I was just a glimmer of a kid-scientist, she'd actually found practical ways to solve Schrödinger's equation on molecules—a formula that had been around since 1923, that made perfect sense, but that could never be solved for the descriptions of things as complex as chiral molecules.

The equation went like this:

$$H\psi = E\psi$$

Simple as pie! (Or psi.) It described molecular phenomena perfectly, but no one could get it to work practically. Lorraine Revent Atwater did. In 1965, at a time when computers were like electronic dinosaurs compared to our present versions, she calculated approximate properties of molecules using Schrödinger. She got it to work. She'd stay up all night calculating, she told me, then she'd fill in the results on the blackboard behind her, like a baseball scoreboard. Each morning she'd post a new set of "scores."

Back in 1965, listening to the Jefferson Airplane, I read an article in *Science* about L.R. and the Schrödinger breakthrough. So when I finally met her, I chalked one up myself: I'd met a brain woman who was thought of as cold. This told me she was no-nonsense, the real thing—a theorist who didn't apologize for the detached, classical beauties of theory, the way my friend Q had. When I felt desolate, I thought of her. For though she'd never been intimate pals with me, or offered me wild enthusiasm for my ideas, she stood steadily by me. And she gave me hope. After all, she *existed*.

She looked up suddenly—a large, hook-nosed woman with short thinning grey-brown hair and an air of physical perfunctoriness. Great radiant eyes behind her wire-rim glasses. She didn't miss a beat, but jumped right in: no small talk.

"Think about it, Esme—the problem is theological, isn't it? A question of seeing it wrong because you've shifted your origin."

"Yeah. But I think it's God who keeps jumping around, not us."

She offered me, with enormous delicacy, a partially eaten ham sandwich. I wolfed it down.

"You need to be a perissodactyl. You know"—she winked and waggled her fingers at me—"have fingers or toes in odd places, to spin *this* Frisbee."

"The tetrahedrals *could* use a kind of special torque, couldn't they?" I swallowed the last of the sandwich and she handed me a dented Coke can and I swigged from it. "Or, you're right—maybe a perissodactyl, something providing the spin that's morphically unfamiliar, a new kind of God? I see why you say the problem's theological!"

"Right," she said, nodding, smiling. She paused. "I don't know if I'd call it *torque* exactly."

"No?" I crumpled up the Coke can in my fist, took careful but show-off aim and watched my empty hit the edge too hard and bounce off. I shook my head and shrugged.

"We're just about at the same place with this stuff, aren't we?" I said. "Though we didn't think this would happen."

"I think so. You got third-order dispersion forces, mixed electromagnetic forces all producing the same results."

"And at shorter distances, calculations lead to large discriminations, of the order of the thermal energy. Easily interpreted in terms of specific atom–atom reactions."

We lapsed into silence, running over the spinning architectures in our heads.

Then she crumpled up a piece of paper, took aim, and hit the wastebasket, with just a little more spin than I'd applied. The paper wad danced around the circumference of the basket, wobbled, fell in.

She smiled again. "Torque," she said.

"I think we're close."

"We're close to the three-center attachment theory of Ogston. Whether our model has implications for chiral selectivity or for homo-chiral preferences in natural selection remains open to question."

"Nevertheless."

"Nevertheless."

We sat and talked some more; I thanked her for "lunch." As I went out the door, she called me back.

"Does it bother you that we're neck-and-neck here, Esme?"

"No," I said, honestly. "Does it bother *you*?"

She sighed, looked away for a second, picking at her teeth with a paper clip. She had big teeth. She looked like Eleanor Roosevelt, I thought suddenly. Then she faced me.

"I've lived longer than you," she said very slowly. She sounded exhausted. "I've worked for years on this problem. Years. One feels things one wishes one didn't. Possessiveness. Defensiveness. But one tries to put things in perspective."

"It *does* bother you, then."

She smiled her odd radiant smile. Her glasses glittered.

"Yes," she said.

Halfway home, I remembered the lab I'd been scheduled to teach that afternoon. I'd forgotten completely about it. If I'd thought of it sooner, I might have called Rocky. She'd have found a grad student to supervise. I pressed down on the accelerator. Oddly, I didn't feel bad at all. I felt absolutely nothing but the desire to pick Ollie up at school, give her a kiss, take her home, and get dinner, build a brave little fire in the fireplace, make hot chocolate, put her to bed in her flannel nightgown with the blue dancing stars, take out my yellow legal pads, my leaky pens, sit down in front of the fire, and go to work. Writing my own versions of bedtime stories—fantastic worlds, reached by leaps of faith, then returned from: hand over hand, across the reversed bridge of proof.

"Jesus, what's up with you anyway, Prof?"

I'd come slogging in to school, late for my ten A.M. Organic class as it turned out. I'd given a disconnected, blurry lecture—and now, opening the lab door, I saw Rocky standing before me like a Judgment Day angel.

I dropped my briefcase and an armful of papers on a counter and walked over and took her hand and shook it.

"Congratulate me. I'm *that* close to chiral recognition."

She dropped my hand. "Too bad you weren't that close for *class* recognition at your lab yesterday. People were *not* happy, man. Especially that asshole, Donald Brandeman. I stood up and made up some lies for you—but you promised those test scores yesterday."

"Shit. That's *right*. I haven't even *looked* at those tests."

Rocky stared at me. "What's goin' on?"

I hoisted myself wearily up and balanced on a counter, a faucet fixture jutting into my back. "Jay took off. He's gone."

Her face swerved out of its expression, unsure. It occurred to me again how young she was. I watched her trying to figure out what to say.

"For *good*?"

"I don't know, but it's been five days and he hasn't sent flowers."

She didn't laugh. The enormous distance I felt from everything focused itself now, here, on the distance between us. I felt as if I was waking up from an odd and very exhausting dream. Here was this *girl,* this kid—what had I been doing, trying to teach her science, lab procedure? Why was I wasting precious research time here in my own funded space, explaining things, correcting her errors, taking her painstakingly through procedures? *She's no good to me* I thought, then I stopped myself. I looked just beyond her and noticed what she'd been doing. She'd set up the lab for sequencing, she had the spinners going, she had a couple of radiographs ready to pop out. The room hummed. Totally in control, I thought. How had this happened? How had this distracted, Walkman-wired, sweet-faced delinquent turned into a practicing scientist in less than two months?

She laughed, right on cue, as if she had a wiretap on my synapses.

"You taught me all this, Prof," she said. "Remember?"

*At night, Ollie and I sit in front of the fire. The heat and light attract us—we eat our meals and do paperwork before it. Ollie, sprawled on her stomach, with a sheet of white construction paper in front of her, draws wings on our house.*

*"It can go up," she tells me.*

*"Where does it go, Ollie, when it goes up?"*

*She stares for a long time at the crayoned shapes, biting her lips.*

*"Where the blue starts, then up to Lucy."*

*"Can you draw Lucy?"*

*She looks at me, astonished at my ignorance.*

*"Lucy can-not fit into our eyes."*

*"But who is Lucy?"*

*"She is here because she is a diamond."*

*"What kind of diamond is she?"*

*She wrinkles her nose at me and laughs.*

*"You know. Diamond that keeps our world inside it."*

*She brushes wisps of hair from her eyes and inhales loudly through her nose, then out again. She still has a cold.*

*I sketch diamonds for a while in the margins of my calculations on a yellow legal pad. I make them three-dimensional cones whose adjoining bases form a circle. I begin to spin the diamonds, glittering, one by one down the right-hand margin. A log shifts suddenly in the grate, and sparks pop and sizzle upward, airborne; one lands on Ollie's flying house and I reach over and smother it with my legal pad. She squeals, a combination of fear and delight:*

*"The fire grows trees inside my house. See?"*

Later, after bedtime stories, when she'd finally drifted off to sleep, I moved quietly around her room, picking up toys, putting clothes in drawers. I filled the humidifier with cool water, lifting it, like a transparent suitcase, back into its cradle. I found a piece of paper on the floor on which Ollie had printed her name in huge letters, along with a series of numbers. I tacked these papers on the corkboard over her drawing table and adjusted the night light: a yodeling frog in spats.

I returned to the dying fire, poked at it a bit, threw on another log, then curled up in the old corduroy-covered chair I'd picked up at a rummage sale somewhere. I was exhausted. I thought about Lucy and diamonds for a while, then Ollie. I'd come to realize that the glimpses of the working public school I'd gotten the day I went to visit Gloria Walther at Sixth Street School were glimpses of a museum. They were all museums now, the public schools. Storehouses of artifacts of a lost past, along with statues of public citizens, bronze rolls of heroes' names, names of parents who paid for public school along with water and roads. Now, forgotten kids, children of minorities and maids, and troubled and confused children, learned their lessons in a museum, stood up to recite in a museum.

I kept seeing the private schools' splendorous campuses—computer banks, soccer meadows, stocked libraries. A poster on the wall: an open book at the end of the rainbow. READING MEANS A GOLDEN FUTURE. I had to find a new school for Ollie.

I jumped as the phone rang.

"It's Jay."

I glanced at the hearth: Ollie's flying house, singed, a ragged bullet hole where the ember hit.

"Hello, Jay."

"I've made a decision, Esme. I want to come by and pick up my stuff and move out."

The fire popped.

"E-Esme?"

"Yeah."

"I'm trying . . . I'm t-telling you that I'm moving out."

"OK."

"Jesus Christ. Is that all you've g-got to say? *OK?*"

"What do you want me to say?"

*"Jesus!"*

"OK. Where *are* you? Who are you with?"

"I'm in W-West L.A. . . . at Paloma's."

I looked across the room to the hallway that led to our bedroom. I laughed. "Paloma."

"Yeah, P-Paloma."

"I don't get it, Jay."

"Of course you don't get it! You would never *g-get* Paloma because she's completely unlike you. She has *f-feelings.* Like, she took me in . . ."

"To her bed."

"Who says we're s-sleeping together? And why are *you* p-pretending that that's what's bothering you? You don't care who I sleep with. I know you still got the hots for whoever-the-fuck-he-was. Right? Paloma is a s-sweet ordinary woman, not a s-scientist or an int-tellectual. Just a good person."

"Well that's *insightful.* You can't be a good person *and* a scientist. Everyone knows *that.*"

There was a long sigh.

"Esme, listen. When I'm with you I feel invisible—l-like I don't exist."

"Jesus, Jay, you *have been* invisible—you're never home—you don't talk to Ollie when you are."

"I don't know what to s-*say* to Ollie. She makes no sense to me."

"Maybe you ought to try to make sense to *her.*"

Another long sigh. "I c-called to say two things: I'm m-moving out and I have some plans for Ollie."

"Ollie?"

"I want to s-spend some time with her. M-maybe even, when things get more settled, have her c-come and live with me."

"You want Ollie to live with you?"

Everything in the room seemed to recede: I watched the fire in the fireplace, the intricate, moving shadows of the miniature Moorish arches and columns of the hallway, the hanging plants, the bookshelves, all retreating. I was beginning to understand something enormous, something huge, a terrible shape the whole world might fit into.

"Jay? How would you take care of her? You're at work twenty hours a day."

"She's my d-daughter, Esme. I can take c-care of her."

"You'd hire a housekeeper? *Tell* me."

"I said, I can t-take care of her. I want some time to spend with her. My time with her, un-p-poisoned by you. I want to get her some help."

"Help?" Straight man: in the unfunniest routine he'd ever created.

"We're talking about a child who is s-seriously disturbed, Esme."

"Tell me what you're planning to do for this seriously disturbed child?"

"I'm going to put her in a school for d-dysfunctional kids. I'm going to get professionals to work with her. You know, work on her speech, her p-powers of e-expression, her . . . behavior."

"Jay, you don't spend enough time with her to know if she's dysfunctional."

"Esme. Your d-daughter is not a normal kid—it's *obvious* to everyone but you. She needs h-help. And, frankly, Esme, s-so do you."

"And *you*? Do *you* need help?"

He took a breath. "P-Paloma's giving me all the h-help I need."

After we'd hung up on each other, I sat down again and stared at the cage of neon embers in the grate. The fire still sputtered and popped—it had a life and it was not eager to relinquish it. I sat for a long time; the fire went out and it got cold in the room. And still I sat.

# Chapter 15

Donald Brandeman was waiting outside the door of my lab. I saw him as I came in the main entrance, and I had to walk the entire length of the hall, my heels echoing, staring at him.

He slumped against the doorframe. He was wearing sunglasses; he was trying to look like some actor or other, one of those bandanna-headed, one-earring types with dead eyes and a two-day growth of beard. He was even smoking a cigarette. I'd have found all this drag hilarious if he hadn't looked quite so malevolent.

"Good morning, Donald." I tried to brush by him. He straightened up and blocked the door. I smelled something—liquor? I stared into the black lenses: something twitched behind them. He wasn't exactly drunk, but maybe *bolstered* a little—a few beers?

"I need to know my goddam grade."

He pushed a printed form in my face. I took it from him: "Midterm Grade Report."

"I gave all my profs a copy of this—two, no, maybe three weeks ago. And they all filled it out, every one of them, and returned it. Except you."

"God—academics are anal, don't you think?"

Something twitched again behind the shades. When he spoke again his voice sounded hoarse, as if he might begin to cry.

"Maybe I need to break this *down* for you, Professor. I'm on the swim team, OK? Mid-semester the athletics department sends out grade requests to all my course instructors to see if I'm keeping up my average. This form is important to me. And it's important to my coach. Obviously, it's not important to *you*. You never gave any of us back our tests, you never gave out midterm grades. You don't even bother to show up for lab these days."

"Those are really neat sunglasses, Donald, did I mention that at all? I used to have a maiden aunt—Twissy was her name, Aunt Twiss? She had a pair just like yours. In fact, she was wearing them the day she died—did I ever tell you *how* Twiss died? No? Well, she aspirated a Bac-O. You know those little sprinkly buggers on salads? She'd been trying to sniff the lettuce to see if it was fresh and she snorked one right up her nostril and it got in her lung. She started choking, making weird noises like this: 'Snaaagh, snaaagh!'—and suddenly a big fat guy came racing over from just behind the pie rack, screaming '*Heimlich!* Heimlich!' and he started hugging her like a giant vise. He cracked all her ribs and cut off her air supply. He killed her dead, Donald, that big fat guy. By trying to save her life, don't you see. Apparently he'd only seen the Heimlich maneuver performed once in a movie and he didn't realize he was suffocating her. Too bad for Twiss, huh? But she kept those shades on the whole time, Donald. Laid out there at HoJo's by the pie twirler, wearing those chic babies. Like yours, Donald, as I said. It's amazing. Your nose is kind of shaped like hers too, now that I see it close up. Stay away from Bac-Os, Donald. That's my advice to you."

"You are deranged, Professor."

"I hope so, Donald. I hope so. It's a state I've worked hard to achieve. Now, if you'll excuse me . . ."

I lunged for the door. He blocked me again.

"What about my grade, Professor?"

"Which grade? The A-plus you think you deserve—or the F I intend to give you?"

"F? Why would I get an F? My lab grades have been in the high eighties. What are you talking about?"

"I know very well what your lab grades have been, Donald, but you see, I grade on *attitude* as much as accomplishment and I think your attitude has been that of a really jolly serial killer. I just don't *like* you, Donald."

"Wait a minute! You're telling me that you're flunking me because you don't *like* me?"

"Donald, you're fast. But not fast enough."

I winked and slipped around him. He pulled back; his face was white.

"When will I get this . . . grade? So I can begin taking action?"

"I'll just go look at your file now, Donald. This could take some time."

I winked again. And shut the door.

I sat in the lab for a while grading lab tests. Donald Brandeman's average was, as he'd said, a B and I wrote that letter after his name, after some lengthy and blasphemous hesitation.

I finished the other grades; then I heard Rocky coming in. She stood in the doorway, staring at me. She looked distraught.

"Hi, Rock," I called. Then I dropped some things. My grade book, my keys, a whole rack of tubes came crashing down.

"Jesus, how did I do that?"

She rushed over to help me pick up. Her face close up was panicked.

"Prof, what's wrong with you?"

"Rocky, what's the big deal? I dropped my keys and a couple of tubes. Stop looking at me like I'm ready for the psych ward, OK?"

She started to cry. Her hair fell over her face and her thin shoulders shook.

"I just saw that guy, that blond guy? Donald Brandeman? In the hall. He was on his way to Faber's office. He said he had a fight with you and then he said some . . . real terrible shit . . . about you."

"Oh yeah? I hope you decked him."

She looked up through her tears.

"Well, yeah, actually, man, I did."

I backed out of the safety shower, where I'd been crawling after a rolling tube, and looked at her.

"You hit him?"

"I blind-sided him. He didn't even see it coming. I dropped him."

She grinned, her face wet with tears.

"You know, one of *these*." She mimed a lightning left to the jaw. "Blam! wham! Down he goes! Man, he's a *pussy,* that guy, you know? He sits there like *this,* holding his jaw and whining that I *broke* it and that he can't swim anymore this semester."

"Jesus. Between you and me, we've nailed this poor sucker for the semester."

I started to laugh and then she laughed too, a little halfheartedly. Then I grabbed her by the shoulders and we looked at each other, sitting there on the floor together, and we really started going off. We laughed so long and hard that I got the hiccups and she started weeping again.

I tried to hold my breath but my diaphragm would not stop convulsing.

"Wait. Lemme get some water."

She got up and ran me a flask full of lukewarm tap. I drank it but my chest kept heaving and she sobbed as I hiccuped. Then we started laughing again. She blew her nose as I collapsed finally on the floor, my arms and legs outstretched like a kid making snow angels—my grade book and tubes around me, hiccuping and laughing.

Neither one of us heard the lab door open. It wasn't until Faber actually stood over us that we noticed him.

"Professor Charbonneau, have you been drinking?"

Rocky and I bounced off the same wall, then looked up in slow motion at him. It was obvious that he didn't often encounter faculty members lying on the floor.

"No. I'm not drunk. I was just discussing [heeeekk!] ah, midterm grades with my assistant [heeeekk!], Ms. Salinas, here . . . and I had a little fall [heeek!]."

Rocky and I started off again. We couldn't help it.

He started to say something, then thought better of it.

"Could I see you in my office, Professor? As soon as you . . . gather yourself up?"

As soon as the door shut, we went off again. We just couldn't stop.

I knocked and he called to me to come in. He was still a bit shaken from our encounter in the lab, trying to appear as if he hadn't been waiting for me. He put down the phone receiver, looking distracted, pawed through some notes on his desk—then looked up and nodded, indicating the chair in front of his desk.

I sat, hiccuping a little into my collar. His wandering eye focused on me briefly, piercingly, then rolled off.

"Esme, I'm *confused*. I'd like to leap to what may seem like a radical conclusion here and state boldly that if you need professional *help*, if you have a drug or alcohol problem, there are programs that I can look into . . ."

I tried to ambush a large hiccup in my throat and made a gurgling, strangling noise.

He started to get up from his chair and the thought of the fictitious

Aunt Twiss and the Heimlich leapt to mind, which made me choke more. I held up a hand to stay him and gradually got control.

"I'm not an alcoholic. I'm not a drug user. I'm a scientist."

"I'm sorry, I . . ."

I gasped and another piercing hiccup followed this intake of breath. I swallowed carefully and continued.

"I'm a *scientist.* I know you think I've been irresponsible and I admit that I *have been,* in the matter of meeting my classes. I've been erratic in my schedule, *yes.* But I've been having *visions,* these last months. I feared them once but now I see—"

"I'm sorry. You're not making sense, Esme."

"I have a TOE, Dr. Faber. I know that you didn't hire me to be a theoretician, but I've been working on questions of chirality in space. I've consulted Lorraine Atwater at USC. I'm on the right track here, in fact, as of the last week or so, I think I'm—"

"Esme. Please. What are you trying to say?"

I jumped up and approached his desk. He recoiled instinctively.

"Dr. Faber, I need some time. A little time to work this theory out." I grabbed the edge of his desk and leaned across. "I have been given a *gift.*"

He shook his head. He crouched in his chair, ready to spring, staring at me with, for once, both eyes. Had I cured his optical problem?

"It's like chinning yourself on the topmost rung of the ladder to heaven. You lift yourself up and just get this *flash,* a glimpse of the angels and the reaches of paradise, all making *sense* suddenly—a flash. And then your grip gives and you fall back down into the dark."

He cleared his throat. "Please sit down, Esme. You're very excited."

I threw up my hands and sat down. "Of course I am. Of course I'm excited. I've seen it! The post-ambidextrous universe!"

I sat down, breathing heavily. I realized with relief that my hiccups were gone.

Faber cleared his throat again. He lifted a manila folder—a file?—

from the papers on his desk. He peered inside it, then looked at me.

"Some weeks ago, as you know, Donald Brandeman made several rather serious allegations about your conduct in the laboratory. And we had the question about the 'politics' of your lectures. I was inclined at the time to dismiss all this, given your record at Harvard and your teaching reputation—but since then, Esme . . . your strange behavior . . ."

"What strange behavior?"

"You know as well as I do that you've been consistently late for classes and laboratories, often not showing up at lab at all. You have failed to provide substitute instructors to cover your absences. You did not register midterm grades. I was also informed by personnel that you took the highly irregular step of hiring an undergraduate as your lab assistant, using grant funds. A Miss"—he peered into the file again—"Rocio Salinas."

"I hired Rocky because she is the best young scientist I know. More imaginative and finally more capable than any of my graduate students."

He looked up. "The young woman who was just . . . lying on the lab floor next to you?"

I smiled. *"That's* the one!"

He looked down again. "It's against university policy. We have also had complaints about the presence of your child in the radioactive areas of the Oberman labs. I hope I don't have to remind you, Esme, as a mother, about the inherent dangers for children of low levels of—"

"I take care to ensure my child's safety in the lab. She is restricted to the outer area, where there's about as much radiation as she'd get on a flight to Chicago."

"Nevertheless, we're talking about a number of imprudent decisions made willy-nilly, if you ask *me.* This is highly disturbing behavior. And since you yourself brought up the subject of chemistry theory, I will reiterate what *you* said. You were not hired to theorize; you were hired to do biochemical research in the area of single-gene-deficiency disease, most specifically Alpha$_1$ Antitrypsin Deficiency."

There was a silence.

"I need some time, Dr. Faber. To work out this theory."

"I am warning you, Esme. Failure to appear at your regularly scheduled lecture and lab meetings will be looked upon as breach of your teaching contract. These students pay a lot of tuition to learn certain things from you. I am not in a position to hire someone else at this late date. I have to inform you that continued unexplained and un-provided-for absences will lead to your suspension by this university."

I stood up. "This is all about *students,* right? Nothing to do with the two million in grant money invested in my lab—or the pressure to find a cure for $a_1AT$, right?"

He looked morosely at me. "I'm not denying that you have *another* serious responsibility to NIH, Derridex, and everyone else involved in your lab. *Of course* I'm concerned about that."

"No *shit.*"

"Get your midterm grades in, Esme. Teach your courses. And *yes,* do your lab research. Otherwise you leave me no alternative."

"You didn't hear anything I said. Did you?"

Both his eyes were focused on me. Now I was positive I'd cured his wandering eye.

"Esme, please. I'm talking about *no alternative.*"

I turned in the doorway. "Right," I said. "I know. I haven't any either."

He laughed, not a pleasant sound. "Esme," he said, "does it strike you as just *slightly* ironic that you sat in this office not long ago, going on about the lack of moral standards among science students? And now here you are, *abandoning* your teaching duties to these very students?"

"How can I possibly teach anybody about *morality* if I abandon my own values? You and I both know that you can find someone to fill in temporarily for me in Organic. These are extraordinary circumstances! And I've clarified my moral position these last months. I'm not made to be a *crusader;* the best example I can give students is my own thinking. Hawking said—"

He interrupted me. "Oh my my my. Oh, Esme, Esme. You and Stephen Hawking. You and Einstein. You and Newton. Do you think maybe you're living in a *fantasy* world?"

I smiled sweetly. "So were *they.*"

His phone began to ring.

"I'm sorry," we said together, as if we'd rehearsed this final moment, worked it out months ago—perhaps around the time I'd first arrived at UGC: the real thing, a successful woman scientist.

# Part Three

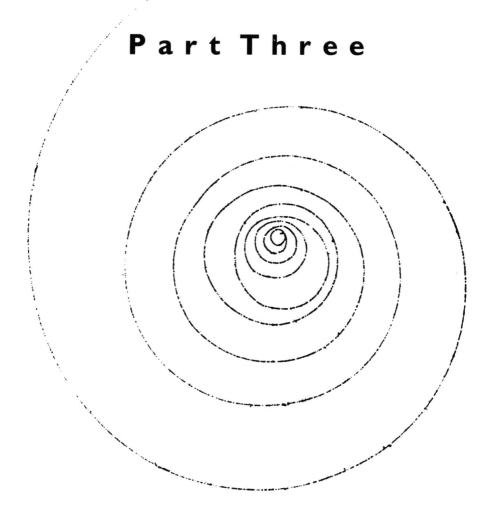

*After the wind an earthquake . . . And after the
earthquake a fire . . . and after the fire a still small
voice.*

I Kings 19:11–12

# Chapter 16

I made my way to a table that was near the stage but slightly obscured by a pillar. I thought it made a good vantage point. When the waitress came, I ordered a rum and Coke, since the house wine looked like scarlet hair tonic.

I got a few stares, a woman by herself at a nightclub table, but after a while everyone stopped stealing little surreptitious glances at me and I became invisible again. I sipped the rum and Coke. It reminded me of grad school and postdoc parties, and I thought of Jesse again, then put him out of my mind. As soon as my glass was half empty, the waitress, in punk attire, appeared at my elbow.

"C'getcha somethin' else?"

"Sure, another one of *these*. Great rum!"

She looked at me, tongued her gum into the opposite cheek, then winked.

"Like that rum, huh? I'll see the bartender fixes you up right. He's my pal."

"Hey, thanks."

Actually I had forgotten in my nostalgic haze that, in fact, rum wasn't my favorite, but so what, I thought. It was sort of like the

*185*

taste of certain cough syrups one remembered from one's childhood; the terrible flavor was comforting.

Suddenly, there was a second drink before me; the waitress winked again and was gone. Then the room went very dark, the table candles lit people's faces upward ghoulishly. The spot hit the stage, the three-piece band rattled and honked, there was a silvery clash of cymbals and the toupee'd emcee slouched out.

"I'd like to say that we have a really unusual group of performers tonight. A lot of them write their own stuff, so don't go to the rest rooms and read the doors till the show's over, it might spoil some of these hot jokes!" He showed his teeth and there was the familiar rim shot on the drums.

He buzz-sawed on and I stopped listening. A very young, pimply guy hurried out—he looked like a high school kid—the first stand-up of the night. It was painful. He made bad joke after bad joke; no one would laugh. I laughed a little, hollowly, and people turned around and stared at me. Then someone behind me growled, "Take a walk, lame-o!" and the poor boy, sweating and bowing again and again and crying thank you to no one, relinquished the stage to a very large Tootsie-ish woman. Midway through her routine ("Don't make any jokes about mother-in-laws, I *am* your mother-in-law!"), I began picturing us, the audience, as a vast compact sea of particles, all possessing negative inertial mass. (A simple concept—it means that if a force pushes on the particle, it moves in a direction *opposite* to the way in which the force is urging. You know, like when your mother nagged at you as a kid and you did just the opposite of what she wanted?) The stand-ups, as they arrived one by one and stood heroically, gladiator-ish, in the dazzling ray of light, tried pushing this mass, the audience, with their naked embarrassing need to be funny ("Please laugh at me, I'm funny, I'm funny, don't you think?") and the audience not only resisted, they moved in the other direction—

active disapproval, boos, rude comments, heckling. It was amazing how neatly the paradigm worked. I was on the fourth rum and Coke now, and my brain whirled with bad analogies.

"What a buncha *dogs* tonight!" I heard someone behind me mutter as the Tootsie-woman started doing a little soft-shoe. I loved her suddenly, she reminded me of a ghost who'd floated in straight from the vaudeville stage; though she was extremely heavy and carried a great wedding-cake wig on her head, she was light on her feet and she danced with a natural dip and girlish quickstep and sway. She seemed lost in reverie as she moved—for just that second I believed people were charmed—and then the catcalls and whoops of ridicule started and she opened her eyes very lazily, like an old sea turtle, fixed the house with a death stare, and croaked into the mike, "Bugger you all!," soft-shoe-ing with enormous dignity into the wings. I clapped heartily for her, but my applause was drowned out by jeers.

Fear snaked through me. When would he come on? After this next jittery, Lenny Bruce–ish fellow or two or so down the stretch? Whenever he appeared, I knew he was in for trouble, and the thought of him suffering onstage filled me with dread. I'd begun the day facing Faber; then Rocky had driven home with me and suggested she baby-sit and I take the night off. "Go to a movie, have a massage," she'd cried, pushing me out the door. "You gotta relax." So I came here, to the Club Sez Who on the Strip. If not to relax, to at least relieve my heart of some weighty anxiety: I just had to see that Jay was alive, I told myself. That's all. Anyway, that had been my plan a while back when I'd first seated myself. I'd intended to see if he was OK, then slip unobtrusively out. This still seemed like a workable idea, but this crowd was going to make it all harder, I could see. I could remember this future easily.

The Lenny Bruce guy was holding his own. He had a nervous high-pitched laugh, contagious, and whenever he broke up after a long spacey riff, the audience would titter a bit too. Finally he got off a few decent one-liners and people started warming up. One or two even clapped.

"Commitment? Yeah, this town's so incapable of commitment, people are afraid to use their turn signals!"

"Yeah, my friends thought I got it easier—my Jewish mother moved to Miami. Now she *faxes* me guilt."

People chuckled and buzzed to each other. I could see Lenny breathing easier.

"Yeah, so how do you give a blonde a CAT scan? Shine a flashlight in her ear, right? Am I right? Forgive me, all you blondes in the audience, but you know people got to wonder. Are you or aren't you? I mean *real* blondes. I asked a date of mine to prove she was a real blonde and she got right up and showed it to me . . . yeah, the hair on her chest."

The audience roared; they were with him now. He was beaming.

"Hey, I was satisfied, right? She could have gotten insulted and hit me with her jock strap! . . . Yeah, I was lucky . . . yeah."

Smoke swirled in the air and I began thinking about a cigarette again. When the urge got too strong, I redirected my thoughts to chirality. In our world there exists a chiral right-handed twin of nicotine called dextro-nicotine, not found in tobacco plants. It has been synthesized, and guess what: It is far far less toxic than old left-handed death-nicotine. I briefly, drunkenly, played with the notion of synthesizing and marketing dextro-nicotine cigarettes: Virginia Switch. What a genius idea, I thought, and smiled to myself as Lenny lifted the mike off its stand and pranced about, triumphant. Then I remembered that it was the *tars* that got you cancer—the nicotine only addicted you.

Then, I caught a glimpse of movement in the wings, just beyond Lenny. I saw his face. He was next. I could see him moving his lips, he was repeating his jokes, like he always did, getting the timing just right. Or, in his case, just wrong. I drank down the last of my drink, and my faithful pal the waitress appeared again.

Lenny left in a flurry of enthusiastic applause and the band gave him a glittery spiral of rim shots. Then Jay was standing there. He didn't say anything for what seemed an eternity. He looked tired and (I squinted, I was having a little trouble seeing through the layers of smoke) he looked sad. A tall, thin, worried-looking guy.

"Hi everybody." He peered out at the audience, squinting into the lights. "Hi," he said again and there were a couple of groans. He snapped to finally.

"Well, I'm Jay *Talkman,* they call me Talkman 'cause I'm really *wired*! Hah, hah." There was silence, terrible premeditated silence. I considered chuckling, but he knew my laugh too well.

"Well, anyway, folks, I see we've got a *tough crowd* tonight—but hey, you don't scare me, my last gig was for Caligula." (A few snorts.) "He was a great guy; he wanted to feed me to the lions but they were on a corn-free diet. Hah, hah."

"Hey," yelled the guy in back of me, "the lions didn't wanna get sick!"

Jay ignored the guy. "So, anyway, folks, they did things back in Rome a little differently than they do them now—and I think they did them right! For one thing, when *their* senators screwed up, they made them sit in the bath and b-bleed to death. In the U.S. we do it differently—when our senators screw up, *we* take the bath *and* they bleed *us* to death."

A few people made appreciative noises, I laughed carefully, in a disguised register. But then the guy in back chimed in again:

"Whyn't you drown *yourself* in the goddam bathtub, you stupid dickhead!"

Jay swallowed. "But L.A., hey L.A., what a c-city! We all hate it, we all l-l-love it. I mean, is this a g-great city, or what?"

I swallowed. The worst had happened, it was all coming apart: He was starting to stutter.

"Hey! Are you a great d-d-d-dickhead, or what?"

"I really love this c-city. Even when I get up in the morning and see smog, I'm happy here. R-really, I am. If there's an i-inversion layer—"

"A *what,* d-d-d-dickhead?"

Jay smiled into the lights. I could see sweat streaming down his face. "An . . . ah, i-i-inversion layer—"

A few other drunks were joining in now. "A *what,* d-d-dickhead? A wh-wh-*what*?"

I got up. I don't know how it happened but I was on my feet, brushing tables and mumbling "Excuse *me*" and I was stumbling up the steps to the stage in the dark. I fell down and bumped my knee, but I kept moving. Then I was onstage. The lights were white-bright, blinding, and for a second, I froze. I always think I'm just a mind: I had a body. A visible form for people to look at and judge. Black jeans and sweater, little black heels. I felt enormous.

The hecklers were yelling things I couldn't understand. Then I saw Jay looking at me. He had backed away from the mike. I could never describe the look he was giving me. I suppose if your wife died, then suddenly showed up in bed with you and a new lover, it might approach that gaze. But I'd recovered myself now; nothing could stop me. I marched to the mike. Out of the corner of my eye, I could see the emcee gesturing at Jay, *What gives?*

I stood in front of the mike. The room reeled before me, then slowed down. The hecklers were wild, whistling, stomping and making kissing noises.

"H-hey," someone cried, "maybe your f-f-fuckin' *girlfriend* is funnier than you."

"Shut up," I said into the mike.

My voice surprised me. It was bigger and calmer than I thought possible, given my state of mind.

"Shut *up*," I repeated, and the room actually fell silent.

"You like that word '*dickhead*,' huh? You think that's a funny word, *dickhead*?"

I squinted out into the audience trying to find the dread heckler. My words echoed.

"This is my husband. Standing right here. Yeah." It was eerily silent. "Here's his problem. He's too *smart* for you—talk about dickheads, you guys need to pull jockstraps over your ears to keep your thoughts straight! You need a condom to keep your head dry when it rains! Hey, *you're* such a dickhead that when you come, your I.Q. drops forty points! Which means, in fact, you can only come *twice*!"

I was dimly aware of laughter but my fury hadn't abated enough for me to really hear it. Where does this shit come from? I wondered, shocked, in the back of my mind.

"You know, I just wanna tell you jerks something. My husband" —I gestured again at Jay, who looked paralyzed—"*Jay*, gets up here and tries to entertain you. Tries to be funny—but what can you do when people just don't *get* it? Hey, I'm a biochemist—I know what it's like! He uses a phrase like 'inversion layer' and that bozo over there thinks an inversion layer is when he barfs in his Cheerios."

Laughter. Then: "Hey *Mrs*. Dickhead, why don't you sit down? On my face! We'll talk some *biology*!"

"Hey Slick!" I cried. "Don't give me any *shit*. I know who *you* are. You couldn't take high school biology because they wanted to put you on the *syllabus*."

"E-Esme?"

I heard him, but I didn't turn.

"You wanna know something? As a biochemist, I can tell by looking at you, pal, your DNA is DOA. I can look at you, pal, and see what went wrong with the family genetics. Oh yeah, old Uncle Walt, he was a great guy but he kept trying to fuck trees. And all those cousins intermarrying . . ."

People were laughing, but now Jay was standing beside me.

"P-please get off the *stage,* Esme!"

"Hey, Mrs. Dickhead, if you're a scientist, what's the Second Law of Thermodynamics?"

I glanced at Jay. I couldn't quite bring him into focus.

"You want to know what the Second Law of Thermodynamics is? The Second Law of Thermodynamics is like Murphy's Law: Everything eventually screws up."

"Look," I said, swaying a little, "I can explain it. The Second Law of Thermodynamics." I paused. The three beautiful, hopeless Laws, the holy trinity of dissolution, presented themselves glittering before my mind's eye. Maybe I could actually make them clear to these raucous Goths?

"If a rain of glass fragments fell from the ceiling right now, none of them would form into beautiful wineglasses in your hands, right? The pieces shatter into worse shatter. We call that entropy. How everything works, or doesn't work. Things keep breaking down, things move in the direction of greater chaos, that's how we know we're still alive. People age, people get sick, relationships fall apart . . ." I finally looked at Jay, who stood stock-still, his gaze riveted on me. I turned back to the audience. "But what you come here to see, what you came here to see tonight, was the Second Law, the breakdown. You all came to see people fall apart—see things shatter—and hey, you got it!" I opened my arms wide. "Before your eyes—entropy! The Second Law! And what about you—you all? Look at you there, the guy in the front row here, drunk, slobbering on your tie: Second Law. Look at this: You and your girlfriend look like you got hung up on a power line by your hair. Second Law. Excuse me, *you* look like a victim of designer drive-by—yes. We're all going to hell because of a thermodynamic principle; now, isn't that *funny*? Nothing *that* good is going to happen to you again and a *whole lot* of bad *is*."

"Esme."

I looked at him.

"We're g-getting off the s-stage now."

And somehow, we did. He freed my sweaty hold on the mike; the band started playing. People began clapping and whistling, still looking at us strangely. I nodded at everyone; I was having trouble walking.

As he steered me by a group at a table, a guy jumped up to shake Jay's hand.

"Great *bit*—the wife coming up like that! Very odd, but it flies."

Another guy poked me in the side as I lumbered by. "Hey," he growled, "what's a quark?"

I stared at him.

"A fart in the bathtub!" he hollered. "You don't even know that one?"

"C-come *on!*" cried Jay, and tugged harder.

We stumbled out together, into the chilly night, the bright lights of the Strip.

# Chapter 17

Entropy. It was the same force Lorraine Revent Atwater and I were attempting to elude on our computer screens; the luminous graphics-created molecules danced in their axes, within the alternating vector lines. If we pushed them fractally, fast enough, we might, cosmologically speaking, create a local naked singularity, that is to say, a human-made version of the start-up singularity. What does this mean? It means that we had big plans for those chiral particles. We were trying to connect them (tie them up with?) Super String Theory, with the Big Bang. But that's another story.

It was a windless night, but Jay and I stood in an eerie vacuum of weird feelings outside the Sez Who? Lights from the honking cars on the Strip flickered over us; sightseers and cruising kids shouted and called to each other. The huge billboard Marlboro man high up over the Strip puffed white smoke from his coffin nail, staring squarely into the face of Death: *Howdy pardner.* Jay bent slightly, his hands in his jacket pockets, leaning toward me the way one leans (patiently, condescendingly) towards a child or an old person. I realized, with the slow-rotating take of the very drunk, that he was looking at me disapprovingly; I began to gather that much. In fact, I further gathered, leaning back at him, peering, that he looked really pissed off.

He spoke slowly, as if English were my second language.

"Esme, t-tell me. *Where* in all your d-delusions, did you get the idea that you could . . . d-do what you just did?"

He stopped and ran a hand across his eyes.

I'd been standing by, smiling dreamily, and now I reeled back as if he'd slapped me, teetering a bit on my heels. I caught myself.

"Wait a second, *what* did you say?"

"You d-destroyed me up there!"

"Jay! *I* can't believe . . . I was *trying* to help you."

His face twisted. "I don't need *h-help*."

"Those people were making fun of you. I couldn't stand it—"

"That's my *act,* stupid! I act like a b-bad s-stand-up, don't you get it?"

"No, I don't. And I don't think *they* did either."

"Well, Christ, how *c-could* they get it, with you ch-charging up onstage—how could they—"

"Jay, I'm sorry. I lost control . . . I tried to"—I paused and looked around me—"help with the humor. And Jay, you have to admit—I was a little *funny*. People were laughing."

"Esme. People were laughing *at* you. Th-there's a difference."

"Well, shit, you oughta know."

"This is my b-business! What do you know about it? *Nothing!* Do you kn-know what I was going to d-do next? The f-follow-up I do, when I g-get heckled like that is t-to use my st-stutter. I *use* the stutter! And it's really f-funny."

"I'm sorry."

He threw me a quick, bitter glance.

"You're so far out of t-touch you don't even know it, Esme. Plus you're stinking drunk. Your kind of help I don't need. *Ollie* doesn't need this k-kind of help. You're c-crazy, Esme. And if what you did tonight isn't proof, I don't know what is."

I took a deep breath, trying to slow things down.

"Jay. I couldn't stand the way those people were mocking you."

My throat was dry and my shin began throbbing. I reached down and felt around and winced. I'd bruised it badly climbing onto the stage. As I bent over I felt the tears overflowing down my face. They surprised me. Everything this evening had been a surprise to me.

"W-where's your car?"

"Over there."

I pointed and he set off in the direction of the parking lot behind the club, me limping behind.

We stood in front of the jeep as I rummaged in my purse for the ticket to give to the parking attendant. I could feel myself sobering up. I began to shake with cold. I felt perfectly calm now, but the tears kept falling.

"Jay. I came up onstage because I love you. I came to this club tonight because I love you."

"Too *late,* Esme. And a *l-lie.* You don't *get it,* do you?" He flinched, then spat the words out. "I tried to understand *you.* I even r-read your science books. You never tried to know *me.*"

"Why do you think I'm here tonight? Because I—"

"Being f-funny was the only thing I had that was mine. I was a s-stand-up, it was mine. *Now* you've taken that away, too. You were trying to make me look like a *fool.*"

He turned his back on me, talked over his shoulder. His left leg shook as if it were running on a separate engine of anger. The attendant pulled up in my car and I handed him a bill.

"Can you drive?"

"Drive? Why wouldn't I be able to drive?"

He sighed. "Do you want me to d-drive you home?"

"Of course not."

I let myself into the car with injured dignity, then rolled down the window as Jay knocked on it.

"You're *funnier* than m-me, Esme. You're s-smarter than me. OK? Does th-that make you happy?"

"No," I said, "that doesn't make me happy."

He put his head down on the car roof for a second, then lifted it, cocked it, and looked in at me.

"Wh-what were you t-trying to do tonight?"

I closed my eyes, then opened them again. "I wanted to save you —something I had neither the power nor right to do. I tried to do something really dumb—an act of chivalry. Do you know what I mean?"

He stared, then his mouth twisted and he pulled away.

"Go h-home, Esme," he said. "Sleep it off."

# Chapter 18

"So you realized that you loved him—and then you, like, screwed it up," said Rocky. "I mean, that's what you're saying."

"I screwed it up? How?"

"How? How? Your husband is standing on a stage in front of a club filled with people . . ." She stopped to scratch her eyes and feel around for her glass. It was two-thirty in the morning. "And you leap up from your seat and jump up onto the stage, grab the mike from his hands and begin tellin' jokes. And you ask me *how*?"

"I did not tell jokes. I talked about the Second Law of Thermodynamics." I stared at the bottom of my glass. "And I told them off."

"Yeah, well. You sort of . . . hijacked his act, right? Did you think he'd be real *happy* about your stealing his thunder?"

"Well it wasn't exactly thunder, it was more like static. I stole his static."

"Let's go back. To the part where you suddenly go leaping up." She laughed and shook her head, obviously enjoying this. "You got this feeling inside for him, right? Real desire to protect him."

"I'm tired," I said. "It's almost three."

Rocky poured herself more tequila.

"I've never heard of such a thing as what you did tonight. It's fucking amazing to me. But how can you, who are a damn smart person, be so fuckin' *stupid*? *This* is the question we gotta answer! This is the question!"

"Yeah, well, if you come up with a definitive answer let me know. Maybe I wouldn't have to think about theory anymore."

Rocky dropped her head to one side, drunk but hanging in there.

"Why *are* you dicking around with this theory, Prof? We got so much work in the lab—I don't get it! This $a_1AT$'s enough to keep me busy night and day and you're out there in the stars somewhere, even when you *do* come in."

She propped up her head with her hand and grinned lopsidedly at me.

"I miss you. The lab seems really empty these days."

I raised my glass and sang: "I've grown accustomed to your *blots*!"

Rocky snorted and emptied her glass. I looked at mine halfheartedly. I'd been drinking, off and on, since eight or nine. When I'd come limping in after midnight, Rocky took in my agitated state and broke out an old bottle of Cuervo Gold of Jay's she found in the pantry. We toasted him with the first swallow, lifting our faceted glasses to the dim yellow-domed kitchen light.

Now the bottle was half empty. Oreos and Doritos littered the table, and a fat low red candle had burned down into its hollow.

"To theory!" cried Rocky. "Fuck it."

We clicked glasses and drank, then winced at the cactusy taste. I coughed a little.

"Rocky—why do you stay on in the lab?"

She wrapped a long spiral of hair around her finger, looked at it, then let it go; slowly, slowly it repositioned itself.

"I like the procedures. I like very much knowing, for just once in my life, *exactly* what's going to happen."

"Me too. That's precisely why I chose science. From the time I was a little kid, I loved the sense it gave me, not so much that there were answers, as that certain things always happened the same way and you could count on them."

I sat up and rubbed my eyes.

"And then, at Harvard, I had this professor, Q—right, I know I've mentioned him to you—who kept insisting that the answers be plugged into fairy tales, you know: The holy crusaders set off to save the babies. Or the Genome Project: We're going to decode the language of life and thus end all human suffering, and triumph over death. Well, that's admirable, but what if it's not true? It takes the incorruptibility of the answers away. There are hardly any disinterested researchers anymore. Scientists are invested in these biotech companies up the old wazoo. I care a lot about those kids with gene deficiencies, but there's not that much that can actually be cured. You know why? There is no *normal* gene sequence that we can use *as a standard*. All sequences are unique—*shit*. No more crippled babies, no more death. *Shit*."

Rocky shook her head woozily, grinning. She pulled a Baggie from a jacket draped over the back of her chair, plopped it on the table, spat on a paper, and began rolling a joint. She spun it nimbly between her fingers into a cylinder, lit it, inhaled, sucked on it again, and passed it to me. I took a hit.

"I've *always* loved theory. Which I turn to again and again because there seems to be so little order at all in the universe, not since relativity's real implications hit, anyway, and everybody's making up voodoo hypotheses, but at least they're humble, you know what I mean? Theoretical physicists and chemists don't feel like they're *designing* futures—they can't even define what the future is, or the past. Nobody dares talk about Laws anymore, there are only models, *suggestions* of the way it *might* be possibly, in special circumstances. And then too, the observer unquestionably alters what is observed. They talk about *God*, Rocky, about finding God."

"Wow," squeaked Rocky. Her voice had gone tight as a drum and she squinted at me, then released a huge billow of smoke from her nostrils. "Wow. God!"

"No, look, I'm serious. And you know when scientists look for God, they *really* haven't a clue. Which is a good state for a scientist to be in: *Clueless.* Starting from scratch."

I swayed unsteadily, then slumped back down in my chair, exhausted.

Then I got up into a kneeling position.

"I mean, *OK,* the theory people use metaphors too! God knows they've got eleven dimensions squeezed up like Cheez Whiz in Super Strings. . . . I know this biologist, Richard Lewontin? He made the distinction clear for me: There's a difference between useful metaphors that allow the mind closer to a verifiable reality, and metaphors that are *identities,* that become the thing itself."

I stood up on my chair, waving my glass. "They stole Descartes's *clock*!" I shouted, almost falling. "Now they're *selling* Descartes's clock!"

I paused and regained my balance. "Rocky!" I cried, swaying. "Who owns the story of the future? Who owns the Bedtime Story?"

"You know what?" Rocky interrupted. I sat down, deflated, and she handed me the joint. "You know *what*? I'm the first one in my family to go to college."

I held the joint to my lips, then stopped. I'd had enough for one night. I handed it back.

"Is that true, Rock?"

"Yeah! It's a real smart family, my family, but no higher education. Except my mother's sister in Guatemala. She's a teacher. Everybody works in the store—the grocery store in Pacoima. But not anymore little Rocio! I go to school. They sent me. They put their hard-earned money behind me." She looked up at the ceiling. Smoke, in a blue torrent, poured out of her red mouth. "I was good with numbers.

That's all. I could add *up* things in my head. Now I gotta be sure I don't flunk out, 'cause my family, they think I'm so *great.*"

"You *are,* Rocky," I said. "There's no grad student who could do the job you do."

She beamed at me. "I learn *fast,* huh? Too bad I forget just as *quick.*"

"Rocky," I said. "You *are* the lab right now. You're *it.*"

"But what about $a_1AT$?" she asked. "You given up on that?"

I held the roach, pincerlike, between my fingers; she shook her head and I stubbed it out.

"I think about it every day. Just because I'm not in the lab doesn't mean it's not on my mind. I just can't stand Faber's shadow all over me."

"Yeah, I know. Bad, huh?"

"Yeah, it's bad."

"Well yeah. I know that. But sometimes I think, What about *me?* What about *me,* Prof? You plucked me off my motorcycle, got me hooked—and now, now you shake me off like water from a dog's butt."

"Rocky, don't you start on me too. I can't take it, I swear."

"Well, fuck you, Professor. I have feelings too. You taught me a whole new way of looking at science, you taught me laboratory procedures, you were my teacher *and* my friend, at least I thought you were my friend. But then you just, like, walked out the door. What kind of friend leaves a partner high and dry?"

"Me. I'm terrible—a terrible wife who messes up her husband's life, a bad mother who won't get her weird kid professional help, an incompetent teacher who doesn't teach, and a lousy lousy friend and lab partner who's never there. That's me, right? Did I sum it all up? Did I miss anything?"

Rocky laughed. "Yeah. You missed yourself. You're messing up yourself. You think that you're thinking for yourself but you're just thinking *in reaction* to everybody else. You're pissed off at the schools in L.A., you're pissed off at Q and Faber, you're pissed at Jay, at big-bucks science, money metaphors, but you run away, you don't face up, man. Then you get yourself in trouble. Climbing around out in the galaxies ain't gonna do nothin' for it. That's why I thought when you got up on that stage tonight it was *great,* you actually got real for once. You kicked *ass.*"

"Yeah, and *you* know what's real, right? *You* really can tell me about the world from your vantage point: after dark in the back seat! Cholos, frat boys, what does it matter, right?"

I meant this humorously, or I thought I did, but it sure didn't fly.

Her face turned dark. "I don't fuck cholos!"

She leaped up, knocking the chair over.

"I don't fuck frat boys, for the history books, either. I ain't fucked *anybody* since I started this goddam *convent* job, working for Mother Superior."

Her mouth turned down, like a little kid's, like Ollie's, and she started to cry.

"Rocky, oh God, wait. I'm sorry."

She threw herself from her chair and went crashing around the room, picking up her jacket and bag, her cast-off bracelets, a jeweled belt, shoes.

"No. You're right. Hey, I don't belong in your lab. I'm not that far anyhow from Pacoima. I got no right takin' up your space, huh? You got better things to do now anyway, right? You're fuckin' *Einstein.* And me, I fuck *cholos!*"

"Rocky. Don't do this, please. I'm sorry. I just can't say anything right tonight. I'm not *funny,* I'm just not funny. Don't go, Rocky, you're in no condition to drive!"

"I just sobered up."

I shook my head and laughed. "Jesus," I said. "This is goddam entropy, the Second Law."

Rocky walked up to me, bent over, and put her face in mine as I sat in my chair. "No," she said. Her brown eyes looked huge from the dope, the pupils were dilated, tears glittered on her cheeks, and her hair was wild, it seemed to have grown longer and wilder through the force of her anger.

"This ain't no Second Law. This is Rocky's *First* Law, which says that if you treat people like shit, after a while they gonna treat you *ditto*."

The door slammed. There was the sound of an ignition, then a screeching turn, loud acceleration off into the night. I sat for a while and then I went in to check on Ollie. She was sleeping on her side, holding her dragon tight. Then I went into the bathroom, turned on the light, and looked in the mirror. And there she was: the trouble-maker, the great theorist, stand-up physicist. I didn't cry, I didn't do anything. I stared at myself. I remembered how Q had kept me feeling safe all those years. Remarkable, I thought. I couldn't make Rocky feel safe for one semester.

I walked around the house, checking windows, locking doors, turning off the lights. I turned the phone machine on and I poured myself a large glass of water. I went back to the mirror and lifted the glass in a toast.

"Chirality," I said aloud and drank it down.

Dimly, through a haze of impressions: Ollie standing sentinellike at the side of the bed, the phone ringing; I came awake. I patted Ollie on the head and felt around on the floor for the bedside clock. I read its luminous dial (caused by a form of radioactivity known as alpha decay) and gasped. Noon. The room was dark, the curtains were drawn.

"Shit," I said to Ollie's serious face. "My lab."

"Shit," said Ollie. "My lab."

"Sweetheart, how long have you been up?"

"Two cookies fell on the raisins. Ollie danced and danced in her box."

"Great. Since nine, huh?"

I felt I'd swallowed a dump truck's load of sand, that same truck had backed up and poured some into my eyes for good measure. The phone rang again. I picked it up warily.

"Hello."

"Hello? Professor Charbonneau? This is Mrs. Vickers, Dr. Faber's secretary. He would like to speak with you, if you can just hold one—"

"Ah, that won't be necessary, Mrs. Vickers. Just tell him I discovered a cure for cancer *and* AIDS this morning. That's why I couldn't make it to my lab."

"I beg your pardon? I—"

"Thanks, Mrs. Vickers."

I hung up.

"Well, Ollie," I said, "it's just you and me, kiddo."

And it was. Just Ollie and me. We had breakfast, then we went to the store and stocked up on groceries. I bought enough for two or three weeks. Then we went to the children's bookstore and the toy store and stocked up there too. I still felt light-headed and I had to stop every so often and breathe deeply, tell myself I was all right.

When we got home, I fixed lunch; then Ollie took a nap.

"No school today, sweetie," I said. "And no school tomorrow."

She fell asleep almost immediately, holding her new book, *Max, the Bad-Talking Parrot.*

I took my legal pads into my study, turned on the computer, sat staring for a while, then lay down on the floor and fell into a deep sound sleep.

----------------

# Chapter 19

Imaginary Lecture:

Michael Faraday, or Avenging a Style of Thought

*When everything is chaos, Ollie, I like to think about Michael Faraday. Patron Saint of the Oddly Made, the Lispers, the Spinners, the Galaxy Leapers.*

*He was Einstein's hero and Maxwell's; Einstein kept a picture of Faraday on his wall. Why? Because, as Maxwell, who translated his ideas into math, said, "Faraday, in his mind's eye, saw lines of force traversing all space." He was a visionary. He discovered electromagnetic rotations, he discovered induction and the magneto-optical effect and diamagnetism. His ideas were the foundations for electromagnetic theory, even Einstein's notions of field theory. He anticipated Einstein's view of gravitation. But he had no math, no scientific language. He had no formal education.*

*He was a blacksmith's son, born in 1791, of parents so poor that he ended up a child of the streets in pre-Dickens London. Close to homeless. But he made his own way. His family was proud and religious; they belonged to the Scottish Sandemanian sect, an austere, fundamentalist, plain-style faith that preached self-improvement.*

*After an early, skimpy education in a country school, Faraday became*
*a bookbinder's apprentice in London and educated himself by reading*
*the texts he bound. He taught himself to write. But people laughed*
*at him: He had a severe speech impediment, he couldn't say the letter*
*"r" at all. And when he learned to write, he couldn't get his mind*
*around punctuation and spelling. He began to attend public lectures*
*on science and through these lectures grew to idolize Sir Humphry*
*Davy, a Royal Institution scientist. He carefully copied out Davy's*
*lectures, bound them at work, and presented them to Davy as a gift.*
*He began to dog Davy's steps, begging for a job in his lab. We have*
*Davy's comment, when a Royal Society associate suggested hiring*
*Faraday "to wash bottles," just to get rid of him: Davy insisted that*
*the boy could be used for "something better than that." Something*
*about Faraday haunted him—he was sad, comic, yet* arresting: *a*
*skinny, fire-eyed youth scrambling after him in the street, chattering*
*in his r-less language, gesturing.*

*Faraday started at the Royal Institution, Davy's lab, in 1813 as a*
*lab assistant, working for a menial wage. In three years he was writing*
*research papers, and eventually he became director and the greatest*
*experimental physicist of the time. He learned everything about the*
*laboratory, from cleaning flasks to wiring magnetic coils. He carefully*
*observed and took notes on every experiment. It became clear to his*
*colleagues that his mind worked differently than others'. Here's Far-*
*aday himself:*

> Do not suppose that I was a very deep thinker, or was marked
> as a precocious person. I was a very lively imaginative person,
> and could believe in the "Arabian Nights" as easily as in the
> "Encyclopedia." But facts were important to me, and saved me.

*How odd. Faraday, for all his talk of the* facts, *paid no attention*
*to them at all. He just let his mind walk, never allowed predisposed*

*ideas to get in his way. Because he knew no math, the academy ignored him. Faraday's religion forbade representation in signs or symbols, plus he said he had trouble remembering formulae. So he talked and wrote about what he saw—and he saw things other people didn't see.*

*He wanted to share these things; he particularly wanted ordinary people, his people, poor people, to understand science. Every Christmas he gave a special, public Children's Science Lecture: Little kids and amateurs came. People contrasted his funny, startling, unforgettable language in explaining scientific phenomena with Davy's more pretentious, dead diction. I suppose he was like a rock star or a stand-up comic on the lecture stage—bouncing around, his whole body animated by his thought. He'd work audiences into a terrific excitement. It isn't clear if his speech impediment disappeared when he lectured. I like to think it didn't—I like to think that he bopped around, sounding like a hopped-up genius Elmer Fudd.*

*The public is always hungry for Science Stories, but Faraday did not take his examples from contemporary culture; he invented analogies, he got his audience to stretch their imaginations. Faraday's style of thought was "scattered," they all said—but, even more interesting, his thoughts moved free of "reasoning," free of prior frameworks of thought. "Intuitive," they said. Faraday knew how his own mind worked. He moved, in his thinking, toward what he called lateral action, without giving any single idea hierarchical priority. Things clarified themselves through unpredictable "thought selections." He allowed chaos into his head. Principles, observations, and facts all whirled there, in and out of the chaos Faraday by dispensing with the need to immediately "understand," evolved a coherent model. Facts, he said, saved him—but it was not the word "facts," perhaps, that he meant to emphasize. It was the verb "to save." His mind saved things (not in the sense of keeping, but in the sense of salvation), spinning them out of unarticulated space, darkness. Without math, his comprehension was mathematical—he traveled with the light waves, then brought them back into language, the linear, back through the mirror, saved.*

*I imagine him in the lab; he sprinkles iron filings over a piece of paper resting on top of a bar magnet, then records the patterns of the magnetic field lines traced around the magnetic poles. Beautiful starbursts, sprays, spirals, fingerprint whorls. Then he lifts up his head, imagining the waves and whorls moving outward, transversing all matter, running through the universe.*

*He thought like a child. He took a hike one August and stood looking at a waterfall: watching a rainbow at the bottom of the falls, superimposed over the chaos. He saw things spatially. The chaos didn't bother him: The image sprang from it—and he saw things simultaneously. Or four-dimensionally, just as he saw ghostly waves, the pattern of field lines, everywhere, even inside magnets. What he worked out showed the deep abiding connection between electricity and magnetism—only fully revealed when the two are set in relative motion. Thus he stepped into contemporary physics. This beautiful symbiosis would be shown off by the field concept. In 1865, when James Clerk Maxwell thought up a system of equations that articulated this electromagnetic relationship, it was easy to predict the future. Our whole technological world (electricity, lights, TV, computers, satellites) depends on what these equations tell us about the interactive behavior, the marriage, of electricity and magnetism:* the electromagnetic field. *You could only tell what they were capable of when you got them moving around each other, arguing, making up, finally connecting. The waves of the electromagnetic field (Maxwell said) were a form of light. And you might be able to guess where the waves went from there. Into the mind of a patent officer, junior grade, in Switzerland. Then into the mind of Niels Bohr, into a theory he called complementarity.*

*Oh, I like to think about Michael Faraday. I like to imagine him thinking his patchwork thoughts, putting seemingly unlike concepts together—shocking the world with his strange running commentary.*

*The first lab is the child's mind: before conditioning, even before consciousness. Children, even right-handed nondyslexic children, write words backwards. Maybe they can see "through" things, maybe they only see the "curve" of the words (OUT–TUO) around in space, around corners. The lab is where sense is made first, not in school. The lab can be a sandbox, a stream bottom, dust motes in light-filled air.*

*When you grow up to be a scientist, you study the parts of the cell; light; elements; you count chromosomes. You discern the structure of DNA, and you tally reflips and markers, alleles and enzymes that work like molecular scissors. You draw pictures and take notes; you look again, through a powerful microscope, at the structure of DNA, the double helical structure. Then one day, you set your gaze a notch up over your cold cup of coffee, you crane your stiff neck, lean back, and gaze up a little into the galaxy and notice the mirror symmetry in the world of whirling planets. You notice the symmetry because of the asymmetry also discernible there.*

*Then it must be true: What Nature does in a left-handed way she can also do in a right-handed way! Our sun circles through the galaxy on such an axis that its planets trace spiraling helical paths of other-handedness! Astronomical asymmetry: How did this happen in our galaxy? Are other planets, orbiting other suns, describing spirals of reverse handedness? The human heart beats on the left, but there are examples of hearts working away on the right side. Mother Nature allows it, you see, in differing quantities, the existence of both types of handedness: the ambidextrous universe.*

*This is how you begin to imagine things that few people believe are actually there. You peek into the wild, subatomic world—where particles move right through walls and disappear. Quantum electro-dynamics makes Mother Nature look crazy, a real nut case, from the perspective of common sense. Yet the theories agree completely with experiment.*

*When I watch how you think, sweetheart, I compare your cerebral skitter and leap to Faraday's "lateral action." And I ask myself, What teacher is going to pay attention to this phenomenon, assuming she would even notice? You fit into no category. You can read and write, so you're not dyslexic. (It was not words he couldn't grasp, it was the superimposed organization: grammar, syntax, punctuation—how the story was told. So he had to tell it his way—to invent his own way through words.)*

*"Learning-disabled," that's what you are—because you don't talk like others, or think like them. And you're "gifted": an equal curse. Of course there's the right and left brain, but I believe in the ambidextrous, asymmetric prelateralized brain. Like Faraday's.*

*When I was growing up, I wanted words to be less confusing. Language defines itself spatially like this: left-right reversal understood by us in terms of our bilateral symmetry. Stuck there, you see. In the mirror, opposite the enantiomer. How I loved, in high school, the precise spatial language of three-space coordinate geometry! What a relief from the endless* flatland *of words. I dream in a language that is spatial, that is cubist, hyper-dimensions of thought and speech. But the language isn't math, or geometry. It's Ollie's speech, Ollie's waterfall of words.*

*So I like to think of Michael Faraday, little street urchin, running after a scholarly gentleman in the street, speaking gibberish. I don't like to think about how he left the world, mad and sequestered, the waves having finally overwhelmed him. As we close the door on the world for a while, Ollie, perhaps he'll be our guardian angel. Perhaps we'll feel the waves begin to hum and gently oscillate—above, below, around us? Verbs: to think, to Faraday. Perchance to dream.*

# Chapter 20

Then this sweet interlude of false peace: Ollie and I alone together for three, four, five days? I lost track. With food, music, drawing paper, toys. Cozy fires in the fireplace, fudge. We lay on the floor together in pajamas, talking, coloring. We trimmed the plants and watered them, baked cookies. We slept together in the big bed. Nose to nose, she stared cross-eyed at me, thinking hard. "Mom," she said, and patted my face solemnly. Then smiled her lopsided smile. "Ollie and Mamma."

I refused to answer the phone. Disembodied voices talked away behind the door of my study, following the high-pitched beep. With a certain amount of morbid satisfaction, I noted the increasing urgency in these floating voices as the days rolled by. Occasionally, I'd stand outside my study door, eavesdropping on whoever was calling. Students, friends, Faber's secretary—even, once, Jay. But I would not pick up the receiver.

It rained—unusual for Los Angeles—which provided an even stronger sense of haven for us. The rain beat on the roof and trees and burbled in the downspouts all night. The air, when I opened the front shutters on the fifth or sixth day, was incredibly fresh, cleansed and shimmering. The sidewalks and bricks gave off a hosed-down, steamy smell; there were terraced puddles on the lawn. There was a nostalgic smell of washed linen, baked bread. Chlorophyll. Leaf patterns moved on the wooden porch and over its ceiling beams. I was beginning to feel restored. I yawned and stretched. I'd been working on my theory at night, after Ollie went to sleep; now I was so close to what I wanted that I knew I had to call L.R.

I turned back to the room, where Ollie sat in a rhomboid of sunlight in the lotus position, drinking from a yellow twin-handled Yogi Bear plastic cup. We'd been drawing together—whatever she suggested. We each tried a hand at her visions. We'd drawn the "X's that fly," lizards pulling "some deep egg ponds," walking streetlight trees, the "gas station guy opening his mouth," "scary" waves and stars "giving sharpness to the clouds," and "very very green and loud spoons."

I tore off another sheet from the big drawing tablet. I couldn't resist giving her a little test. Everyone else is testing her, I thought.

I pencil-sketch some flat shapes that are symmetric and therefore not reversed by the mirror. I draw circles, squares, ellipses, equilateral triangles, and, for good gambling measure, diamonds, hearts, spades, clubs. She comments on the diamond—she loves that shape. When you draw a line of a certain length, there is a center point of symmetry—a single place that divides the figure into identical halves. But when you choose plane shapes, like the ones I did, you move into the two-dimensional world. Nevertheless, all these shapes can be bisected by a line of symmetry, which divides the shape into exact, mirror-image halves. I ask Ollie to show me where to sever a line and she does. We slice the diamond, her favorite. Then I ask her to look at the other shapes and she takes a pencil and divides them, square, circle, triangle, into their twin halves.

Then I show her asymmetric plane figures, I draw the mysterious ones: rhomboid, swastika, and spiral. If you try to bisect these guys into mirror image halves, no matter how hard you try—it won't work. They're asymmetric. I demonstrate this to Ollie: I try to divide the shapes equally and show how it doesn't work. She takes the pencil from my hand and tries herself, then looks up at me and frowns. She understands, it just won't do. She looks back at the symmetrical shapes, then tries again. No go. "No, Mom," she says. She points to the different halves.

Then I try to draw three-dimensional solids. Lines have a *point* of symmetry, figures have a *line* of symmetry, 3-D solids have a *plane* of symmetry. I draw a circle. I draw a cylinder. This is harder. We're into plane geometry now. If you think of a plane of symmetry as a reflecting surface, half the figure and its reflection restore the original shape. It has rotational depth. I get a hand mirror, cut an orange in half and show Ollie how it makes itself whole again, reflected. She watches carefully. I think she's with me. Then I draw an asymmetric solid: one that can never be made to click with its reflection. The helix, the curve of the spiral staircase—I draw that, in the form of a candy cane and the red stripe that winds around it. You can't divide that 3-D helix, that spiral, into mirror halves, no matter how hard you try. So she can see that the mirror image is exactly like the asymmetric solid, except that it goes the other way. Now we're into *my* stuff. Enantiomers. Or enantiomorphs. I show her her own hands. Look, they're just alike, but asymmetric. Her shoes are enantio-morphs. Her ears. She laughs as I wiggle my ears at her. Does she understand? I know she does. Ollie frowns and she draws more shapes; some are actually three-dimensional, and she bisects the sym-metrical ones. I watch her. She hums a little.

"Ollie *line*. Ollie *line*. Ollie cut. Ollie's pieces *fly*."

Left and right, mirror reversals. All this doesn't sound that hard, really. But amazing events in twentieth-century physics—the over-throw of parity and the magical corkscrew of DNA—are tied up with this looking-glass stuff. I show Ollie a piece of string. Maybe it *looks* symmetrical, but each strand twists into a helix that will dance the opposite way when reflected. I'm not sure she understands. Her face scrunches up in thought. While she's looking at the unraveled string in the mirror, I get up, find my address book, and dial Lorraine Atwater. She answers on the third ring.

"Hi, L.R. It's Esme." I take a deep breath. "You know . . . I think it works. There was an error in our ab initio calculations—but when that's corrected, you get the . . . It *happens*."

There was her barklike laugh.

"You know what I did last night? I went over and over the calculations. What have you *got*?"

I opened my legal pad. We went to work. We stayed on the phone for nearly thirty minutes, both talking at once after a while, yelling, we were so excited. Then the doorbell rang.

Ollie glanced at the door. I smiled reassuringly over the receiver at her.

"L.R.? I gotta go. Someone's at the door. I'll call you back."

I peeked out through the curtains and saw an irritated-looking woman in a very ugly, shiny, navy-blue suit, standing on one foot and then the other. She was about twenty-five but she looked old and used, bad skin, greasy hair. I thought she might be a graduate student, but I didn't recognize her.

I opened the door and she leaped forward, as if she meant me harm; I recoiled instinctively. Her eyes narrowed with a sudden fierce pleasure. I noticed that she was wearing a Happy Face pin on her lapel. HAVE A NICE DAY!

"Esme Tallich?"

"Yes?"

She dropped a manila envelope in my hands, grimaced passionately, like her terrible button face, then was gone.

I leaned against the doorjamb, watching her click-click on her heels around the shining puddles to her VW parked at the curb.

"Thanks a *lot*!" I called after her, but she didn't turn around.

I tore open the envelope and the papers slid out into my hands. I stared at the top sheet. Jay was divorcing me, on grounds of incompatibility. I turned over a page. He was asking the court for full custody of his daughter, Olivia Tallich.

I sat down hard on the porch steps. I watched and heard the ugly young woman shift out of neutral into first and roar off in her VW. A number of other cars passed. Then I got up and went back inside. Ollie was drawing the string. She'd carefully separated all the symmetric shapes from the asymmetric; they were divided by a long half-erased wobbly line. Now she was making a drawing of the unraveled string. As she worked, she sucked on the orange half; it was attached like a suction cup to her mouth. Juice dribbled down her chin.

She looked up at me and laughed. The orange half dropped. I hugged her, smelling her sweet orange smell, and I lifted my finger, drew an imaginary line from the top of her head down the center of her body, bisecting her. Then she did the same to me. I wiggled my ears again, but she looked at me solemnly.

"Mom, I am seeing ears. They are jumping with line bees."

The sun rose higher in the sky and we still sat there on the braided rug, out of time, talking about our shapes. Ollie and Esme, Esme and Ollie; for just this moment no one could touch us: safe on the other side of the mirror.

# Chapter 21

I opened the front door on Mrs. Kraft (my talkative elderly neighbor and occasional baby-sitter). I held a finger to my lips. Ollie was taking a late-morning nap and she was a light sleeper.

"Why isn't the little stinker in school?" Mrs. K. asked in a loud stage whisper, her little birdlike head bobbing on her neck, her bright inquisitive eyes taking in the room. She winked at me. I used to wink back at her every single time until I finally realized she had a facial tic.

"She's been exhausted lately." I smiled, and covered my lips with my finger again. "Let her sleep, OK? I'll probably be home before she wakes up."

After Mrs. K. had settled herself, winking, in front of her soap operas with a diet Pepsi, I went into my study, shut the door, and played back the accumulated voices of concern and judgment. The tape ran around its track, the Greek chorus intoned.

Students' voices: superficially solicitous, then annoyed. "Professor, my grade." "Professor, my paper." Two colleagues from the biochemistry department, inquiring politely as to my whereabouts and presumably, my state of mind. Faber's secretary (several times, her tone getting sharper and sharper); then Faber himself ("Since you are not returning my calls, I have no choice but to leave this message on your recording machine. I've been in consultation with the dean and it is my sad task to inform you that as of Wednesday your contract with this university is suspended until further notice. I regret very much having had to take this step," blah, blah); Susan Dubs, a friend and fellow mother at Sixth Street School; Ollie's kindergarten teacher, sounding confused—Was *Olive* well? she asked after a long hesitation; *beep*, Jay—who paused dramatically, then called out "Esme? Esme?" as if I was deliberately refusing to acknowledge him, then left a terse sentence about the divorce papers. Rocky next, leaving a cool memorandum: She'd clear her stuff out of the lab, she'd leave the key on the hook by the door, she'd see me around sometime. Three hangups; a message from Jay's dentist: His teeth were due to be cleaned. Before the tape ran out, cutting off his message, I heard a smoky, weighted voice, East Coast accent.

"Esme. Jesse. I was just thinking—" followed by a series of loud beeps. The tape was full.

Well, I thought, not bad. In one elliptical turn I'd lost my job, my husband, and the best lab assistant I'd ever had, *and* had my steamy fantasy life offhandedly amputated.

I sat down at my messy desk and put my head in my hands. Then I jumped up, talking to myself, grabbed my bag, and hit the door.

I stood on the porch, staring blindly in front of me. Then: Take them all away, God, I prayed. Except her.

I turned into the Paramount lot and stopped at the guard booth, where, as I'd expected, Sherman was on duty. We stared each other down, combat veterans; then he rolled his eyes, and with a quick brutal gesture waved me through.

I parked and found my way to Jay's building. A red bulb burned over the entrance to the soundstage, indicating that a taping was in progress. There was a director's trailer next to the soundstage and I walked up the steps and opened the door.

No one looked up as I came in. The director, a nervous man in glasses and a plaid shirt, huddled with Jay and the A.D., while crew members milled around them.

I glanced at the wall of monitors. On the screens was a montage of shots, all focusing on a cluster of very small people—dwarfs or midgets. I stared at the nearest monitor. Several of the dwarfs looked up at the dangling boom as one of their group pointed at it. They were dressed in strange costumes, vaguely Elizabethan—doublets and jerkins and hose. The costumes exaggerated their physical oddness, which was a matter not just of diminutive size but of queer altered symmetry: great hands, barrel torsos, overdeveloped biceps and legs—as if they'd all tried to grow laterally. One of their number stood to the side; he had a long pale face and a high Mayan forehead. He looked tragic and refined, like one of Picasso's *saltimbanques*. One held a bouquet of shaggy mums, another an enormous lollipop. There was a wave of laughter from the studio audience, then another, sounding unintentionally cruel.

I wondered what show they were taping and, as if she'd read my thoughts, one of the production assistants moved in front of the monitors, sipping coffee and murmuring, "I mean, *I* could never guess which one is directly descended from an original Munchkin, could you, Tina? Are they gonna stump those deadheads on the panel, or what?"

A crew member came up behind her and put his arms around her. "Who'd you rather fuck? Me or a Munchkin?"

She pulled away, making a face.

"In case you haven't heard, Kellogg, *size* has nothing to do with it."

I walked up to Jay and tapped him on the shoulder. He turned slowly, still talking to the director, and then he froze.

"Hey, Jay. I got your papers. I'd like to talk to you."

He shook his head. "Not *now,* Esme."

"This will only take a minute."

The director looked at me over his glasses, then turned to Jay.

"Jay, take a little break, it's fine. We're just going to go over that last shot—stay close where we can find you."

He turned away and Jay glared at me. Without a word, he spun on his heel, stalked over to the trailer doorway. I followed.

We stood on the steps and faced each other. Then he looked away. The sound of studio laughter filled the room behind us.

"Yes?"

"I just wanted to ask you face to face: Why are you asking for full custody of Ollie?"

Audience laughter.

"I *told* you—I want to p-put her in a special school, I want her to have a ch-chance to be a normal child."

"So you're going to put her in an institution."

Laughter.

"*Not* an institution, a *s-school,* can you grasp the difference? She's not going to be put in a straitjacket, she's going to be working with p-professionals who will help her. And I s-suggest, Esme"—he looked into my eyes for the first time since I'd arrived—"that you get some p-professional help too. I mean it."

"Jay, I don't want a penny of alimony, I'll give you the house, Jay, *anything*—OK? Just stop trying to hurt me like this."

He laughed. There was another swell of audience mirth, backing him up.

"Wake *up,* Esme! I c-called UGC to talk to you and I was told by the department secretary that you've been s-suspended from your job. Apparently you've been fucking up there too. How are *you* going to support Ollie? And k-keep the house? Have you thought about th-that?"

I tried to catch his eye.

"Jay. The TOE came together. As a model, it works. Lorraine Atwater and I—"

"God damn your T-TOE!" he yelled, and a production assistant coming up the steps glanced, shocked, at my sandals.

"Listen to me! If this thing is what we think, I'll be able to teach anywhere I choose. Jay, it's something I *had* to do. And Ollie . . ."
He was looking out at the lot and I moved around and down a step so that I was looking up into his face.

"Jay, Ollie is fine. She sees the world in a very sophisticated spatial fashion. I went over mirror-symmetrical and asymmetrical shapes with her and she picked them right out. Then she organized them all—"

"Jesus, Esme! When are you going to st-stop this shit! Trying to make your own kid your . . . experiment. S-so what if she understands the theory of relativity? She can't t-talk to her parents, she can't t-talk to other kids. She's in a world of her own, Esme."

More laughter.

"She talks to me, Jay. All the time."

The director's assistant stood in the doorway.

"Jay. Time."

He started to turn and I grabbed his arm.

"Jay. Don't put her through this."

"D-don't contact me again. Except through the lawyer. His n-name's on the papers."

He pushed inside, into the swelling laughter, then turned around. We looked at each other for a long minute. Then he closed his eyes, very slowly opened them, whirled around and was gone.


I stepped down and walked toward the parking lot. I nearly ran head-on into Paloma, who was hurrying toward the trailer carrying a number of grease-spotted white bags filled with what smelled unmistakably like Chinese food.

We stared at each other. Then she started to move around me. I stopped her.

"How are you doin', Paloma? What's new?"

"Hello . . . Esme."

"Got some egg rolls there, Paloma? You bringing those to my husband?"

"If you'll *excuse* me, Esme—"

"You wanna take my kid, right? Bring her up? *My* kid—who you think is cuckoo, right?"

"Esme, listen to me, OK? I can't help it your daughter is not *normal.* The sooner she gets into a . . . you know, *special environment,* the better. Then she might have a chance to be . . . like other normal, you know, *happy* kids."

"That's *true.* Maybe she could grow up to be like *you,* Paloma! You've met Ollie—what? *Once?* Right?"

"Esme, I *don't* want to talk to you. Let me—"

"You stay away from Ollie. Do you hear me? Don't you *touch* Ollie, don't you even *think* about her!"

Paloma backed away from me and stumbled, dropping one of the bags. White-lidded foil cartons spilled onto the grass. She opened her mouth wide.

"Jay!"

It was amazing. He was there in an instant. I don't ever remember him moving that fast the whole time I'd known him. He must have been watching from the door.

"P-Paloma?"

She took his arm. She began to cry.

"J-Jesus fucking C-Christ, Esme!"

He couldn't look at me.

"Well," I said. "Here's my best wishes to you both."

A plastic bag of fortune cookies lay next to my foot. I stomped on it and ground it in with my heel.

I smiled at them.

"Now," I said, "you've got what you deserve—*no* future! Or about the same future *you* have as a stand-up, Jay."

I kicked one of the foil containers toward them as I turned to go. They jumped back, staring at it.

"Too bad, Jay," I said. "A depressing aspect of all this is you used to at least *try* to be funny."

I waved to Sherman from my car on my way out, and he froze a second, then actually smiled and waved back to me.

When I got home there was a message on my machine from Lorraine Revent Atwater. She'd decided to go away for a while, the message said. She needed some more time to "refine her thinking." She left no forwarding number, but she said she'd call me soon from the East Coast.

I played her message back twice, listening closely for some hint of emotional content—was she upset, tired, pissed off with me (like everyone else), or just preoccupied? But her tone was steady and uncompromising in its banality: Hello, Esme. It's been swell. Good-bye, Esme.

I waited till Ollie was tucked in that night and then paced the floor of my study. At one point I tried L.R.'s number at home, but her recorded response was equally opaque. She was out of town. She'd be returning soon. Please leave a message after the beep.

The magnitude of what we'd come up with seemed undercut suddenly by feelings of doubt: What if L.R. had found something shockingly wrong with my calculations, so wrong she was embarrassed to tell me—no. What if . . . I stopped myself. I sat down in my desk chair, but I could not relax.

I'd taken enormous risks. I'd sacrificed my status quo for this work. I'd actually thought I was doing what no woman scientist had ever done: writing my own life. I'd waited for L.R. to take the lead, given her age and experience, in determining where to submit our results for publication, deciding who should be notified and in what order. Now, in her wake, I wasn't sure how to proceed: On my own? Solo but noting both our names? *How?*

For the first time in all the previous dark twisting weeks, I let myself weep for myself, my life. What had I done, where was this going to end? I'd been unstable, unrepentant, heartless, single-minded about my goal. But somehow I'd had faith; the world of theory is touched by God, it had provided me a halo tunnel—I'd felt blessed, invincible. Now the walls were starting to fall and there was no longer that sense of invincibility, the giddiness of privileged vision.

Earlier, through a friend at UGC Law School, I'd located a lawyer who agreed to represent me. I was terrified that Jay was going to sue for temporary custody of Ollie while the divorce was in progress.

On the phone the lawyer had asked me several questions, about my marriage and Ollie, and though I sensed her sympathy and willingness to understand, I felt she'd had trouble grasping the heart of the conflict between Jay and me—our polar views of Ollie. I arranged a time the next day to meet with her and I set myself the goal of appearing strong and collected by the time the meeting took place.

The next morning Ollie chattered away at breakfast, then climbed down from her chair, picked up her crayons, and settled on the floor to draw while I did the dishes.

"Mom," she called after a while, propping herself up on her elbows. Then she beckoned with one hand, urgently.

"These are the same ones turned."

I wiped my hands on the dish towel, then knelt beside her. She had been drawing the shapes I'd shown her: first the symmetric, then the asymmetric. Her renderings were careful and exact, lined up on the page—but then she had flipped them. That is to say, she'd shown how two enantiomorphic (one left, one right) polygons could be superimposed. That was easy. But since the other day's science lesson, she'd been obsessed with two enantiomorphic corkscrews, one left-handed, one right-handed. To imagine superimposing these two guys you'd have to be able to visualize four dimensions—that is, to see them not in a Euclidean, 3-D manner, but topologically. One of them would have to be cranked around, rotated, flipped over in a fourth dimension (disappearing!) and then it would reappear as the "other side." If you had 4-D eyes you could view the corkscrew as a left helix from one spot and as a right helix from another. Ollie had drawn a loop from "behind" the left-handed corkscrew, knotted it "overhand," then brought it up behind the right-hander.

"I believe you can see this," I said to her bent head. "I believe you see hyperspace."

She looked up at me and nodded. "Ollie is a very turning eye," she said proudly. She got to her feet and began spinning slowly, gradually faster and faster. Then she stopped abruptly, shaking herself like a puppy. She steadied herself, then turned toward me.

"I am Ollie," she said, and smiled. It was extraordinary—the first time I had ever known her to refer to herself in the first person.

"Yes. You're Ollie." I laughed and hugged her and kissed her. She wrinkled up her face and smiled.

"You are most definitely Ollie. The only such Ollie on earth."

An hour or so later, the doorbell rang again. In a zombielike calm, I opened the door. *This* time the messenger was a young black kid; he had a dreamy look on his face and he wore a lime-green satin baseball jacket. He kept checking his watch, annoyed. It was a fake too-gold Rolex—I wondered if he'd been conned into buying it and now it was running badly.

He'd looked up smiling when the door opened and he handed me the envelope in a very delicate, hesitant fashion. As if he knew—or did that slightly cringing behavior come with the territory?

"Have a good one, if you *can,* man!" he called over his shoulder, loping away in his hightops.

I took the papers out to the kitchen, so Ollie couldn't see my face. I sat down and read the words slowly: ". . . temporary custody of Olivia Tallich, during divorce proceedings."

I restacked the papers neatly. I looked up at the clock and went to the phone.

# Chapter 22

The glass door is right in front of me, reading TUO: Walk out, tuo klaw, I think, into the fourth dimension. Did I think Ollie was a genius? No. But I think she saw the world differently from everyone. Was she an autistic savant, one of those strange children with little or no language ability who can paint like Leonardo or add up and multiply columns of figures in their heads? No.

But I thought she really did see things differently—therefore her powers of description were different—therefore language was a tight-rope for her, from here to there—and sometimes she rose up off the tightrope and walked a glittering trail on air. Around, all the way around shape. I wrote her phrases, her word-collages down and I recorded the consistencies—she was always making her own kind of "sense." Whenever we went out—I mean left somewhere, said good-bye, exited—she spoke in more orderly sentences, as if she recognized doorways in experience through which she came and went.

Jean Piaget believed all kids see the world topologically, four-dimensionally, *first,* as infants, before they are *taught* to see things in three-dimensional Euclidean geometric space. Squares, rectangles, tri-angles, you see, don't come to us naturally—we have to internalize the cookie-cutter. But fluid, unending, curving hyperspace—it's our

229

first visual home. That's why a palette, a circle with dots of paint in colors moving clockwise around it, and a *reverse* palette, with the colors going counter, will be looked on as the *same* by those little minds that can "flip" the spheres with no effort. A triangle and a circle look the same—it's the closed curve that likens them in a child's mind. "Handedness" exists only for those minds trapped in space-time.

These thoughts, far extended, kept me busy in the hours before my meeting with the lawyer. Ollie was back in school and I felt lonely —I sat filling up pages of my yellow legal pads.

I'd had a letter from Faber. His tone was still woundedly imperious, but slightly chastened. He was interested in talking to me about continuing my work in the lab, even if I didn't teach. He mentioned my original negotiations with UGC—how surprised they'd all been when I wanted to teach Organic. Maybe, he said, that hadn't been such a good idea after all, though I'd convinced everyone it was. A research specialist like myself needed time to work uninterrupted; I hadn't had that time. Wow, I thought. The funders must have gotten to him. My contract with them still stood. Maybe they'd said: "Cut her some slack, Walter."

I was feeling stronger somehow; it was weird, the more I was threatened, the more I believed I felt strength shoring me up. I got up and stared out the window. It was another beautiful day. Faber was terrified of losing the lab funding. He was going to have to make peace with me. Jay would never get Ollie. Ollie would be fine, I'd find a school for her. Lorraine Atwater would be back soon. Sometime in the future I'd see Jesse again. We'd fall through that gold-lit cloud again. We'd die and go to heaven. I sighed a big sigh. I realized that I loved Jesse. I smiled to myself, then I looked down and noticed my hands shaking.

The lawyer, Terry McMahon, was youngish, brisk, and efficient. She was a graduate of UGC Law School, and we shook hands in that self-consciously solemn manner of the new woman professional, straightening our shoulders, looking each other squarely in the eye.

She offered me coffee, turning to a gleaming white Mocha Maker tucked into a walnut niche behind her desk, beneath shelves of thick leatherbound volumes: torts, precedents. Near the Mocha Maker stood a silver trophy: women's soccer. She lifted the glass pot and poured as the sun came out from a cloud and flooded through her windows. She had long brown hair pinned back, and a strand came loose. She set the half-filled coffee mug down and reanchored it.

We sat down with our mugs of coffee and she went to work.

"So he's made the move for Olivia?"

"*Ollie*. Yes. He's asked the court for temporary custody."

I asked her what would happen next and she told me that under California law, an evaluation of our situation would take place. This was called mediation. A "mediator," usually a therapist, would take a look at the problem, then (most likely) refer each of us to a psychiatrist for separate evaluations. Ollie might receive a court-appointed attorney or a "guardian ad litem."

"If it goes to that point," she added. "This person becomes Ollie's advocate; her best interests will be determined by him or her. However, usually these things are settled in mediation, so it never gets to that stage."

She watched me closely. I was trying not to get upset, as the idea, so alien, of someone else deciding what would happen to Ollie struck me with force.

She sipped her coffee, looking at me over the mug.

"On the phone you said that Ollie is not like other kids—what did you mean by that?"

"I meant that she is different from her peers. Well, she's different from almost *everybody*. She hasn't developed along predictable lines—her speech, her mannerisms, her behavior, everything she does is unconventional."

"You keep using the word 'unconventional' to describe her to me. This implies that you think her behavior is a kind of *choice,* is that true?"

I hesitated. "No. Her behavior is not a choice."

"So her development is not so much unconventional as *unusual,* would you say?"

I nodded, suspicious.

"As a matter of fact, your husband has characterized her behavior as disturbed."

"That's right."

"And what is your response to his characterization?"

"I don't think that he really *knows* Ollie. He doesn't observe her and he doesn't talk to her because her manner frightens him."

"Why?"

"Maybe he lacks imagination?"

"Come *on,* Esme."

"No, I'm *serious.* That's where our views of Ollie differ. Imagination. Hers, his, mine. Ollie imagines *everything* and expresses it. He wants her to imagine things within limits."

"To be fair, his view would strike me as responsible. We cannot, as parents, let our children live in a world of imagination, now can we?"

"Right. Well then, my question to you would be, How do we limit their imaginations? In our responsible fashion? What do we take away? And when? And *how* do we do it? How do we convince them that they don't see what they see—that they see only what we tell them?"

"You're getting a little beyond me here, Esme. Your approach is theoretical—I'm talking about *your* child. Your husband's view is that she needs help to function in the world. Yours is, I take it, that she does not."

I put my mug down on a convenient desktop coaster. A glossy little Audubon: the Least Tern.

"Don't misunderstand me. I've had questions about Ollie always, from the beginning. Her manner is very strange. But I do not think it is pathological. As a matter of fact, I think that she *needs* to be the way she is in order to survive."

"I wonder if you can give me a description of some of Ollie's behavior patterns."

"She likes to spin—around in circles—and she repeats things to herself. She describes her own actions under her breath as she does things. She usually refers to herself in the third person. When she speaks, her word order is primitive but the ideas she expresses are . . . surprising, often complex. She seems to think in images, even shapes. She doesn't seem to like playing with other children much. Her . . . way of expressing herself manages to set her apart from others, children and adults. But she isn't unhappy. She's always think-ing, all the time, and this thinking excites her. She talks to me about what she thinks. Oh yes, she also wears a TV, I mean, something she calls a TV, that she made from a cardboard box, over her head a lot. She thinks the TV is funny."

"This repetitive behavior—the spinning in circles and the word-echoing—have these patterns ever struck you as symptoms of autism?"

"No. They did strike a specialist we visited as something like that. I mean, he didn't think that she was autistic, but he did think that she might have some dysfunction: learning and emotional disability."

"And you, again, disagreed?"

I looked down at the Least Tern, then up at her, sighing.

"Yes."

There was a silence. The telephone on her desk rang twice, mutedly, then stopped.

"I guess you know what I'm going to ask you now. Why, when both your husband and a children's specialist suggest that her behavior is not normal, do you persist in your belief that she is OK?"

"I know my daughter. Better than anyone. I *told* you: She needs to be the way she is in order to survive."

"You mean to survive as *herself*."

"Yes."

"Does Ollie read—or write?"

"Both. She's left-handed so there's some reversal of letters when she writes, but her motor control is normal. She reads quite well. Again, she sees words backwards sometimes. But it's not a major problem. She's been categorized at Sixth Street kindergarten as 'gifted' as well as 'attention-deficient.' "

"Both?"

"Both."

Terry got up suddenly, folded her arms, and walked around her desk. She began to play with a brass letter opener, slapping it into her open palm. A very TV-movie gesture, but she seemed entirely unconscious of this.

"Esme, I don't doubt your sincerity as the mother of this quite exceptional child—I mean, in maintaining that she is special and that her situation must be treated with special attention. But it seems to me that it would be very hard to convince a concerned social worker, or anyone else for that matter, that you had her best interests at heart when you ignored both your husband's and a physician's *and* her school's warnings about her behavior. I think that they would see this as irresponsible on your part."

I looked at my hands. "Do you think it is?"

"Do I think it's irresponsible?" She sat down again, sighing.

"I don't know. On the face of it, it does seem . . . stubborn and unrealistic to me. But irresponsible—I don't know. I just know what *they'll* say."

We talked some more. I told her about my problems at work, my theory, Ollie's spatial abilities. She kept nodding her head, but her eyes changed. I could see that she was making up her mind about me, my story.

Finally, we stood up. It was late and I had to get back home. Her phone kept ringing; it seemed harder for her to ignore it.

She held out her hand, with a touch more personal feeling this time.

"What do you think?" I asked.

"We're going to fight like hell," she said. "But it seems to me that they have powerful ammunition on their side. It may be best for us to emphasize that you are going through a difficult emotional period, what with lab and classroom burdens as well as your high-pressure theory work. That you've not been yourself lately. Otherwise you would have done more to help Ollie."

"Jesus Christ, that's a *lie*. You think that I'm fucked up, too!"

"No, Esme, I don't. But you want to keep Ollie, right?"

"Are you kidding?"

"Well then? Think about it. To them you're a nut case. A woman who is advised by family members and professionals to seek help for her child, and refuses. An unstable teacher who fights with students, misses lectures, and is suspended from her job at a major university for an indefinite period. A researcher who refuses to go to her lab. A person who believes that she has a Theory of Everything in the universe, but hasn't proven it yet, to anyone, anywhere. A woman who justifies her little girl's odd behavior by talking about cosmic events. How does that sound to you? Because that's how you're going to sound to the judge."

I sat back down and put my hand over my eyes.

"Esme. Go home now. Let me think about this. We'll find a way for you to keep Ollie."

I remained frozen for a minute. Then I got up. I looked at her.

"Thanks for the coffee," I said.

She waved good-bye backwards, Italian-style, and I noticed, belatedly, that she was left-handed.

## Chapter 23

The beep sounded and I said, quickly, "Hi, Rocky. Call me, OK? Just wondering how you are."

Then I tried L.R. again and the same old message tape rewound. She was gone, she'd be back.

I put the phone down. It was nearing two in the morning. I'd been drinking tea and eating Bath biscuits and reworking parts of the theory. I'd seen the court psychiatrist earlier in the day and now, exhausted and unable to come up with any more distractions, I began to play back our conversation in my head.

The shrink was a small heavyset man, who looked disconcertingly like Richard Nixon, jowly and furtive-eyed. (Faber looked like Lincoln; was there a connection? Maybe presidential DNA *was* being exhumed and recycled?) When he talked, however, that impression fled. He had a relaxing voice that rose at the end of every sentence; he *intoned* his thoughts. He wore a sort of Navajo-pattern shirt that made him look like a Native American Nixon. I found this image of Nixon—in braids, buckskin, and headband, with a peace pipe—mildly distracting.

Freud's consultation room in Vienna, which I'd visited on my student travels, rose in my mind: the intense deep intimate reds of the couch and the wall hangings, the overstuffed parlorish feel of the room. He'd recreated the ghastly tedium of the middle-class drawing room to reassure his patients. This office, Dr. Lamb's, was overly lit and olive drab, with a military feel to it. I sat in a vinyl chair and picked at imaginary lint on my skirt.

At first he was very noncommittal, our talk almost desultory. I sensed him judging me just under the surface of his intonation, and I knew that the importance of this interview could not be overestimated in determining Ollie's future, but I felt no uneasiness—and after all, his questions seemed fairly innocuous: How long had Jay and I been married? How did Ollie like school?

Then he moved in, tightening the focus. Could I explain my TOE to him, why did I think that it was so cosmological in implication, who else knew about it? Did I connect this theory to Ollie? He adjusted himself in his chair: Did I think that other people were trying to steal my theory?

He *had* to ask these questions, and I tried my best to answer them, but I knew we were having a different kind of interview now. He asked about my childhood and again I tried to weigh my responses. Yes, my father was French Canadian, an electrical engineer employed by a hydraulics company, my mother a housewife. I said I regretted not being closer to my mother. Had I shown early high intelligence? Did I think of myself as a genius? I was an average person with science aptitude, I said.

Then he swiveled in his chair again and leaned toward me. His singsong style vanished. He spoke quickly, almost harshly. I'd been suspended from my position at UGC. I'd taken Ollie out of school for two weeks for no urgent reason—what was it like when Ollie and I were alone together during those two weeks?

"We relaxed," I said, staring back at his fixed expression. "We slept late and made big breakfasts and drew crayon pictures. We sang.

We built fires in the fireplace and toasted marshmallows. It was like camping out."

"Esme. Do you believe that your life is getting better—or does everything seem on a downhill course?"

I sighed. "Well, you know, Dr. Lamb, the world—any closed system—is entropic. I believe things inevitably break—"

"Please. I'm not asking for a physics theory. I'm asking your opinion of your own life."

"I think my life is getting better."

"And can you tell me why?"

"Because my daughter seems more connected to the world than ever before. Because I've discovered, with another scientist, a breakthrough theory. Because Jay is gone and . . ."

I stopped and he was silent for a second.

"Jay hurts me."

"Not physically."

"No," I said, "emotionally."

"Tell me, Esme, have you ever been violent with Jay—or Ollie? Have you ever threatened either of them physically?"

I was so shocked that I couldn't answer immediately.

"Violent? Of course not. I'm not a violent person." I looked down at my trembling hands. "I'm an impulsive person, I'm extremely opinionated, I sometimes put people off with my sense of humor—but I've never been violent, Doctor."

Now as I stood up, stiff and chilled, picking up my papers, I saw his face again as he questioned me. I felt that he'd decided that I had done something monstrous.

I went to bed, preoccupied, and almost immediately, it seemed, the alarm went off. I fished it up from the floor and stared at it: seven-fifteen A.M. I curled back up under the covers. Ollie didn't have to be at school till eight-forty-five. I slept another half hour or so and then the phone rang.

It was Terry McMahon.

"Esme. I didn't wake you, did I?"

I sat up in bed and pushed my hair out of my eyes.

"No, no. Of course not."

"Good. Because we have to talk, Esme. I want to ask you how you think that I can represent you here if you don't level with me about everything?"

I sat up straighter, terrified. "What?"

"You must know what I mean. We're talking about physical threats here, we're talking about attempted assault—"

"What?"

Ollie wandered in, sleepy-eyed, her wispy pink hair standing straight up on her head, looking personally affronted by my loud shocked voice. She sat on the rug by the bed, staring at me.

"Come on, Esme. Don't act so surprised. *Surely* you remember appearing uninvited at Jay's workplace, threatening his friend Paloma Jenz with physical violence if she had anything to do with Ollie, then throwing or—*kicking,* I guess it was—an unidentified object at them both?"

"Moo goo gai pan."

"I beg your pardon?"

"Moo goo gai pan! *That's* what I kicked in their direction. A carton of moo goo gai pan."

"I'm sorry. Are you saying that you threatened them with *Chinese food*?"

"Well, if *that* was an assault, then the weapon was a carton of Chinese. Yes."

There was a long silence.

"I don't get it."

"Well, Jesus, Terry, neither do I. I mean, Paloma had already spilled the food on the ground. I kicked at one of the cartons and it moved roughly in their direction. But I don't think you can inflict major wounds with moo goo gai pan. If you know what I mean."

She cleared her throat. "Maybe, then, you should explain to me what you were doing on the Paramount lot in the first place. And while you're at it, clarify for me your presence onstage at the . . . let's see, *Club Sez Who* on a recent evening—when Jay charges that you forced your way onstage, seized the microphone from him, and proceeded to babble incoherently at the crowd . . . destroying his act and frightening the clientele."

I started to laugh. I don't know why, but I felt vindicated, amused, by Jay's desperation—that he had to resort to this shit.

"Esme?"

"Yeah." I told her that I had gone out to Paramount to talk to Jay, since I knew he'd be there. I told her about our conversation, about Paloma and the bags of food.

"Well, then, please tell me about the Club Sez Who."

Ollie stood up and went into the bathroom. I could see her reflected in the full-length mirror, hoisting herself up on the toilet.

"I was a little drunk. Make that *very* drunk. I'd gone to see Jay's act. He was *dying* onstage. I don't know. I admit it, I lost control. I went up on the stage to help him. I wanted to tell off the hecklers in the audience, but instead I ended up explaining the Second Law of Thermodynamics to them."

"Oh."

"Jay was furious. After we left the club and I sobered up a little, I saw his face and understood the enormity of my mistake. But, God, you know: I had good intentions. I wanted to ease his suffering in some way. I've gone through *years* of his terrible routines."

Ollie flushed the toilet and returned to sit on the rug, minus her underpants. She grinned at me and began picking her nose.

"Terry? I've got to get going. I've got to take Ollie to school."

"Wait, wait. Wait. Jay has requested a visit with Ollie this after-noon. After school. Can you arrange this? He also requested that you not be present at the house when he picks her up. He wants to visit with her for two or three hours. Take her to dinner."

A lightninglike cold passed, glittered through me. "Do I have to agree to this?"

I looked up and saw Ollie, who'd wandered off, reflected in the bathroom mirror: half naked, spinning. I watched her twirl too close to the sink. "Ollie," I called out. "Be careful!"

"If you want to appear reasonable to the court and you don't want to generate sympathy for him, yes, I would say, yes, you have to agree. Do you have any reason to deny him a visit?"

"Hey, of course not. Can *you* think of one? I mean, what a good sport, huh?"

She said nothing.

"Fine," I said. "I can get Mrs. K. to be here when he comes, and he can leave her on the porch when he brings her back home and I won't come out till he's in his car." I held the receiver away from my mouth. "Ollie—watch *out*!"

"Esme?"

"Yes."

"Is there anything else I should know? I mean, so that I'm not taken up short like this again. You swear you didn't hurl sushi or something at somebody else, right?"

"Nah. Just some bagels and lox."

"Esme?"

"Yeah?"

"You know, this really *isn't* funny."

"I know. I know that, Terry."

Driving Ollie to school, I remembered the shrink. No wonder he'd grilled me about violence. I should have pelted him with bok choy, I thought. But somehow, this time, I couldn't work up a laugh. And Ollie sat, one hand held dramatically against her forehead, which she *had* bumped. There was a tiny swelling—we'd put a boo-boo strip on it. I eased up on the accelerator, but somehow the car seemed to go faster and faster.

Mrs. K. arrived and I left the house before four, kissing Ollie good-bye and holding her close for a long moment. I sang her a song about a flying cat and then she drew her finger down the middle of my face "bisecting" me. I did the same to her. "Good-bye, Mother," she said clearly. "I'll miss you!" I hugged her again. "I'll miss you!" she called after me. "I'll miss you, Mommy!" Then I drove to the lab.

I nearly reeled when I opened the door. Faber had obviously organized regular staffing and maintenance. Everything was clean and kept up —but the power of my memories, pure *lab* memories, almost over-came me. A laboratory is so physical: Everything is touch and ob-servation, measurement and pouring and enzyme-snipping. Your skin remembers tactilely—goose bumps rise, the ends of your fingers tingle, old acid burns shift under the old proud flesh. I couldn't believe the feelings that swelled in me, standing in that doorway. And the smells and sound, acetone, sulfur, and dripping faucets, spinner hum—all jostled for the attention of my senses, pulling me in back into the flicker and swim.

Then I turned and spotted Rocky's key with its red diamond charm attached, hanging on its hook by the door. On a hook next to that was her ratty stained lab coat—and, taped on the wall nearby, a scrawled note in her big loopy hand: LATER, PROF. I pulled the note down and stuffed it in my pocket.

All the ghosts, all the gathering sorrows in the lab began to circle me. Rocky's sorrows and mine, the osmotic presences of all the Or-ganic students I couldn't teach anymore, even poor Donald Brandeman. The accusing faces of the victims of Alpha$_1$ Antitrypsin Deficiency. What am I hiding from? I asked myself. The lab? The students? I don't need to hide anymore. I felt ready to return.

I checked out the freezers, the bases, the spinners, and the Drosophila communities and then I sat down and wrote out an apology to Rocky. Then one to my Organic students:

*Forgive me. It's a lie to try and teach order when your world is coming apart. I'm trying to work this thing out. Forgive me for missing our labs and classes.*

To Rocky I wrote simply: "I miss you. Ollie misses you. She asks for you every day. Come back, please."

After I'd sealed them both (one I'd drop in the mail to Rocky; the other I'd post in the student lounge) I sat down again. It occurred to me that though Ollie hadn't asked much for Jay, when I'd told her he was coming to visit her she'd smiled and laughed and pointed to his Dodgers cap still hanging from the front-hall peg.

Terror ran through me when I thought about her: alone somewhere with Jay. Would he bring her back? Would she be frightened without me? I wondered where they were having dinner—a restaurant? Or at Paloma's house? I held my head. The thoughts stopped.

I pulled some papers out of my bag. I read a little, then began to write.

**Imaginary Lecture,
or Letter to Ollie—Mamma's Theory—**

*Ollie, someday you're going to ask me about this period in both our lives. I'd like you to be able to read my excuse, my theory, the reason for all this unseemly behavior.*

*But I have to go back a little in scientific history. I drew you some pictures before of the four universal forces (in descending order of power): the Nuclear (or Strong) Force; Electromagnetism; the Weak Force; and Gravity.*

*Protons and neutrons are held in the nucleus of an atom by the Strong Force. Electromagnetism (Faraday's baby!) binds electrons to the nucleus, atoms to molecules, molecules to liquids or solids. See how this works? Then good old gravity, as you know (the force with which one mass attracts another mass), keeps us on earth.*

*The force involved in weak nuclear interactions, has been a kind of mystery. We know this force exists because of certain particle dances that are slow (if you can call a ten-billionth of a second slow)—slower, indeed, than if the electromagnetic or the strong nuclear forces were calling the shots. Scientists, some time ago, found that particles acted weirdly in weak interactions with each other. They acted as if they were being tugged more in one direction than another. Was it possible that parity, the perfect mirror symmetry that everyone wanted to believe in—the universe's elegant consistency from top to bottom—was being violated here?*

*Let's go back to 1956. Enter two young Chinese-American physicists, Lee and Yang. These guys thought up a series of tests to check the conservation of parity in weak interactions—to see if weak interactions separated right from left. Their published paper (when it was finally understood!) shook the foundations of quantum theory because they said absolutely that parity was violated.*

*Then there were experiments to prove or disprove their theory. Another Chinese-American, Ms. Chien-shiung Wu, professor of physics at Columbia, performed the tests that clinched the hypothesis. (Though she was not included in their Nobel Prize!) Her experiment is a little complicated to explain, but it all hinged on this: If, after her testing, the number of electrons she was using divided evenly into two sets, some zooming north and some zooming south, parity would be proven and completely preserved. If this process, however, showed a "handedness" (a larger number of electrons galloping in one direction than in the other), parity would be history. Ms. Wu's experiment showed what no one in the history of science had been able to demonstrate before: a way of "labeling the ends of a magnetic axis," or that the universe definitely had a* handedness. *Zip! More electrons zoomed to one end than the other.*

*The theoretical scientific community was in shock. Wolfgang Pauli, the great physicist, said: "I am not so much shocked by the fact that the Lord prefers the left hand as by the fact that he still strongly appears to be left-handed symmetric when he expresses himself strongly." In other words, why is the strong nuclear force so right-and-left symmetric in interaction, and the weak so definitely* handed? *Another scientist commented that what Lee, Yang, and Wu had found out was that space was a weak left-eyed giant. Not a cyclops, with the eye in the middle, but a weak* left-eyed cyclops. *That should give an astronaut pause, no?*

*What does all this have to do with my theory? Well, we still haven't taken in all the implications of the Weak Force. If the Weak Force seems to be saying that nature is asymmetric, many scientists do not want to listen. They want their universe balanced, rational. But Roger Penrose, a cosmologist colleague of Stephen Hawking's doesn't care that the universe is asymmetric; in fact he has no trouble at all believing in fundamental asymmetry.*

*There's a lot of talk that it was an "asymmetric underlying field" that caused the Big Bang to produce more matter than antimatter, which is the way our world's set up. They think this underlying field might be a Superweak force. Or broken symmetry. Or there's an even deeper asymmetry—Roger Penrose's notion. His theory is an asymmetric geometric structure called* twistor space.

*He invented twistors—and they're fun, you'd like this, Ollie: asymmetric geometric shapes underlying everything. Twistors are structures that can define the motions, spins and bumps and grinds, of massless particles. They are the "points" of four complex dimensions. If we could see them in ordinary Euclidean three-space they'd look like a twisted family of circles, lying on each other like stacked doughnuts or used tires. Twistors are helical, as their name implies, and their* helical *nature explains the chirality of particles, the violation of parity in weak interactions, the difference between positive and negative charges, and maybe even the Unstoppable Arrow, the one-way direction of time. Penrose thinks of twistors as the underside of the universe. I think of them as huge bright mattress springs or fields of Oz-like tornadoes. Anyway, Penrose believes he's discovered a nonambidextrous universe.*

*Now, the Superstring guys, on the other hand, believe that particles like fermions or quarks have tiny one-dimensional line pieces, or strings. A couple of physicists had the idea of combining these snippets with Superstrings: open, massless, incredibly strong strings moving in and out of all spatial dimensions. This is a TOE, not a GUT (Grand Unified Theory), and it underscores Einstein's theory of gravity because the vibration of the strings demands gravity interaction.*

*The latest version of String Theory is* heterotic *string theory, combining string and superstring theory. Many, many dimensions fold up in these strings; ripples go around loops. Chirality and positive-negative charges are explained. But it would require far larger supercolliders than the ones we now have to prove heterotic string theory.*

*What L.R. and I hit on, moving our asymmetric chiral molecules through space, was a kind of adjacent calculation, regarding particles without mass. Our chiral molecules recognized each other and this demonstrated certain proclivities of the weak force interaction and mass—but if you take mass away, move into hyperspace, into four dimensions (get out of space-time), and apply Penrose's twistors, you avoid the infinities (or "ghosts") that have plagued particle theory.*

*We began to derive values of particle masses—on a primitive level, of course, because our technology is not up to the real assessment— but we derived the first, the beginnings. But the end result hinted at a successful TOE, linking Penrose's asymmetric geometry with String Theory. Interpreting the world in such a way that gravity, the only one of the four forces of nature to remain unexplained by quantum theory, could be quantized.*

*Ollie, it's there, it's in place. Experiment will prove or disprove or elaborate on it: But it is odd and beautiful, it works and it's* mine. And L.R.'s, *I thought belatedly.*

I stopped writing and rubbed my eyes. It was late, I had to lock up and go. Across the room, a spinner set by a computerized timer turned itself off with a shudder. I looked at my watch. Jay would be bringing Ollie back soon.

The wall phone began to ring. I considered not answering it. I figured it was probably a student or a postdoc, looking for information or a colleague. Or worse, Faber.

After four rings, I gave up and picked it up.

There was a lot of static on the line; it sounded like a satellite transmission. Then the static cleared and I heard a voice calling my name.

It was Michele Mueller, an old friend of mine from Cambridge. We'd gone to Harvard together, different majors. She was in journalism and we'd probably never have met except that she grabbed me one day outside the Organic lab and began querying me about everything from quarks to neutrinos, which I knew very little about at the time, but we went for espresso and ended up talking about women in science, and became fast friends. Later, she became fascinated with the work going on in Q's lab and had written a series of articles for the *Crimson* about the biochem scene. Now she worked at a very influential academic journal called *Theory Abstracts*.

"I can hardly hear you," I called into the shifting sizzle.

We chatted, or shouted at each other a bit, catching up. She complained about trying to reach me for two days. Nobody answered at home and so she'd finally tried the lab—what was I doing, trying to hide from my demanding public? Then a pause.

"So, Esme. You were working on that chirality theory, right?"

"Right. I still am." A little ripple of fear.

"Well, you know something? I don't want to lower the boom on you—and I'm really going against the Commandment of Confidentiality here, but I felt, as an old friend, I should alert you to the fact that one of the older novas out there on your coast, L. R. Atwater, has sent us abstracts from a manuscript that looks hot—and according to my editor in chief concerns itself with *chirality* and the Weak Force. You know, the staffers can't see her envelope till right before publication. But he told me it's not just Q-and-A stuff, it's *hard*, it could even be approaching a TOE. I thought you should know anyway, that—"

"Michele?"

"What?"

"You're saying that it's from *L.R., Lorraine* Atwater?"

"Yeah. Old L.R.—Lorraine, Lorrie, *Ms.* Atwater. Whatever."

"She sent you an article on—"

"Chirality. My editor said. Chirality and the Weak Force. I was rather proud, Esme, that I remembered you mentioning the last time we talked, that you were doing some work in that area, too. So I knew you'd be intrigued. Think she's hit pay dirt? Her name in lights?"

I looked at a hood, the yellow-and-black nuclear triangles. I rubbed my eyes again.

"Michele? You know what? I gotta go now or I'll miss Ollie."

There was a squeal. "How *is* she, Esme? Why don't you ever send pictures of her? I'm dying to see—"

I hung up. I looked down at the papers before me, all my painstaking scribblings to Ollie. *Mamma's Theory.* I looked straight ahead again and then laughed. *Mamma's Theory.* I laughed again, louder; the sound echoing off the lab walls. Then I slowly tore the sheets of paper up.

I drove around till it was time for Ollie's return. Scooped. I drove, watching the bumper lights in front of me, the turn signals, traffic lights. I drove like an automaton—I registered nothing of my surroundings. Once, cars honked behind me and I realized I'd been sitting before a green light for seconds. Scooped. Then I looked up and realized I was nearing my street.

I turned into my driveway, parked, and put my head on the steering wheel. I knew I had to get out of the car, get into the house, get the lights on before Jay arrived with Ollie—but I couldn't move. Scooped, you poor sad-assed dolt—and by a colleague. A woman. My head throbbed. I'd *helped* her. I'd helped her finish it—I'd pushed her over the top. I lifted my head, then forced myself to open the car door and get out. I staggered a little as I walked to the house. The porch steps seemed enormous; it took all my strength to climb them.

Inside the house, I walked around numbly, turning on lights, pulling down shades. I picked up Ollie's dragon from the braided rug. She must have dropped it on her way out with Jay. I knew she'd miss it by now. I propped it in a little red plastic chair in the entranceway, then glanced at the clock over the mantel. It was late. It was nearly eight. He was supposed to have brought her back by seven-forty-five. I held my head. Had I gotten the time wrong? Had I screwed that up, too? A pile of my legal pads sat on the coffee table and I grabbed them up suddenly and threw them against the wall. They landed next to Ollie's box "TV," propped in a corner. Scooped. Rosalind Franklin, Mileva Maric. I beat my fists against my temples. Shit, I'd looked up to her—she was my inspiration, Atwater—a great woman scientist! My *inspiration.* Still, some part of me couldn't quite believe this had happened, could not believe that L.R. had done such a thing. I couldn't accept it. Maybe, I thought, she'd tried to call me. Maybe I should check the machine. Maybe this can all be cleared up.

The phone rang and I jumped, then ran for it.

"Hello, Esme."

"Jay—where *are* you? You're late, aren't you? Wasn't Ollie supposed to be back before eight?"

"Yeah I guess she *was*, but that's of little consequence now."

My heart stopped, then slowly began again.

"What do you mean, Jay?"

"What I mean, Esme, is that I'm not bringing Ollie back."

I tried to speak, but nothing would come out of my mouth. Then I shouted.

"Jay? What have you done with her?"

"Isn't that funny, Esme. That was just the question I was about to ask you. For starters, there's this *b-bump* on her head—above her eye? *Where* did that c-*come* from, Esme?"

"Oh God, oh God, Jay, please. Don't do this. Don't do this to Ollie and me. I beg you. I told you before—you can have *everything* if you just leave us in peace. Oh God, please bring her home to me now."

I knelt down next to the telephone table, gasping, praying to the god of the drowning.

"Esme, it's a m-*mark* on my daughter. I am *required*, my lawyer says, to check this out. He's *insisting*. I don't know what's g-going on with you these days." His voice went high suddenly. "*Jesus*. Coming after Paloma and me the other day on the lot? I don't get you." His voice went calm again. "I can tell you what's going to h-happen. I called my lawyer and he's going to call *your* lawyer. We're going to ask for a special c-court evaluation here and I'm going to take t-t-temporary custody."

I took a deep shaking breath. I sensed that he was about to hang up and I knew I had to keep him on the phone. The room was spinning and the receiver was my only stationary point. I held on for dear life, forcing my voice to be calm.

"Jay, listen. Jay, Ollie bumped her head on the bathroom sink this morning. *You know* how she spins around? She just banged into it—she was dizzy and—"

"No, I d-don't *get it,* Esme. Nothing like that ever happened to her b-before, when *I* was around! I just keep th-thinking about what I saw in your face when you came after Paloma at Paramount the other day . . ."

"Jay—Jesus! You *know* me, you know I'd never hit Ollie. Why are you doing this? Why are you trying to hurt me like this? And *Ollie*—because you have no *idea* how this is going to hurt her, Jay . . ."

"Esme, I did you the c-courtesy of *calling* you to tell you this. I didn't *have* to do this, Christ knows. I thought I'd be f-f-fair . . ."

"You *can't* keep her—you don't have custody! I do!"

"Possession, Esme, is n-nine tenths of the law. And if there is any question of violence, the court isn't going to side with you n-now, are they?"

"Jay, please. We said we *loved* each other once—please, listen to me. Let me have her back."

"Love was another l-lifetime. Love was before you shut me out of your life."

Tears poured down my face.

"So now you're going to shut Ollie out of *mine*?"

There was silence.

"Jay. I'm going to come over there and get her. I'm going to leave now."

"Esme, listen. You come over here and I'll have to call the police."

"Do what you want. I'm coming to get her."

"Esme. There's s-something else—really disturbing. Ollie told me that you *cut* her."

"*Cut* her?"

"She was sitting right in f-front of me and she said, 'Mamma cut me,' and drew a line with her finger right down the middle of her face."

"Oh Jesus, Jay, that's *mirror symmetry*—I taught her how to *bisect* some shapes. Jay, she's describing a *game* we play . . ."

"I'm very *sorry*, Esme. Your b-behavior's too weird, too u-unpredictable to—"

"Jay, I'm on my way over."

"Th-then you'll make this worse than it h-has to be!"

We both hung up. I got off the floor, then fell down again, sobbing. The phone rang again almost immediately and I stumbled, grabbing for it, pulling the cord, and the phone slid off the table and crashed to the floor. I fumbled the receiver into my grasp.

"Esme?"

"Jay? Jay?"

"No, Esme, it's Terry McMahon. Are you all right? You've heard?"

"Jesus, you told me to let her go. You told me to let him take her tonight! Now look what he's done!"

I was screaming into the phone. I heard myself, but I didn't care.

"Esme. How did she get a bruise on her head?"

"Oh my God. I can't believe you! You're on his side! She *bumped* her head on the sink today. She was spinning like she always does, spinning, and she bumped . . ."

I started to sob, I couldn't talk anymore. I leaned forward, almost touching my head to my knees, and I kept sobbing.

"OK, Esme, OK. Please listen to me. I *believe* you. Esme?"

I took a gasping breath and sat up again.

"Tell me what I do to get her back, Terry. That's all I want to hear from you now."

"Well. His lawyer told me that they're going to ask for a 4602 evaluation—"

"A what? Jesus, what's that?"

"That's Civil Code 4602, which means they're asking for an evaluation of Ollie's situation, based on their charge that she's being abused by you—and in the meantime, they're taking custody."

I started to sob again.

"Listen, Esme, 4602 just means they'll get another court-appointed psychiatrist to evaluate Ollie and he'll also talk to you guys, her doctors and teachers and so on. I'm sure it will become obvious that she belongs with you. They're going to watch for what they call 'the primary emotional bond' here."

"I'm going over there to get her, Terry."

"Esme. You must, under no circumstances, try to take Ollie back by force. Listen to me. It will *destroy* your chances of ever getting her back. The court will be convinced that you are unstable."

"But he stole her! He kidnapped her from me! What about his *stability*? Where is the justice here?"

"Esme. You have got to hold on. The court will rectify all of this, I really believe that. In the meantime, you must not do anything to jeopardize getting Ollie back."

"I don't *know* what I'm going to do," I said. "I don't know what is going to happen. I wish I could tell you but I can't."

I hung up.

The phone began ringing again right away, but I ignored it. I lay on the floor trying to get my breath. Ollie's dragon sat in its red chair near my head and I reached up and pulled it to me, rocking back and forth on the floor, holding it to my heart.

# Chapter 24

I turned off on a side street and drove slowly, my head half out the window, peering at the phosphorescent numbers painted on the curb, talking to myself. I'd stopped crying now and was a little calmer. It helped to be doing something: driving a car, looking for house numbers, moving through space.

News was on the radio; a weatherman predicting rain again. Unseasonable weather: Storms and lightning. Due soon. I braked: 5-0-5-2, that was it. I drove past the house and parked toward the middle of the block on the other side of the street. I switched off the ignition and sat quietly in the reflection of a street lamp. It hit me how tired I was—my whole body ached—but this was an observation completely unconnected to any action. I knew I wouldn't sleep again till Ollie was safe with me.

I looked back over my shoulder at the house, a little gingerbread-chalet thing—carved shutters and ceramic trolls on the lawn. There'll be a welcome mat with a smiling face on it, I thought viciously. I thought of Ollie inside that house, in the guest bed, or in a sleeping bag. We'd never been separated before, not even for a night.

I got out of the car, locked it, and crossed the street. I turned in the walk and climbed the steps. I was reaching for the doorbell when

Jay came out, pulling the door carefully shut behind him with a jingling sound.

We looked at each other. The front light was on and it outlined his whole body. A fugitive caught in a searchlight: terrified.

"I'm *asking* you to leave," he said. "Paloma's calling the p-police right now, Esme. They'll be r-right here."

His voice sounded high and unsure. He stood with his arms folded across his chest and this made him look fragile, as if he were covering a wound. By contrast, my voice, when I spoke, sounded deep to me —oddly calm and reassuring.

"It's all right, Jay. Just let me see her."

"Are you c-c-crazy? Do you know what time it is? Ollie's in bed!" There was a pause.

"I'm tellin' you—leave now, Esme. The c-cops are on their way." I moved to the right and tried to see around him into the house; he shifted quickly, blocking my line of sight.

"She's awake, isn't she? I *know* she can't be asleep, Jay. For God's sake, let me see her. *Please.* I'll forget this happened, Jay—if you just let me take her home now."

"Esme." He rolled his eyes and laughed and shook his head, lifting his palms up to an invisible witness. "What is it g-gonna take to convince you? Ollie is staying with *me*."

I moved in closer. I looked him directly in the eye. I was a bit shorter than Jay, but I felt at least his size, maybe bigger, as I faced him.

"No," I said, "she isn't."

He swallowed. "Get out of here, Esme. Unless you w-*want* to go to jail."

I looked down suddenly and saw the smiling-face welcome mat under my feet and laughed.

"Go ahead," he said, "laugh. They'll be here any s-second."

There was a sound from the back of the house—a muffled cry, I thought, and I tried to push past Jay. He shoved me away and I stumbled backwards, almost falling down the steps. I regained my balance and grabbed him by the lapels of his jacket, pulling his face close to mine.

"Jay," I said. We were eyeball-to-eyeball. I could smell the cloying lime-y aftershave he wore for Paloma. "Listen."

He looked back at me as if he might, for a second, listen—then something else crossed his face and he wrenched out of my grip and pushed me backwards again, harder. This time I *did* fall down the steps, but as I lost my balance, I grabbed him and took him down with me.

We landed hard on the grass—me on my back—and I felt something metal, a sprinkler head? a troll? dig into my spine. But this was a distant, unfocused pain. The precise focus of my immediate pain was Jay. I wanted to kill him. And he wanted to kill me.

He wrapped his hands around my throat, choking me, and I kneed him in the balls and he let up. We rolled around on the grass, both of us sobbing, cursing, hitting blindly at each other.

"Get out of here. Get the fuck *out* of here, Esme."

"Give her to me, Jay. Give her to me and I'll go."

"No, *you* go. *Go*, Esme, get out!"

We butted heads accidentally and this momentarily stunned us. We lay dazed on the grass as the police cruiser pulled up, lights flashing, radio squawking.

We struggled to get up as the car doors slammed and two enormous LAPD cops materialized on either side of us.

"Let's break this up now, folks," one of them said, and I felt purposeful hands under my shoulders, lifting me to my feet.

Jay and I stood, swaying, grass-stained and rumpled-looking, the cops looming over us.

"Which one of you called for help?" they asked, and Jay put his hand over his heart and grimaced like a cardiac victim.

"I d-did, officer. This w-woman here—"

"This your place of residence?"

"Well, yes. I'm staying with a f-friend."

"Your friend is the owner of the house?"

"Yes. I called you because my d-daughter and I are staying here with my f-friend and this . . . my . . . w-wife, soon to be ex-wife, has come here to threaten us and try to take my daughter."

They asked for names and we gave them and showed I.D. They asked for the name of the owner of the house. I looked at the cop on my left. He looked paternal; he was large, resigned in the eyes, but kind. The other guy was younger, but less intelligent, a little brutish, and bored.

"Officers, please listen to me. My daughter was living with me until this evening when my husband here took her away, in effect kidnapped her. I came over here to get her back."

The cops exchanged a tired oh-shit look. Not a domestic, they were thinking, not tonight—not a goddam custody battle.

"My lawyer feels that my d-daughter should be kept from this woman—there's a q-question of abuse. I've requested full c-custody from the court. She just *attacked* me here—right in front of the *house*!"

The young cop looked at me.

"Ma'am, if the court and your lawyers are settling this matter, we have no power but to leave things as they are and to request at this time that you vacate the premises."

I turned to the older cop. "Please. My little girl is inside there. They took her away from me. She's never been away from me a whole night before . . ." I broke down and began to cry. "Please, please help me. Please help me, I beg you."

The older cop nodded to the younger one, who took Jay off to one side of the yard. Then the older guy walked me over to a spot under a tree.

"Esme? That your name? Esme, I can't help you here. The one who's got the kid is the one we're supposed to hold with, unless I see the guy's drunk or abusive, whatever. Now I suggest that you go on home and call your lawyer and get to work on getting your child back through the courts. That's the only way to do it. Anything else is going to get you in a load of trouble."

I was crying so hard that I couldn't speak. I struggled to get my breath—but the tears sprang from me. He put a hand on my arm and gave me a tissue.

"Hold on. Hold on, Esme."

I pushed at my face with the tissue.

"I can't leave without her. My God, my God—where would I go?"

He looked startled. "Home!"

"Don't you see?" I cried. "I can't go back there—*everything* I see there reminds me of her!"

Across the yard I heard laughter: Jay and the other cop. I smelled cigarette smoke:—they were bullshitting together. I turned and ran for the house.

"Ollie!" I screamed. "Ollie! Mamma is here, Mamma is here, sweetheart!"

Hands fell on me and my arms were jerked back behind me with a snap and I was spun around. The young cop stared at me, a look of annoyance combined with clinical disinterest: another nut case.

"Come on, ma'am," he said without moving his lips. "Let's go. Where's your car?"

I nodded up the street; he glanced that way and I pulled away again.

"Ollie! Mamma will be back! I promise!"

He bent my arm again and hurried me in front of him. I could feel his fury.

"You scream and run like that again and I'll handcuff you and book you for trespassing and disturbing the peace. And you'll *never* see your daughter again. You got it?"

I didn't answer. The older cop walked behind us. I thought that he felt sorry for me. I hoped he did. I hoped that he'd think about me the rest of the night, for the rest of his life. But after they'd checked out my driver's license and registration, shone a flashlight in my eyes, sat me behind the wheel with many admonitions, escorted me out of the neighborhood, I knew he wouldn't remember anything about me past the next radio call, the next nut case, the next lost cause.

So I drove. I drove for miles and I don't remember a single destination. I zoomed through the strange lit caverns of underpasses and through tunnels and around cloverleafs. Cars pulled up next to mine on the freeway, people gestured at me, then fell back, but I don't know why. I think that I was talking loudly to myself, sobbing hysterically. I looked up at the lit exit signs but I could not read them. I got off the freeway and on a long dark road: miles of derricks, then the ocean at one point. A gas station. Then I was back downtown. It was the blue-grey hour before sunrise; I was in Chinatown, there were people hurrying to the street markets, there were smells of fish and coffee. I felt hungry but when I thought of eating, my stomach lurched. The sun came up in Chinatown and I parked the car and sat. I was almost out of gas.

I watched the sun swell and turn over Chinatown on its great pink axis. The car windows were rose colored. People hurried in front of my windshield—they seemed to float in their bright red pants and army jackets and genderless ponytails. Newspapers and flowers and Styrofoam cups of coffee floated by and I sat and stared. At one point a man knocked on my window, offering me an orange branch filled with whistling, bobbing, singing, wind-up birds. I shook my head no and then I thought, Ollie would like that, but he was gone and then

I realized I'd forgotten for one second that Ollie was no longer with me. I put my head back on the headrest and I waited, but forgetfulness did not come again. So I got out of the car and began to walk.

I'd walked several blocks before I realized I had a coffee cup in my hand. I didn't remember buying it or drinking it, but the cup was empty. I had somehow wandered clear of Chinatown—I looked up at the street signs and saw I was nearing Fourth and Wall.

In front of warehouses and on street corners, in alleyways, there were people huddling and sleeping on piles of rubbish. People with faces darkened and toughened by wind and exposure, rooting through garbage or panhandling. Some of them crawled in and out of cardboard boxes or packing crates. I saw a gaunt woman with pocked skin, pushing her three children ahead of her down the street. On her back a filthy hand-lettered sign read: WE ARE HUNGRY. PLEASE HELP. THANK YOU.

I ran after her. She turned when she heard me coming up behind her, fear in her face. I saw that her left eye was blackened, and a long seamed cut like a surgical incision festered on her throat. She looked like a hatchet, something hewn from stone or shattered bone. She drew her lips back, showing her teeth like an animal, then closed them tight suddenly, pursing her lips—she did this again and again, like a mad dignitary in a receiving line: smiling, not smiling, smiling.

She stared at me and gathered her children to her, smiling, not smiling. The oldest was a little boy about seven, with an Afro, in shorts and a torn, filthy jacket. He was humming to himself. *Ollie,* I thought, *Ollie,* then stopped myself and looked at her retarded girl of five with a knee-length Ninja Turtles T-shirt on and nothing else, not even shoes, and the skinny light-skinned baby with a bubble of snot at his nose and listless black eyes.

"Whaddyou want?" Her voice was oddly gentle, soft, the harsh words dreamily stretched out. "You from the Social Service?"

"No," I said. "I'm not from Social Services."

I pulled a clump of bills from my bag and held it out to her. She reached out for it, then hesitated.

"You come to take my kids?"

"No."

She took the bills, looked at them, then secreted them somewhere in her ragged coat.

I looked around. We were standing in front of a low Spanish-style building with a huge sign reading CHRISTIAN SUPER-LIGHT MISSION on it. A net of colored Christmas lights, many burned out, blinked off and on across its façade.

"Someone took my little girl away," I said suddenly, and began to cry.

She nodded. She was still holding her children to her.

I wiped my tears on my sleeve, trying to change the subject. I nodded toward the mission.

"You stay here?"

She looked at me wild-eyed, her lips still moving. "You from the *mission,* is that right?" She began to edge away from me.

"I'm not. I swear it."

She spat into the street. Her lips stopped. "They try to take my kids, like all 'em do. Take the mother in, then pack these off and send to foster. You from Social Service you said, right? You come for my kids?"

"No."

We stared at each other.

"Where your girl?" she asked finally.

"My husband took her."

She laughed, showing her broken teeth. "You come from the mission?"

"No."

"You go in those missions: They *Bible-beaters* in there."

"My husband took her—didn't even give me a chance to talk to her. The son of a bitch, he won't let me even see her."

"Son of a bitch. Uh-hum. That's right, baby."

The baby had started crying and she lifted it on her shoulder and nuzzled it.

"I'm going to die if I don't get her back."

"He came after me. He's gonna cut my babies too, he say."

The little boy pulled away from her suddenly and tugged at her coat. His voice was high and lisping.

"Can we go up there to McDonald's? Huh? Huh?"

"What's going to happen now?"

She blinked.

"McDonald's."

We walked up the littered street toward the Golden Arches. The family stayed together, a careful unit, and I walked a little behind.

"Listen," I called after her as we walked, "did you know that a single quark is afloat in a crowded sea of continuously appearing and disappearing virtual pairs of quarks?"

"Uh-hum. Uh-hum," she said softly. "You from Social Service, right?"

"Quark," said the little retarded girl, "quark quark quark!"

*O Aspasia, Annie Jump Cannon, Elizabeth of Bohemia, Elizabeth Fulhame ("the ingenious and lively Ms. Fulhame on the reduction of gold salts by light") . . . O Isabella Bird Bishop, O St. Nicerata, O Ellen Swallow, O Theana.*

We marched, me bringing up the rear, toward the Golden Arches.

On the steps of the Magellan Hotel, I watched the storm clouds gather. The air was full of high-flying green electricity: Rain was on its way. The old battered men on the steps spat and complained; the wind picked up and tousled their ratty hair, blew trash across the street. Where would all these people go if it rained? Inside, I'd settled with the desk clerk (if you could call a man in a metal cage in charge of opening doors a desk clerk)—the Family would stay at the Magellan for five more days, which is what the Mother had wanted to do— and then? I didn't know. I no longer had a salary. I had grant money for my work in the lab but I didn't know if I was ever going back to the lab. The Mother liked the Magellan because she believed the desk kept out the Social Service and the missionaries, plus the ghost of her mother came once every two days. Also it was close to McDonald's. Maybe in the next month or so, when my money ran out, when I slipped through the safety net into the street, I'd end up there too. With Ollie?

I'd been at the Magellan for a little while. After we'd dined at McDonald's, the Mother had pointed out the Magellan as a refuge she'd sought when she could afford it and we went there. They settled in a "suite" of ugly brown rooms with a toilet and a sink in a closet. I sat down in a chair in a room across the hall from theirs—and I *stopped*. It was a kind of catatonia; I sat there in the chair and I don't know how much time passed. I was aware of them moving about their room, the doors open, TV blaring . . . but I was made of stone. For the moment, my headlong flight had ceased. I'd go in and out of consciousness. Sometimes I'd come to and the woman would be danc- ing soundlessly in my room. Once I jolted awake: she was standing over me. She touched my face—then my hair.

"Fire-red. Fire-red." Then she frowned.

"Lemme see your *teeth*." She pulled up my upper lip and stared at my front teeth. Her face was very close to mine, a frown of concen- tration on it. Her breath was sweet but overripe, like apricots.

"No *false?*"

I shook my head.

She touched my front teeth, her finger felt like a zap of electricity, then let the lip drop: "I know somebody put a *di*-mon right *there*."

She walked away, across the hall, and took a chicken leg from a bucket on the table, then stood chewing on it, tearing at the flesh, staring across the hall at me.

When I finally shook myself and stood up, I was used to the stained walls, the bare bulb overhead; I'd lost all sense of time. Was it Wednesday, Thursday? Another week? I took a step, unsteadily—I had to go get Ollie. I washed my face, staring at myself in the rippling piece of dark mirror over the standing drain that was a sink—I saw how ghastly I looked. I rinsed my mouth and tried to clean my nails. Down the hall I could hear two drunken men shouting at each other. Then came the powerful smell of disinfectant and the clank of a pail: housekeeping.

I went downstairs and outside and stood on the steps of the Magellan Hotel in the wind and sobbed for Ollie. The numbness of her loss had splintered now into specific pains: The pain of not being able to touch her, to hold her, to nuzzle through her fragrant fine hair. The pain of not hearing her voice, of not seeing her face startle like a bird into each of its familiar and subtle expressions, not bathing her, not feeding her, not putting her to sleep. My shoulders shook and I had to sit down on the top step and hold myself, to stop the sobbing.

I had two dollars left in my pocket. I tried to remember where my car was, but I couldn't. I wiped my eyes. I heard a ruckus behind me in the hotel lobby, turned around and saw the Family making its way through the dim stained interior. The Mother was shouting something and the kids, pulled along in her wake, looked exhausted and resigned.

They brushed past me on the top step and I touched the Mother's arm. She looked strangely at me. She didn't remember me though I'd just said good-bye to her upstairs. I'd asked her name and the names of her children, but she said they didn't call each other by name and she certainly didn't ask mine.

"Hi," I said. "What's going on?"

"We got to go," she said and rolled her eyes. "They let in some Social Service person up there."

"You're leaving?"

"Wait a minute, *you* Social Service too!"

"No, I'm not. Wait, there's no Social Service person upstairs!"

"I gotta go now."

"Wait," I said. "Come back here, please. Just promise me you'll come back and stay, OK? It's going to *rain*."

I grabbed her sleeve; she was already on her way, the baby asleep on her shoulder.

"Don't go, please."

She pulled away; the baby opened its eyes and stared dully at me over her shoulder. I took the hand of the little boy. He looked at me, terrified.

"Bring your mommy back here later, to the room. It's all paid for."

He continued to stare at me. His mother called him and he ran. She called him Brother.

Halfway down the block, she stopped, turned around and looked directly at me.

"When my mamma *call* to me, I'll come back here! It might be sooner, it might be *later*," she yelled at me. "You think you can tell nobody what to do? No you *can't*, you burnin' Red, you can't tell *nobody*!" Then she whirled around and shuffled off.

One of the old men on the step craned around and looked up at me. "Goddam fucking bitch," he said. Then: "Goddam fucking wind." And as he spoke I felt the first drizzling drops on my face. I walked past him down the steps; he held out his grizzled hand and I gave him a dollar. Then it started to pour.

I boarded the bus a few blocks away and fell exhausted into a seat. The other passengers stared at me. I was soaking wet and I was still wearing a paper crown from McDonald's on my head and I realized I'd been talking to myself. I waved at the staring faces and they quickly looked away. Somehow this made me laugh, rather loudly, and the woman sitting across from me moved to a different seat, nearer the driver.

I stared out the window at the passing city; after a while I understood that the bus was going to go within blocks of UGC. At the main gate stop, I got off in the driving rain and walked past the guard in his neon slicker, busy in his booth, then trudged toward Oberman Hall. My shoes were filled with water and my hair was streaming. Soaking bits of the yellow tissue crown stuck to my hair and eyelashes. I stopped at one point and leaned against a tree. Then the rain came down even harder; I had to squint to see. At last I could make out the outlines of the science and research buildings and I heard myself sobbing as I pushed my body toward the lab.

I fell against the wall inside Oberman Hall, panting. When I pushed open the door, the lights were on and there was loud music. Rocky was there, dressed up in glittery leggings and a jeweled black leather jacket, lots of makeup with about sixteen gold earrings. There was her big red book bag on the floor, half filled with texts and slides.

She came around a pillar, leaned against it, and stared at me. Then she hurried over and took my arm.

"He took Ollie."

"Who did? Jay?"

I nodded and started to sob and then I got control. I put my head back and breathed through my nose. Rocky pulled up a chair, sat me in it, then held up a hand for me to wait and turned off her tape deck.

I felt a sense of horror telling her what had happened, because now the events had become a narrative, a story, and this somehow distanced me from Ollie, set the unthinkable into predictable anecdotal sequence. But I had to talk to someone.

Rocky blinked her eyes and shook her head at me.

"You look like you died," she said, and didn't laugh. "I mean it. You look as if someone shot you in the back seven hours ago and you've been walking around ever since, losing blood and your memory."

"Blood, maybe," I said. "But I remember everything."

She got up and went to the hot-drinks machine and came back with two cups of coffee. I drank mine down eagerly, even though it burned my throat. I heard Rocky rummaging around in the shelves and this time she returned with a pile of old towels. I set my coffee down and she threw one over my head. I dried my hair. Then, still shaking with cold, I wrapped myself in the remaining towels and went back to the coffee.

"Jesus," she said again, "you look like shit."

I toasted her with the plastic cup. "You're back."

She looked away.

"No," she said. "I'm not. I just came in tonight to pick up my *stuff*." She shrugged and looked around, scratching her arm and sipping her coffee. "My books and tape deck and stuff—I'm *leavin'*."

"What do you mean?"

"I mean, I'm *leavin'*. I'm droppin' out of school, going back to work in the family store for a while."

I sat up, spilling the last of my coffee. "What are you *talking* about?"

"*Hey*, Professor. *You're* the one who said I wasn't no good at *sci*-ence, just good at *fuck*-ing!"

"I didn't say—"

"Hey Prof, I'm just throwin' *shade* on you. You hurt my feelings that night but . . . that's not it. I made this decision based on, you know, my *life*."

"Rocky, don't be *funny*."

"My *life*. My GPA ain't that hot overall, this place costs big money and . . ." She looked at me. "There's someone new in my life."

"Rocky. *No*."

I watched her as she took a stick of gum out of her jacket pocket, unwrapped it with maddening slowness, then popped it in her mouth.

"Rocky, you're not going to do it, are you? You're not going to *throw* this away?"

I tried to get her to look at me. She stuck out her lower jaw, stretching the gum inside her mouth. Her eyes were fluttering, half closed.

"How *many* grad students have I had in here? You're a *kid* and you're way *beyond* them. You're so gifted, Rocky." I paused to get my breath. "Who the hell *is* it, anyway? Another *Troy*? Or *Lance*?"

She snorted. "No. It ain't *Lance* or Troy." She chewed, watching me.

"I admit it: Science is important to me. You taught me a lot. But I need to have that same feeling I have in here . . . in other places."

There was silence. She shrugged again and stared into space, her jaws working. I blew my nose. She looked at me.

"You understand?"

"What's to understand? You're in love with some guy and—"

"Woman."

We looked at each other.

"Woman. I'm in love with some woman. I got a new *girlfriend*."

I shook suddenly with cold and she blinked, surprised, as if I'd flinched in revulsion. "Girlfriend?"

"Yeah." She laughed at my face. "You never *guessed*, Prof? That I hang out on *both* sides? God, you're major *uncool*."

I put down my cup awkwardly; towels slid from my shoulders. "Who is she?" I asked, major-uncoolly.

"*Who* she is doesn't matter. I love her. She's not like me. She's quiet, she's deep. But the thing is I have this feeling with her which is very much the way I used to feel *in here* with you."

"So are saying that you never cared about science, you just—"

"No," she said. "It wasn't all *you*, don't get excited, man. What I liked was the fact that two women, two of us, could work together like that. I liked that, Prof. I liked the work and I liked the idea of the two women. So what you said about cholos hurt me—but let me tell you, not as much as it hurt me to go into the graduate admissions office, where they looked at me like some kind of little *puta*! And I thought to myself in there, Why do I need to borrow forty thousand so I can go to grad school in biochemistry or molecular biology and end up working in a *paint factory?* Who's gonna hire *me* afterwards?"

I rubbed my sleeve across my runny nose and felt tears starting up again. "You would *not* end up . . ."

She folded her arms in front of her and snapped her gum with authority. Her look silenced me.

"I'm not *you*. Harvard connections and all that. If I do this, it's just gonna be the way *I* say. That's all."

The tears ran down my face and I put my head down.

After a bit she got up and knelt beside me and put her arms around me. She smelled like gardenias and Doublemint. I put my head on her shoulder and we held each other. Then she sat back on her heels and pushed her long hair out of her eyes.

"I found your note to me in here. The night guard let me in and hey, there it was."

Gum snap.

"Thanks for writing it."

I'd forgotten the notes I'd left; I'd forgotten everything, it seemed. Centuries ago (a sharp but muffled pain) I'd found out I'd been scooped by L.R., standing in this room.

I covered my face with my hands again. Gum snap—I felt her shake her hair. "You want me to kidnap Ollie back from Jay?"

I laughed into my hands—it felt odd to laugh. I looked up. "I want you to come back here to work."

"You know, I can't do that right now. I gotta think."

There was another pause. She stared at me, cracking her gum, thinking. We were still kneeling.

"You ever see a *scientist* with an ass like *this?*" She turned around and waggled her rear end. "And hey, so help me, they can *kiss* it, man!"

"You were *born* to be in science, Rocky."

She laughed. "I was born to cause trouble. Like you."

She leaned over again and kissed me on the lips. Then she pulled away, a little frightened. I reached for her and hugged her.

"I love you," I said. "I need you to help me."

She shook her head dazedly and smiled. "You mean you're coming back *here*?"

"I don't know." I stood up. Rocky stood up too. "I need a ride home. Can you drop me?"

"Sure," she said. "You're on my way."

As we turned up my block, I saw that all the lights were burning inside my house. I couldn't remember if I'd left them on when I'd taken off for Jay's. I saw a silhouette moving inside. My heart moved—Ollie? Had Jay reconsidered and brought her back?

I leapt out of Rocky's car, beckoning to her to follow, ran up the steps, and jammed my key in the door. Someone was in the hallway; a large shape stood there as I opened the door. I pulled my key free of the lock and stared. It was Q.

# Chapter 25

I don't know who was more shocked. We stood staring without speaking. Then Rocky came up behind me and then my mother, wearing a blue silk bathrobe, appeared in the entryway behind Q. Then everyone spoke at once.

I was asking them what they were doing there and they were carrying on about the way I looked, and where had I been, and where were Jay and Ollie? Rocky was trying to say good-bye to me, having sensed family weather. Finally everyone stopped talking and Rocky hugged me, once, hard, and loped off across the lawn.

They pulled me into the house, where, despite the enormous distraction of their presence, a tidal wave of grief overtook me.

Her dragon still sat in the red chair where I'd put it the other night. Her yellow rain boots stood side by side near the umbrella stand. Her "TV" box in the corner. Her dreamy, startling little face looked out from photographs everywhere: on the walls, the coffee table, everywhere I turned. Sobs rose in my throat, but I caught them, one by one. I pulled myself back up straight. They were staring at me.

My mother stepped forward. She had that resolute I-can-fix-it look on her face that I remembered from childhood. It was a look that I'd come, over many years, to understand never existed in pure form. It always appeared in combination with a swift glance of accusation; so it was really the I-can-fix-it—you-did-it-again-didn't-you-you-hapless-jerk look.

"Esme, my God, what's wrong with you?"

We went into the living room together and sat down and I told them the story, or stories: the breakup, my suspension from UGC, the custody battle, Jay's kidnapping of Ollie.

They listened sympathetically, exclaiming in the appropriate places, but once again, I felt the stubborn alarmed judgment of me going on just below the surface of their concern—what had happened to me, the protégée, the postdoc star? How had I done this to myself?

Q's eyes flickered over me again and again: the torn, still-soaked jeans I'd had on for three—four?—days now; the ratty plaid shirt; my damp dirty hair hanging in my face; my filthy fingernails and sandals. He breathed sonorously, filling the room, a sound I remembered well. He looked older to me, but he'd acquired a kind of ruddy gleam, a patina of well-being. They're good for each other, I thought, startled, and I stared for a second at them as a *unit,* as if they'd been placed behind glass in a museum: Last Happy Marriage on Earth, Late Twentieth Century, Cambridge.

He stared back at me. God, I remembered those deceptively mild, inquiring eyes: *How do you confirm this hypothesis, Ms. Charbonneau?* or *How do you explain the discrepancy here between your results and the results in the textbook? What an intriguing theory, Esme, but even Mendel does not support you here.* I looked back into those eyes, trying to remain unshaken. He wanted to know, I supposed, the exact nature of my pathology. And more important, how could he have miscalculated? He'd bet on me, he'd put faith in me.

"But what I don't understand clearly," he said, inhaling noisily through his nose, "is why you stopped going to your lab."

"I'm going to make some hot cocoa for everyone," Millie announced gaily. She stood up and hurried out to the kitchen. I noticed that she wiped a tear away with the back of her hand as she rose.

"Professor Quandahl," I began, and he held up his hand. For one awful moment, I thought he might ask me to call him Dad, and I froze.

"*Ken,*" he said, "please."

"How about 'Q'? I mean, I'd like to call you Q, OK?"

He nodded indifferently. He didn't care what I called him, he just wanted an answer.

"I stopped going to the lab because I was sick of the pressure on me to perform some goddam miracle for funding. And . . . there was another reason. Over the last couple of years, I've turned to theory. And theory began to obsess me, I mean, to the exclusion of my other work. I developed, with"—I paused; it was hard for me to say this name—"Lorraine Atwater, a theory of everything, a TOE. And it flew, Q, I'm serious. I'm serious," I repeated to his amazed expression. "However, it happens that Atwater just scooped me," I added in a small voice.

He sat, staring intently at me, breathing in loud rasps, his nostrils flaring.

"You're not *shocked* at my being scooped, are you? Come on, you know this kind of thing goes on all the time, right? Prof—Q, I mean, people take other people's research, other people's ideas, routinely, don't they? Honcho professors take grad students' and postdocs' research and call it all their own as a matter of course, don't they?"

He lifted an eyebrow. "Esme, you were a great help to me on albinism—your research was invaluable. Do you feel I used material you should have been credited for?"

"No—I'm just aware of how it happens, how the hierarchy stays in place."

We stared at each other in silence for a minute, neither one of us eager to plunge into the swirling vortex before us.

"I'd like to ask *you* a question, at the risk of sounding rude. What are you and Millie doing here?"

My mother came back before he could answer, carrying a laden tray: a hand-painted china teapot (which Jay had given me for our last anniversary), cups, napkins. The delicious insipid smell of chocolate filled the room.

How did she do it? *Cocoa! Goddam cocoa!* I almost burst out laughing, but that kind of explosion would inevitably lead me to more weeping, I knew. I restrained myself and smiled at her.

She set the tray down on the coffee table; Q moved to help her. Then she sat down on the couch, lifted the top daintily off the china teapot, and stirred the steaming contents with a silver spoon, looking at me all the while.

"We wrote to you, Esme, don't you remember? Didn't you get the letter? Kendall"—she glanced over at him—"had a conference in San Francisco three days ago. We told you we'd rent a car and drive down from there for a visit. We just assumed you'd gotten the note. Luckily the elderly woman next door"—"Mrs. K.," I murmured—"had a key and let us in."

I glanced guiltily at a far corner of the room; somewhere in that direction was a cardboard box containing stacks of unopened mail. From the last few weeks. She was watching me closely.

"That's weird. I don't remember a letter like that."

"Well. I think it's weird too, Esme." She put the top back on the teapot and shook her head. "I find . . . all of this . . . very weird. Very disturbing."

She carefully picked up a cup and poured hot chocolate into it in a steady stream.

I felt anger, a spool of red shadows, unwinding fast in me. I stopped the spool.

"What exactly is weird, Mother?" She held out the cup to me and

I took it. My hands were shaking so badly again that the cup rattled noisily in the saucer.

"Esme. Kendall and I are shocked to find you in this . . . condition. You look like a . . . derelict, your marriage has fallen apart, our grandchild has become the pawn in this dispute between you and Jay . . ."

"Pawn? Wait, Mother, that implies that *both* Jay and I are playing a game." I set my cup down with a bang and she jumped. "Jay may be trying to play a game. I'm not. I'm not playing a game. This is *Ollie* we're talking . . ."

I started to cry again. Goddammit, I thought, but the tears cascaded down. I shook my head and dabbed at my eyes with a napkin.

"This is *Ollie*. He *took* her from me. He lied and told his lawyer I'd . . . hurt her."

Q sat forward, setting his cup down.

"What is he claiming you did to her?"

"He's saying that I . . . hit her. She had a little bump where she hit her head on the sink and he said I did that. Prior to that he said I was irresponsible because I didn't agree with him that she needed to be treated like a dysfunctional kid."

"Dear, is there a chance that he's right about Ollie? I don't mean the *bruise*, I mean the . . . dysfunction."

I looked back at her in fury.

"Of course there's a chance that he is right. There was also a chance that I'm right. Who knows? All *I* know is that my daughter has always seemed like herself to me. She just needs time to grow and let the world get used to who she is."

"But there were . . . problems? In school, with other children, language development—isn't this right?"

"Yes and no, Mom. Mostly no. I don't know how to say this so that you'll stop looking at me like I'm some kind of fucking child-abuser, but I know my kid, OK?"

Q frowned at me. "Esme, please don't speak in that manner to your mother."

I stood up. "Please don't speak like that to my *mother*? You're going to tell me how to address my mother now? It wasn't enough that you ran my life for five or six years and made me think I had to be fucking Joan of Arc, now you're going to tell me how to talk to my *mother*? Jesus, how arrogant are you? And by the way, my *mother* and I never talk at all, so there's really no precedent. She and I have never been close, have we, *Mom*?"

She just looked at me.

I sat down again, talking to Q, who was glaring at me.

"I'll tell you what really sucks about all this. She could have helped me so much this last year when I was debating what to do about Ollie. I wanted to know about my own early childhood, of which I remember little. I thought it might shed some light on Ollie's behavior. I wrote her letters, but she never told me anything. Isn't that right?"

"It's hard to know *what* you want, Esme." She put her cup down.

"Yeah. Hard for *you*. Your mind's been elsewhere for my whole life!"

"Esme, I'm not like you. You want answers to everything; that's how your mind works. When you were in therapy, in graduate school, you bombarded me with letters too. I don't like supplying you with *evidence* for some theory you'll derive to justify your own behavior."

"What behavior?"

"Like *now*, the way you're acting now. Finding excuses. If Ollie needs help, Esme, get her help."

"Nothing in my life has prepared me for this. I mean *any* of it, having a child like Ollie, any of it," I said. I took a breath. "I was finding a way, on my own, trying to discover the right place for her. I'd written to a teacher, Gloria Walther—she was Ollie's first kindergarten teacher but was transferred—to ask if she knew of a school that would *recognize* Ollie, help her develop. I'm waiting to hear from her. In the meantime, I'm all alone. Jay took her away from me, Mother. I can't really grieve and I can't let my life go on. I know that she's alive and not that far away but I can't get to her. Do you have any idea how that feels?"

Suddenly her demeanor changed; the erect posture, the carefully held face, altered. She shook a little, as if an electrical surge had passed through her; then she began to cry.

"Yes!" she cried. "I *know* how that feels."

I stared at her, astonished, and Q put an arm around her and patted her hair. He looked over her head at me and something blazed from his face: righteousness, anger, fierce protectiveness? I couldn't tell.

She sat up and dabbed her eyes with her napkin. She looked at me. God, I hated that look. She was always *reasonable*. After she expressed an emotion, she limited it, cauterized it, quickly, perfunctorily. I remembered the mothers of kids I knew: shouting, laughing, weeping. Millie wept a little, now and then, *for form's sake.*

"Esme, I've avoided telling you this because I didn't want to give you fuel for your theories about Ollie. I was an outsider when it came to your upbringing. When you began to exhibit certain tendencies— yes, yes, like those you describe in Ollie—your father panicked. He thought that you were disturbed. We took you to the psychiatrists and child-development people and the advice at that time was always: Give her a normal upbringing, *force* her to be like other kids."

She stopped. We waited, and after drawing a long breath, she went on.

"I disagreed. When you began to . . . move around in circles and talk to yourself, it didn't seem like a disturbance to me. I thought you should not be . . . treated like a disturbed child. But your father . . . You know, Esme, before your father got so sick with emphysema, he was a strong, stubborn man. Your father insisted that he could help you, change you. He thought that I was a bad influence."

She stopped here and said nothing for quite a while. Q wheezed away like a squeezebox and I sat staring at her, as she sat erect, her body slightly turned from me. "You know that there was a popular theory among psychiatrists at that time that autism could be *caused* by the mother? James thought that our bond, the bond between you and me, was . . . He broke it. That bond between you and me." She put her head down. "Do you know what it's like to try and withdraw emotionally from your child?" She looked up again. Her face was naked, grief-stricken.

"That's what they asked me to do. Your father. The therapists. So. Then your father worked with you. Every time he caught you spinning in circles he . . . shook you and brought you back. He insisted that you do regular kid things. He bought you comic books, he taught you to tell jokes. He was *funny*, your father, remember? He tried to make you laugh. When you started to withdraw he went after you. He followed you into that world and he turned your face around and brought you back. He made you talk to him, he made you use words that made sense. 'That doesn't make sense,' he'd say. 'Say it again, Esme, say it again, until you make sense.' Then, you know, not too long after that, he started drinking. He lost his job at Fann Hydraulics and he worked for a while as a toll-taker on the Triboro Bridge. Do you remember that, honey?"

"No," I whispered.

"Well, he worked the night shift and he used to take you with him sometimes."

"No," I said. Then: "Maybe I do remember, but I never knew *where* I was."

The memory washed over me. I must have been four or so, maybe Ollie's age. . . . I remembered being in a tiny space with him. When I remembered it, I always thought that I was recalling a dream, because it appeared to me that we were *in prison,* my father and me, in a cell, behind bars. Beams of light swept over us. I'd always thought the beams were from a nightmare prison watchtower, but now I realized

they were headlights. Now I remembered him talking to me, telling
me to ask for the toll, fifty cents, to hand the change back from a
dollar. "Talk to the people," he'd say. "Say 'Good evening, sir.'"
"Esme, make sense. Answer the lady, Esme, speak up, what do you
say?" "Thank you." "Please." "Pardon?" "Your change, ma'am."
And I remembered too, suddenly, how he bragged about me. I could
make change fast, I picked the math up, even at that early age. He
wanted it both ways, I thought. "Here's my smart little kid. Fast as
lightning, nobody's fool. But look at her, just like all the other kids.
Smart as a toll-taker's daughter, making change (you say the right
word, you pay the toll), handing out the tickets to those who complied,
stamped PAID, you can pass."

"I remember it now," I said.

"Esme, he did all this because he wanted you to be happy, he
wanted you to be normal. *I know* you think that there is no normal,
I know that. But *he* believed it, you see. You and he used to trade
jokes back and forth. Then you just got too fast. He couldn't keep
up. And in school, though he'd tried to keep you out of accelerated
classes—you took off. You started winning all those prizes with
your science projects. He just gave up, you know. But by then, he
was so sick."

She started to weep again. Then stopped herself. Then wept again.

"Why would you want this to happen *again*, Mom?" I noticed how
Q silently reached over and took her hand.

I couldn't imagine how she could have lived through that, condi-
tioned herself, to be the person she'd become to me, day after day.
"No, sweetheart, not now." "No, Mommy can't help." "Mommy
has to go now." "Let go, Esme." I stared at her: Who would we be
now, had we been allowed to love each other?

"I don't know. You said yourself we've never been that close."

"You didn't answer my question. Why would you want me to do
to Ollie what he did to me?"

"Because she has to live in the world, Esme. She can't keep talking just to herself and you. You must see that."

"I know she has to live in the world and talk to other people. I *do* see that. But I've made a lot of people angry trying to protect her," I said. "Because I don't believe that some *expert* can tell me about my own daughter." I paused. "She needed this time in her life to be *safe*: She needed to know I was her mother, that I wouldn't go away."

I got up, walked over, and sat between them. They shrank back a little, both of them, nervous. I sat down between them.

I put my arm around my mother. Then I put my arm around Q. They seemed so old to me, suddenly, so fragile.

"You came because of the letters I wrote, I know that. It wasn't really the conference, was it? You talked to Jay and you were *worried*. It's all OK, really. It's OK."

After a while, my mother stopped crying and I touched the side of her face with my hand. She reached up and took my hand and held it. Then as if that were all the maternal intimacy she could bear for the moment, she let it go. She smiled brightly at me and got up. She went into the bathroom and shut the door. I cleared my throat.

"You know, Q, it's so funny. For the longest time, I *did* think that I was in love with you. You know that. Well, I wasn't in love with you. But you had such power over me—the power that parents have, *totemic* power. In some ways, everything I've done in my field was in reaction to you. Except the theory. That's mine. Or *was*. It freed me of your power over me."

He nodded his head slowly, in time with his labored breathing.

"I've made mistakes," he said finally. "Mistakes of judgment. I was a very lonely man when we worked together and in my loneliness, I confused my work with an emotional life."

He wheezed violently, then caught his breath. "You were right,

Esme, about *some* of the things you said that day in my office. Not all. Not all. I am *not* invested in biotech futures; you were wrong to suggest that. And I find the genome project . . . pretentious. It's true, you've always been impulsive in your judgments."

Still so arrogant I thought, still Q. But this no longer bothered me. In fact, it made me feel a little stronger.

"I *am* impulsive," I said. "But you are, too. You just act on your impulses a little slower, so it looks like measured judgment."

He looked at me, shocked, then amazingly, he laughed a little, hoarsely. "The way you talk to your mother," he murmured. "I don't like it, Esme."

"You don't have to like it, she's not *your* mother." I stared off into middle distance; the bathroom. "She's *my* mother," I said. Then we sat in silence for a time.

"Hey," I said after a minute. "Do you remember a medical fellow named Jesse Falbo? He worked at Harmon-Tannen with us?"

"Maybe," he said, rubbing his eyes. "Wait . . . Oh yes. Jesse. Yes."

"I liked that guy," I said, and thought of that other life, like a dream. "I really did."

# Chapter 26

I stood in the shower, letting the hot water pour over me. I reached up and turned a lever on the shower nozzle and the pour became a spin; the droplets spiraled over and around me and I leaned languorously against the tiled wall, my hair streaming down my back, and I shut my eyes and saw her—the familiar dark figure. She was spinning in the arc of the spray, then turning slower and slower, almost stopping now, and I could see as she slowly rotated—back-of-head to profile, to front—it was no surprise to me that she wore my mother's face. And what I felt, even in the wake of Ollie's loss, for a split second was gratitude. Then I reached for the soap and began to wash myself.

I stood beside the answering machine, filled with dread. Then I pressed the Messages button.

There were three hangups, right in a row, then Michele Mueller, then Terry McMahon, then Terry McMahon again, then the mediator from Family Court wanting to make an appointment with me; then L.R.'s hoarse voice filled the air.

"Esme. I'm so sorry I didn't catch you at home. I'm back in Los Angeles and I'm afraid that I owe you an explanation for my disappearance." (You owe me a tad more than that, I thought grimly.) "The reason I went away was because, I'm afraid, I was feeling some things rather *unworthy* of me." She cleared her throat.

"Esme, you cannot possibly understand what it's like to work for so long on a project and then have someone younger and less experienced come along and redefine it, provide the missing link, just like that. I can only report to you that it is daunting and there is a bitterness that is real and threatens to consume one. That is why I left. When I flew to New York, I had actually considered submitting the TOE to an appropriate journal, under my name only, and leaving it at that. I admit this to you now and I apologize to you for having had this impulse. It was only that, an impulse. I could never have done that. You will be relieved to know that though I submitted the findings to *Theory Abstracts* without your knowledge (and I apologize for this unorthodox step too!), I did not submit them without your name, which will be listed after mine, as co-author of the Theory of Chirality and the Weak Force. The envelope containing our theory with calculations will be opened in the offices of *Theory Abstracts* at eleven A.M. EST, Tuesday the twentieth. I congratulate you, Esme, and I thank you. We deserve to be very proud of ourselves now."

I sank down in my chair. I looked up at a framed picture on the wall: the many-armed god Shiva. Beneath was a brass plaque reading, "The Cosmic Dance of the Universe." L.R. added that I should give her a call when I returned and she would provide me with a copy of her journal submission.

I got up and stopped the tape before the next message and played it again. Then again. Finally, breathing carefully, I let the tape go.

The mediator again. Faber. Then Gloria Walther. Her analysis of Ollie, when Ollie had been in her class at Sixth Street, was that she was highly gifted and had difficulties not uncharacteristic of the gifted. Probably she and I could find a school. Could I call her back?

Then, his voice low, almost a whisper, but urgent: Jay.

"Esme. Please c-call me as soon as possible."

Then Jay again, same message. Followed by a third, a frantic note: "Esme, where *are* y-you? Something is w-w-wrong with Ollie. I don't know what to do for her. She's r-refusing to eat or sleep or even m-move." He coughed, then there was a fumbled echoing hangup of the receiver.

I was up and out of the chair but I stopped in the doorway as the next message materialized:

"Esme. This is Terry McMahon. Where *are* you? I'm calling to inform you that Ollie was taken, an hour or so ago, to Cedars Sinai Medical Center. She hasn't eaten anything for three days now and she is in a kind of fugue-state from which Jay has found it impossible to rouse her. Please call me as soon as you get in."

Then one last one as I stood there frozen: "Esme. Esme. Where are y-you? C-can't you hear me, can't you a-answer? Esme?"

I borrowed Q's rented Firebird and drove fast but carefully, gingerly shifting the unfamiliar gears, trying to concentrate on the traffic, billboards—anything but *her*.

### Letter to Ollie: Schrödinger's Cat

She stood at the top of the basement steps, calling me, the light behind her, like an angel's nimbus. But I knew when I climbed to the top step, she'd be gone. There would be my place set neatly at the table: plate, cup of cold milk, spoon, fork. And warm from the oven: a chop, green vegetable, potatoes. She would not eat with me, the nights he worked late. She would not sit beside me cutting her meat (When did she eat? Later? Standing up at the counter?) or sipping her coffee. But she set my place; she knew exactly what I needed. And waited somewhere in the wings. I ate alone in a kind of regal if ratty splendor: talking to my knife and cup, reading comics, the periodic table, feeding bits of meat to the dog, spilling liberally on myself. Listening always for her step, waiting for her to appear, pull off her apron, sit down beside me. Sometimes, far in the back of the house, I heard her clear her throat, sigh, as if she was listening too.

I could have told her so *much*.

I was ridiculed at school, but *casually*—the other kids barely got interested enough in me to reject me; I was a natural outsider, invisible. Was I invisible to everyone, even my mother?

*Talking to myself, daydreaming, forgetting things, not having the answer the teacher wanted. Obsessed with counting on my dirty bitten nails, walking in circles, lost in contemplation. I saw images superimposed on images: polyhedrons, cathedrals, talking trees, ciphers burning in the margins of my grammar workbook. Lost in the webs and lairs of insects, tracking the sonar of bats, filling jars with cold-lit bugs, rigging up a dry-cell battery, a tank for algae, a star chart, a model of the interior of the sun. Natural objects became familiar but were also graciously strange, they'd make a polite dimensional bow, then flicker in the mirror. Transformed!*

Red traffic light. I braked, I waited.

*I'd figured it out, sitting at my lonely meals, nine, ten years old. There was nothing that I could be kept from thinking about. Nothing that my mind could not track or invent—physics, architecture, comic books. My parents seemed not like parents, more like older siblings, unsure of themselves, emotionally withdrawn or tyrannical—or simply absent. They had, I thought, no power over me. And I could make my own judgments; I didn't have to see what any adult told me to see.*

———

Green light; the traffic surged forward. I shifted, with a little resistance, into first.

*Then I could observe, when I built the DNA model, that no living molecule is self-reproducing—only a whole cell can clone or vary itself—and even then, the proteins of a cell are made by other proteins and without that protein-forming machinery nothing can be made.*

Somebody changes lanes, too fast, without a signal, in front of me. I don't honk at the guy, I speed up behind him. Shift, third.

*Nothing can be made without interconnection, the shuttle and the daring leap of the catalyzers: Stimulated by proteins, brain neurons make new connections, create synapses with other neurons during the learning process, by reaching. The neurons reach out: synaptic plasticity. They have these fingerlike projections, the neurites, and they feel around, test like antennae, stretch, touch, then adhere. The wires connect, but first: the lift out of the familiar. Not the single, self-reproducing, macho spiral we imagine creating us and our thought —no, the crosser, the leaper, the sympathizer, the blesser, the emblematic gesture of praise and affection.*

Quick left turn, close call.

*And the lowly but mighty electron: blessing us by confounding our dimension-drowned minds, driving even Einstein to distraction. Yes, it's a waveform; yes, it has dual wave-particle nature! But this shouldn't imply it's a wave sometimes and a particle sometimes, but that it has the properties of either, depending on circumstances.*

Left turn, two blocks, right turn.

   (Aspasia, Annie Jump Cannon, Sophie Charlotte, Queen of Prussia . . . where is your mother, little girl?)

———

*Because electron waves are waves of probability, like, say, the prob-
ability of more homeless people here in the inner city: people living
in boxes. You can put an electron in a box, slide in a partition—and
assume, according to common sense, that the particle will be in one
side of the box or the other. Wrong. Quantum rules say that the
electron wave is present in* both *sides of the box, because it's true
that when we peek into the box, we are equally likely to find it on
one side of the wall or the other. And this measurement technique
applies to macro particles, the human-sized world too.*

Traffic backup. Honking. We wait.

She patted my face. "Ollie and Mamma," she said.

*Five minutes to Cedars . . . And let us consider Schrödinger's cat:
quantum paradox of the twentieth century. I read this thought-
experiment when I was ten or so, sitting at the kitchen table, and I
was amazed (I still am) at the inherent ghoulishness of its givens. A
cat is placed in a box with a glass flask of cyanide, and a little brass
hammer is balanced above the glass. Also in the box is a radioactive
source, which eventually releases an alpha particle detected by a
Geiger counter, thus triggering the fall of the hammer, which breaks
the cyanide flask and kills the cat. But wait! We have waveforms here,
the same observer-probability measurement paradox as the electron's.
Quantamese, taking in all the eventualities, says we have two over-
lapping waveforms: on one a dead cat comes surfing toward us; on
the other, a live cat. The cat can't be considered either alive or dead,
but* both. *Quantum theory says the cat is* alive-dead. *The cat is a
"ghost-hybrid." The natural universe will not tell us which state she's
in until we observe, we peek in, and we see her, meowing, pacing,
or . . . The question has to be: What is going on inside the box when
nobody is looking? Both, Mother, life and its absence. Alone at the*

*table: She is two. She is invisible, she is dead, she is homeless, she is silent, not like us* and *alike:—she is* both mother and daughter.

Turn into the Cedars parking area—cars everywhere. Don't you see the neon-red Emergency? The same phenomenon occurs every single time an alpha particle is released by a nucleus; watch the radioactive paint on the hands of the luminous clock embedded in the dash-well, *what time is it, alpha decay?* watch that car backing out—Who first looked at her and tried to determine how she would fit in the box, who first said, "No, the world doesn't look like that," who first said, "Medicate," said "Impediment"?

Kick open the door, slam, lock, run. *Ollie,* the partitioned box, *Ollie,* the ghost-hybrid, *Ollie,* the lobby mirrors, *Ollie,* the elevator floor, *Ollie,* the lift out of the familiar, the blessing of the reached, opening door, *Ollie.*

She was in a bed with aluminum sides, like a crib. The sides were half raised, and I lowered the side facing me. She was curled up in the fetal position, her hands folded into each other. Looking closer, I saw the deep black and blue bruises on the left hand: They'd had trouble starting the I.V. line that ran from her palm (her fingers splayed and taped to a balsa-wood rest) to the swinging bottle hung on a hooked pole near the bed. The stenciled polyurethane I.D. band around her right wrist read "OLIVIA TALLICH. 8-19-87." I set the dragon carefully on the pillow beside her.

No sound, except in the halls. No one was in the room but Ollie, I thought at first. Then I saw the other child, so small he couldn't be distinguished from the pillows and sheets around him. Sound asleep. He'd had an operation; his skull was painted with iodine, shaved and bandaged. Sides up. A big bear sat next to him. He, too, had an I.V.

I pulled the sliding curtains shut tight around us. I moved closer to her, almost lying down next to her, and I whispered in her ear.

"Ollie. Ollie. It's Mamma. Ollie."

There was no response. Her breathing stayed regular. Then I thought her left eye jumped a little in her socket. Above that eye was the famous bruise—swelling almost faded, a delicate streak of yellow and slate color above the brow.

"Ollie, sweetheart. Can you hear Mamma?"

"Esme."

He opened the curtains slightly behind me; they rustled on the track, but I did not turn to look at him.

"Esme, she's b-been like this since . . . you know, that night. I didn't know what to . . . I've been *trying* to reach you, where have you been?" His voice broke.

I didn't answer. I felt each breath, in and out, little reassuring wind against my hand.

"She wouldn't eat. Or drink. She wouldn't even l-lie down to sleep. She kept turning and crying and then she just . . . s-stopped. It's like she disappeared. The doctors . . ."

"I don't think I can hear this right now, Jay. Maybe we'll talk later. But I can't talk to you now. I have to ask that you leave us alone, now, just leave us alone here, for a little while."

The curtains slid back and we were enclosed again in that oblong space, a red-gold tent, a safe place. I heard, from the other side of the cosmos, the echoing names of doctors being paged, the squeaky wheels of gurneys passing, people talking. Once I nodded off, just for a second, and then I started, feeling the barely perceptible touch of her finger, moving over my left hand, then back.

"Ollie," I said. I kissed her soft fine hair, then her forehead.

She breathed in and out; I breathed with her. Once, nodding off, I glanced at my watch. It was nearly midnight. But that was all right. I was prepared to wait for a very long time.